THE ARGON FURNACE

Also by Richard L. Graves:
The Black Gold of Malaverde
The Platinum Bullet
Cobalt 60
Quicksilver
C.L.A.W.
Rolling Thunder

THE ARGON FURNACE

A Novel by

RICHARD L. GRAVES

Scarborough House/*Publishers*

c. 1

Scarborough House/*Publishers*
Chelsea, MI 48118

FIRST PUBLISHED IN 1990

Library of Congress Cataloging-in-Publication Data

Graves, Richard L.
    The argon furnace : a novel by / Richard L. Graves.
        p.   cm.
    ISBN 0-8128-4007-0 : $18.95
    I. Title.
PS3557.R289A89   1990
813'.54—dc20   90-35909
                                                          CIP

THE ARGON FURNACE

A band of Japanese-American Navy men
sabotage Japan's progress toward production of a jet fighter plane in World
War II.

prologue

Ringo, Japan, September, 1945

She made her way toward the shrine at the edge of town. Rays
of morning sun sliced through the summer haze, etching the
twisted pines and rocks against an ethereal shoreline. This, she
thought, is peace.

The narrow winding streets of Ringo were unmarked by the
war. Though the great cities were wastelands of ash and rubble,
this tiny fishing village seemed the same as on the first day
she had arrived. Yet, she mused, how much the world had
changed. The little islands of Japan had soared to victory only
to crash in ghastly ruins. The great warships were rusting at
the bottom of the sea or wrecked. Aircraft had flown over the
horizon, never to return. Whole regiments and divisions of
soldiers slept forever in jungles or under coral sands. To her it
seemed a world of ghosts.

It was her duty to report these things to the spirit of her father.
So that morning she had donned her best kimono, the orange
one with the pattern of cranes. It was awkward tying the obi
after so many months — years, in fact — of wearing the atrocious
wartime garb. It was good to feel again the colors blossom
around her after so many dark days. And yet, who knew what
was ahead. Perhaps even darker days. *Shigata ga nai* — It cannot
be helped.

She hurried down the street. From time to time she would
stop to bow and exchange greetings with a neighbor. They all

1

wanted to know the occasion for her kimono. She would simply bow and tell them that it was the day to report to her father's spirit. They understood.

The shrine was on a lane branching away from the main road out of town. It was there on a hillside surrounded by the ubiquitous pines and a few maples. In another month the maples would be showing their autumn red and orange. The trees made a frame for part of the rocky coast and a fragment of the sea. When the leaves were off the trees, the whole sea could be seen spread out below. Her father's shrine faced that way as if on guard. It didn't matter now.

She came to the shrine and stopped to compose herself. Then she clapped her hands, bowed, and addressed her father's spirit. "Father, three years have passed. The war took your life. And now the war has ended. I am sorry I must tell you this on the anniversary of your sacrifice. . .

"Our Emperor has surrendered. A great fleet of American battleships already has sailed into Tokyo Bay. An American army has marched into Tokyo. . ."

As she spoke, a naval officer in dress whites approached quietly behind her. In Ringo no one would have noticed him in particular. He was taller than most, but his appearance was as Japanese as theirs. Nor would the uniform have been out of place. It didn't mean anything now. Not anymore. His name was Tomi Hara. He spoke to her in Japanese.

"Chiyo. . .?"

"Oh!" Not looking at him, she bowed. "You startled me."

"Don't you remember me?"

She looked up. She thought he was a ghost. "Tomi?" Was it an illusion? She reached out and touched his arm. "Is it really you?"

"I'm back. Just as I promised."

"Alive!" She stared at him. Tears welled in her eyes. "I can't believe it!"

He looked the same. Still the same sharp, handsome face. Like a sea eagle, she thought. His skin was darkened by the sun.

It contrasted strikingly against the high collar of his white naval officer's jacket with its rows of colored ribbons.

"I thought you had died long ago," she said. "We heard of great naval battles. When no letters came I thought. . ."

"I knew I would find you here. This is the anniversary of your father's death."

"It is good of you to remember. And to come."

"I had to. How could I forget that night?" The war years hadn't dimmed her beauty. "Nor could I forget you."

She looked down. "I am forgettable."

The memory of their last meeting flooded her mind. "But that night. . ." In her memory's eye the ghostliness of it loomed again. "A night of mysteries. . .of my father's death. . .of shadows and fire."

"A nightmare for you."

"Yes." She looked up at him again. "And for you, also."

"Yes." He smiled sadly. "A nightmare."

"But still, I believe father died as he chose."

Hara nodded. "In battle. A true samurai. He lived the code of *Bushido.*"

"But a battle so strange. Against an enemy that no one lived to tell about." There was a question in her eyes. "Except you. Only you saw. But you disappeared."

"I saw."

"There was an investigation. The Army, the Navy, the civil authorities, they all questioned us. They asked me about you."

"And. . .?"

"That was all. We were told to say nothing at all about what we had seen or heard. It was a great secret."

Hara smiled faintly. "I am sure it was."

"And now you've returned."

"Yes, I'm back. Older. Perhaps wiser."

"The war has changed everything."

"You haven't changed."

"You think so?"

"Just as I remember you. Beautiful."

3

She looked down again. "Thank you. You are the same, too."

"It has been only three years."

"It seems an age."

"If we measure time by events instead of by days, yes, it's been an age."

She looked into his eyes. "I am very glad you have returned."

"I have an *ohn*. I owe it to you."

"You owe me nothing."

"I've come back to tell you about that night..."

"Oh," she interrupted. She rummaged in the sleeve of her kimono. She smiled quickly as she brought out a small red silk bag. "Look!" From the bag she produced a small brass naval insignia. "Remember this?"

"I gave you that."

"Yes. That terrible night. A little badge. So simple." She looked down again, bowing ever so slightly. "But I treasure it." She looked at him again. "I did not tell the investigators about it."

"Why?"

"I was afraid they would take it from me. In all the days since then it has been like a tiny personal shrine for me. A shrine because I thought you..." She fell silent.

"It is worth very little." Except, he thought, the priceless treasures of duty and of sacrifice and of courage and of honor. Of brotherhood. And of death.

"But that is how I remember," she said, looking at the badge. "You were going to face the enemy." Her eyes locked on his again. "I wanted so much to speak my heart, to cry 'No! Stay!' I cast my eyes down. I could not even think to speak. Then I went into my house. When I looked out again, you were gone. Like the shadows. And now you are back."

"It's ended."

"The enemy has won."

"A war is over. We have all lost."

A thought struck her. "But you still wear your uniform?"

"Yes."

"Is it safe?"

4

"It is safe."

"Have you seen the Americans?" she asked hesitantly.

He smiled. "Yes."

"The only ones I ever saw were your two prisoners. It's very different now. Will the Americans come here?" Her eyes dimmed with tears. "I try to be brave. Like father. But I have fear."

"Chiyo, look at me."

"Yes. . .?"

"Look at my cap insignia."

She studied the metal badge. It meant nothing in particular to her. "Yes. . .?"

"Now look at the badge I gave you."

"Yes. They are similar."

"Chiyo, this badge is American." He put his right hand on his breast over three rows of campaign and decoration ribbons. "This is an American naval officer's uniform."

"I don't understand." She shook her head in confusion. "Why? Why do you wear the American uniform?"

His eyes probed hers. "I am American. I am a commander in the United States Navy."

Her thoughts swam in circles. "But how. . .?"

"Let's walk."

He took her gently by the arm and steered her along the path under the pines and maples.

"I will tell you a story." His voice softened, as if he were reciting a folktale to a child. "It begins more than three years ago. August, 1942. This was a time shortly after the Navy — the United States Navy — had defeated the Imperial Japanese fleet at the great Battle of Midway. . ."

Pearl Harbor, August 6, 1942

I

It was hot and humid in the briefing hut. Fans were working but not achieving. Behind the plain wooden rostrum there was a screen. At the back of the hut a projector promised more heat when its lamp went on. At each of the doors on either side of the dais and at the rear of the hut there stood an armed marine. Each managed to look stone cool, belying the sweat straining through his shirt. The audience was small, as wartime briefings went. It was composed of naval officers except for a marine gunnery sergeant, an elderly civilian, a navy yeoman, and another marine sergeant hovering patiently by the projector. The door at the rear opened with a clatter.

" 'Ten-HUT!' "

Admiral Farley Claybourne stalked in, trailing an aide with a briefcase. The audience was on its feet at attention. Claybourne stepped up on the dais and faced them.

"At ease, gentlemen. The smoking lamp is lit." Claybourne glanced at his notes. "Yeoman, for the log, this is the eighteenth meeting of the Naval Special Missions Group. Present are all members except Captain Weymouth, on duty in Australia." He looked up at his audience. "To begin I'd like the group to meet some people we've just brought into the Argon Project. First is Commander James D. Krag."

Krag stood. "Good afternoon." He was a tall, rangy man with iron-gray hair. His deeply lined face had been weathered by tropical sea and sun. He was forty-two. He seemed older than any older man there and tougher than any younger man. The striking thing about him was his eyes, blue and knowing. They gave the impression not only of seeing all, but of understanding.

"Commander Krag arrived yesterday from the Philippines, where he was leading a guerrilla operation against the Japanese on Mindanao. At our request a submarine picked him up, took him to Midway, then he was flown here.

"Next to Commander Krag is Gunnery Sergeant Max Barton, of the Marine Corps. He escaped from a Jap prison compound and managed to join Commander Krag. Gunner. . ."

Barton stood. "Afternoon." He was nearly as tall as Krag but had a wrestler's build and a scarred face. He was thirty-five, but, like Krag, he wore extra years like battle ribbons. Like the marine guards at the doors, he had the quality of rock. The difference was he showed no sweat.

"And next to Sergeant Barton," continued Claybourne, "is Lieutenant Commander Hunley. He's the skipper of *Grayfish*, one of our Gar Class submarines."

Hunley stood. "Gentlemen." He was, perhaps, thirty. Slim, of middling height. He had that faintly aristocratic bearing of Old Navy and Annapolis. And, indeed, he was.

"Thank you, gentlemen. Please sit down. May I have the lights dimmed? First slide, Sergeant."

A very large scale chart of the Western Pacific was projected on the screen at the front of the hut. Claybourne tapped at it with a pointer.

"As you know, task forces under admirals Fletcher and Spruance gave the Nips a broken nose at Midway in June. It was the first naval battle in history decided solely by aircraft. The fleets never saw each other. We sank all four of their fast carriers." He let that sink in, then continued. "As a result the Japanese have pulled their fleet back to the home islands to refit and reorganize. That's done two things for us: it's opened our supply line to Australia, and it's given us an opportunity to start offensive operations sooner than we'd expected."

He turned from the map and looked at his audience. "But let's be very clear about one thing: we didn't win Midway because Japanese planes or personnel were inferior in either quantity or quality. We did *not* — repeat *not* — have air superiority at Midway. That's not to take anything from our fliers. The fact is we had inside information and we were lucky as hell.

"But we can't fight this war on hot tips or on luck. In May in the Coral Sea, we lost a carrier and forty-six percent of our planes. At Midway we were holding all the tactical aces, but we still lost half our planes and a carrier. Those are unacceptable loss rates. We've got to cut our losses and take air control. We've got to stack the cards our way. And we've got to start *now*. That's why we're here. To start, I'll introduce Lieutenant McGlynn, from the Office of Naval Intelligence."

McGlynn was taller than Hunley, younger, and blonder. But he had the same Old Navy look. He accepted the pointer from Claybourne as if it were the Sword of Honor.

"Thank you, Admiral. Next slide, Sergeant."

This was a chart of much smaller scale showing an archipelago. A legend at the bottom described it as the Solomon Islands. "Tomorrow — August 7 — the First Marine Division will land in the Solomon Islands. The main force will hit this island, Guadalcanal, and seize the airstrip. That'll begin our Pacific offensive. Slide, please."

Now the scale of the chart expanded again, showing a range of islands up through the Philippines.

"Frankly, the Solomons battle is going to be nip-and-tuck. But even assuming we're successful in the Solomons, it's still a long road ahead. Based on the experience we, the army, and the Australians are taking in New Guinea, the losses could be appalling. We can't continue to counterattack head-on from land and sea. The offensive against Japan will require *total* air superiority. But, as the Admiral said, we sure don't have it now. Let me show you why."

They saw the triple profile of a blunt-nosed fighter plane. "This is the Mitsubishi A6M3, better known to all as the 'Zero' fighter. I don't have to tell you about the Japanese Zero. It outclimbs, outmaneuvers, and outguns anything we have in action. We *won't* have anything as good for months. But the Japanese aren't waiting for us to catch up. They want to keep a mile ahead. They may do it. Next slide!"

The screen showed profiles of a twin-engined plane.

"This is top secret. It's the Mitsubishi Ki-83.* Code-named 'Zipper.' A dozen prototypes have been built, but it's not in regular production yet. Twin engines: Mitsubishi Ha-211s. Excellent engine. Armament: four cannon. That's right: four — two 30-millimeter and two 20-millimeter. Intelligence says this plane has airspeed as good as our P-38, but *triple* the range. Put that another way: it can stay in action while our boys are back gassing up. It's like having fleets of extra fighters. But that's the *good* news. The bad news is they're modifying this airframe for a new kind of engine. Slide, Sergeant!"

The grainy image of what appeared to be a trash barrel wrapped in tubing was cast on the screen.

"This is it. This is a German engine. We got this picture through the Swiss. The Germans apparently are building it, but they haven't put any planes in the air with it. Not yet. Meanwhile, we learned a month ago that Mitsubishi got designs from the Germans for a new kind of very high performance engine.

"We think it looks something like this. It's called a *ramjet*. No propeller. Just goes along on push from the exhaust. Newton's Third Law in action. In theory, this engine could generate extremely high speeds. And we're not talking about incremental advances. This is a major jump ahead. Now let's see what that means to an aircraft."

---

*The Mitsubishi Ki-83 was still in the prototype stage when Japan surrendered in 1945. It was a sleek, extremely sophisticated design. Some experts believe that had it gone into production it would have made American B-29 raids extremely costly.

The screen showed statistics in two columns comparing the performance prospects of the P-38 with the Ki-83. McGlynn's pointer tapped the Japanese column. "Read 'em and weep. As you can see, the Zipper can outperform the P-38, even with conventional engines. That's bad news. Why? Because we're counting on the P-38 in the Solomons to get altitude on the Zero. It can't outmaneuver the Zero, but it can get over it, dive, and blow it out of the air.

"It'll get one pass, then back up to ceiling. Obviously, a few squadrons of Zippers would take even that edge away from us. Slide, please."

A third column of statistics was added to the other two. "Now the really bad news. Our technical people say that with a jet engine Zipper's ceiling will be more than 45,000 feet. Airspeed: at least 450 miles per hour at altitude. If it gets in the air, it'll totally outclass anything we've got on the drawing board. We're years away." He paused for effect, then said, "Admiral..."

"There it is," said Claybourne, returning to the rostrum. "A super aircraft engine in the hands of the Japanese means control of the air — and the battle — in the Western Pacific for years. Simple as that. Questions?"

"Sir?"

"Question, Commander Krag?"

"Sir, this is all very informative, but where do Sergeant Barton and myself fit in? We're not experts in planes or aircraft engines. I commanded a gunboat that got sunk. Barton's a machine-gun and explosives man."

"I'll give it to you in a nutshell, Krag: Commander Hunley's going to take you and Sergeant Barton to Japan in his submarine."

"Japan?" said Hunley.

"That's right. Japan."

"Yessir," said Hunley. "And when we get there...?"

"There Krag will lead a rather unique mission."

When the Admiral didn't volunteer more information, Krag prompted, "Yessir, a mission. To do what, sir?"

"Why hell, man, to stop that damn Jap engine before it starts."

"Stop it?"

"That's what I said."

"Yessir! Understood sir." Krag stole a glance at Barton. The marine sat like a block, showing no reaction to any of this.

"May I ask what the timetable is, sir?"

Claybourne looked at his wristwatch. "You leave in approximately three hours."

Krag caught his breath. "Three. . .? Could the Admiral perhaps mean three *days*?"

"Hours. We'd make it sooner, but we need cover of darkness."

Krag felt sweat beading his upper lip. "Yessir, but what about briefing? Planning? Training?"

Claybourne was irritated. "You've just gotten the short brief, Krag. When you're aboard *Grayfish,* you and Barton'll get more details and the general plan. Then you'll lay out the on-shore tactical plan. As for training, that's why we brought you and Barton back."

He said it as if any fool should understand. "You've trained for this mission the hard way — behind enemy lines. You've got months of real experience, and you're two of only a handful of people who do. That's critical."

"Yessir. But at this point I'm unclear what two men can accomplish in Japan."

"Oh, you'll have support." Claybourne glanced pointedly at his watch again. "The personnel you'll lead on this mission have been training in depth while we've been getting you back from the Philippines."

"Support. Yessir. And when will we meet these people?"

"Why not now? McGlynn, would you call in the others?"

McGlynn went to a side door, held it ajar tentatively, and peered out. Nothing happened for a moment, then McGlynn shouted "Go!" and jumped aside.

The door slammed all the way open. Five armed Imperial Japanese Navy enlisted men double-timed into the room followed by a Japanese naval officer. The group stomped up on the dais, double-timing in place until the officer called a halt. In Japanese he commanded them to right face toward the audience. There was a uniform gasp, then excited talk.

"Son of a bitch!" said Barton. "Japs!" He was halfway to his feet. Krag pulled him back.

Admiral Claybourne was laughing.

"I think we're gettin' the treatment," Krag said. "Christ, what next?"

Each of the enlisted men carried a Japanese Arisaka rifle with bayonet attached. They wore landing-party gear — ammunition belt, canteen, first-aid kit, and a musette bag carrying God knew what. The officer was armed with a naval dress sword and a Nambu automatic pistol, pistol belt, and ammunition. He issued a command.

Barton, who had a fair command of Japanese, knew it was an order for the men to announce themselves. One by one each stepped forward smartly and said something that only Barton and a few others in the room could understand.

"Chief Petty Officer Toda!" He bowed sharply from the waist.

"Gunner's Mate Sakai."

"Radioman Endo."

"Torpedoman Fujimura."

"Torpedoman Marumoto."

"Lieutenant Hara." He bowed too, then in English said, "Now, tell 'em who you really are."

"Right. I'm Tak Toda, Ensign, U.S. Office of Naval Intelligence."

"Murray Sakai, formerly Los Angeles. Presently, Chief Petty Officer, Office of Naval Intelligence."

"Mike Endo, San Diego, former left halfback at U.S.C., presently Staff Sergeant, Army Military Intelligence Service."

"Sammy Fujimura, Seattle. Steelworker. But now a corporal, Army M.I.S."

"Bob Marumoto, Assistant Professor of Oriental Studies at Yale. Civilian working with O.N.I."

"Thank you, gentlemen. And my name is Tomi Hara, Lieutenant Commander, U.S. Office of Naval Intelligence, presently dolled up as an Imperial Japanese Navy lieutenant, a submarine officer. I've been with O.N.I. for about four years. So I know my way around Japanese naval systems and methods. In case you're wondering, every guy on this squad was born and raised in the United States. But all of us are fluent in Japanese."

He laughed. "I think we look right."

There was a nervous titter in the audience. Krag and Barton didn't smile.

"What do you think, Krag?" Claybourne asked, grinning.

"Fooled me. Impressive, sir."

"Barton?"

"Look like the real thing. But looks are only part of it, sir. What do they know about cover, concealment, tactics, weapons, explosives. . .?"

"We've trained for this for a month," said Hara. "We're ready, willing. . ."

"Yes, yes." Claybourne interrupted. "The original plan was for an all-Nisei group. The men you see here."

"Why change?" asked Krag.

"We didn't have anyone with actual combat experience against the Japanese. We need that extra dimension. This job's too important to risk on untested people when we have an option. You and Barton. You're what we need to fill out the mission. Krag, you're mission commander. Formal orders, the mission statement, and details are sealed until after you sail. McGlynn has them. He'll be sailing with you."

"Understood, sir."

"Permission to speak, sir?" asked Barton.

"Granted."

"I see Arisaka rifles. But where's our automatic rifle? Our machine gun?"

"He's right, sir," said Krag. "We need at least one light machine gun. Nambu, if possible. Two, if we can get 'em."

"We haven't captured any Nambus," said McGlynn. "We had a hard enough time getting Arisaka rifles."

"We need more firepower, no matter what else," said Krag.

"We're not going over there to fight a battle," McGlynn said testily. "We can't risk blowing our cover with an obviously American weapon like a B.A.R."

"You're using two obviously American faces."

"Crazy as it sounds," said McGlynn, "it's easier to get you by the Japanese than to get away with an American B.A.R."

Krag was skeptical. "How do you get us by? In ski masks?"

"We've got a cover story for you and Barton."

"Yeah?"

"You're American pilots." McGlynn said smoothly. "Your plane's crashed at sea. You've been picked up by a Japanese submarine. Hara and his men are taking you ashore for transportation to Naval Headquarters."

Krag's laugh was acid. "The Japanese aren't fools! You think they'll buy a scam like that?"

"We think they'll buy it," said McGlynn.

Hara spoke up. "I think so, too. Japanese military people will find it inconceivable that there's an American military force looking and speaking fluent Japanese. It's just not in their book."

"Says you," muttered Barton.

"How do you know it's not in their book?" Krag asked.

"I'm an intelligence officer."

Barton snorted derisively.

Hara stared hard at him. "We've done a lot of analysis on just this kind of situation, Sergeant. Bob Marumoto here is an authority on Japan. Bob, explain it a little bit."

This Nisei was older than the others, perhaps forty, of middle height. A little gray peppered his cropped hair. He wore round dark-rimmed glasses of Japanese style.

"Well, one thing we know is that the Japanese have some basic cultural misconceptions about Americans. For example, one is that they think our military wouldn't trust orientals any more than the Imperial Navy would trust *gaijin* — foreigners — which is not at all.

"For another thing, they think Americans of Japanese background — like me and these other guys here — have some kind of mystical loyalty to the Emperor, some kind of genetic identification with *Dai Nippon*."

"Don't they?" asked Barton.

Silence chilled the room better than the fans. Then Hara said, "Take it from me, they don't."

"Okay," said Krag, "if what you way is true, the idea might fly." Like a submarine, he thought.

"It's true," said Hara.

"You still need a light machine gun," said Barton. "If there's a showdown, you can't hit 'em with spitballs. Those Arisaka rifles are just one cut above slingshots."

McGlynn sighed. "Any suggestions on the machine gun?"

The Admiral's aide stood up. "The Japanese Nambu Type 99 machine gun is similar to the British Bren gun. They look alike. I believe there are some Brens around Pearl."

Barton nodded. "That'd do. The Japs captured lots of Bren guns from the Brits at Hong Kong and Singapore. They use 'em all through the Philippines."

"We'll check it," said Claybourne. "Anything else?"

"Not at the moment, sir," Krag answered. "I'm sure I'll think of something else the minute we land in Japan."

The Admiral ignored the sarcasm. "Very well." He checked his watch. "If there's nothing else, I suggest you prepare to board *Grayfish*. What kind of shape you in, Hunley?"

"As ordered, sir, the crew has been reduced to minimum. We've off-loaded our torpedoes. Gives us extra space. We've stowed five hundred pounds of TNT in demolition blocks; fifty pounds of RDX. Plenty of timers, fuze, and primacord. Inflatable boats, motors, and gear for landing parties are aboard. We've loaded a lot of cans of paint for some reason. Ship's stores and refueling are complete. We're ready to sail on command, sir."

"Very well." Claybourne glanced at the elderly man who had been sitting quietly to one side. "Oh, Doctor, would you join me

16

outside, please?"

"Certainly."

"Odd-looking bird," Krag whispered to Barton.

"Yeah. I'll bet a buck he's the guy who dreamed up this thing. It's always some guy wearing thick glasses who makes big trouble."

Krag nodded. "Just the kind of double-dome you'd expect to frame a nutty mission like this," he muttered.

Up front, Claybourne said, "Good luck, gentlemen. Carry on." He headed for the rear door.

" 'Ten-HUT!" the aide shouted. There was some half-hearted compliance, then the group broke up.

Krag turned to Hunley. "How long have you been preparing for this?"

"I'm in the same boat as you in more ways than one. We came in from picket duty after Midway. First thing they did was move my deck gun from abaft the conning tower to the foredeck without telling me why. Then they repainted us with a non-kosher camouflage scheme above the waterline without telling me why. That took a while. Then I was ordered to take out my torpedoes, reduce crew, and prepare for a long voyage with extra passengers. That's all I knew. I thought we might be headed for the Philippines. First I heard the word 'Japan' was just now."

"Nothing else?"

"No. And, frankly, I don't like it. *Grayfish* could do a hell of a lot better, in my opinion, by hanging off Yokosuka and nailing a carrier or a cruiser. That's what a submarine's for. Nothing personal, Commander, but being an underwater bus driver isn't my idea of warfare."

"Tell you what: get up a petition to call this thing off, I'll sign it."

"Sure." Hunley grinned. "I'll get right on that."

McGlynn called Krag to the room's wall telephone. Barton sidled over to Marumoto and inspected him. The smaller man's spectacles made him seem scholarly and innocent at the same time.

17

"*Konichi-wa go zai masu*," Barton said — Japanese for "Good afternoon."

"I know English," Marumoto replied.

"And I know Jap. What do we talk in?"

"American."

"Sure. What's your job in this?"

"I'm supposed to be a Japanese torpedoman."

"Yeah, I heard that. But I also heard 'Yale.' Why a Yale Jap civilian on a deal like this?"

Marumoto felt intimidated by the burly marine, but he was determined not to show it. "I'm going along to help the mission. Whatever it takes. But the main thing is I've got more background in Japanese culture than the others. So I help them work on language, customs — details, things that might give them away in a pinch. Our guys all grew up in America. Without some coaching they could reveal themselves in a clutch in a dozen ways."

"Japanese culture, huh?" Barton fingered the edge of the bayonet on Marumoto's rifle. "Know how to use a Jap rifle?"

"I can hit a target."

"I mean the bayonet. Real Japs like the pigsticker. Part of their culture. Japs like to gut military prisoners with bayonets. Civilians, too. You like to stab?"

Marumoto felt anger rising. "Never tried it," he said tightly.

"You ought to. You'd like it. Japs all like it."

"I'm American. I'm a professor at Yale."

"American?" Barton's eyes might have been dead. "Not in my book. . . *Perfesser.*"

"What're you, Barton?"

"Don't smart-ass me, Perfesser. I've slit throats under faces like yours. One more would suit me fine."

Krag shouted from the phone. "Hey! Barton! Army ordnance's got Bren guns and ammo. They're sending two down to *Grayfish.*"

"Great." Barton looked back at Marumoto. "Remember this, Perfesser: I don't like Japs one little bit. You may think you're

18

some kind of American, but you ain't American in my book 'til you prove it to me. I'm watchin' you and" — he jabbed a finger at the other Nisei — "them. I'm like a snake watchin' mice. Pass it on."

II

They rode in Claybourne's sedan.

"What did you think of our little pageant, Doctor Borovitch?"

"It was quite impressive and most encouraging. When I first wrote to the War Department urging an attack on the Japanese facility, I envisioned brave young Caucasians landing somehow in the middle of the night. It never occurred to me that you could produce a team of real Japanese to do the job."

"Not Japanese, Doctor. Nisei. Japanese-Americans. And I have to confess that under some other circumstances the thought might not have occurred to me either. Or, worse, I might have rejected it because of misconceptions, even bigotry."

"What circumstances brought them to your attention?"

"Not so much circumstances as Commander Hara. I've known him since he came out of the Naval Academy. He's one of our special analysts on Japanese naval systems. We've worked together in O.N.I. So, when your letter and the backup file were forwarded to me, I naturally discussed the problem with him. He was the one who suggested an all-Nisei squad. The idea was so obvious I almost cried."

"One hopes it doesn't seem simpler in concept than in execution."

"We went into that at length. That's why we brought in that Yale fellow, the professor. Not only did he do an analysis endorsing the idea, he volunteered to go along."

"Still, I think you were wise to bring in those two experienced men. Krag, is it?"

"Yes. Krag and Barton. They've been touched by fire. They know things you can only know by being touched by fire. They give the Nisei that extra instinct."

19

"What instinct is that?"

"The killer instinct, of course. There's no way to teach it."

"Thank God."

III

Sunset painted the tropical sky salmon pink, fading to maroon. Pearl Harbor was blacked out. *Grayfish* squatted at its berth in the submarine cove, dark and brooding. Sailors worked in the goblin red twilight of night illumination, stowing the last odds and ends needed for a long patrol. If the skeleton submarine crew wondered before why their torpedoes had been removed, they more than wondered now at what obviously was a squad of Orientals who appeared from a darkened bus and quickly made their way below.

At pierside Hunley watched the action. "Ought to be a hell of a trip," he said to Barton.

"Bad enough getting out of Mindanao on one of these things. Never thought I'd ship the other way on one with a squad of Japs."

"Americans, Barton."

"We'll see."

"They're okay," Hunley insisted. "They've trained hard. I'm advised they've been checked and double-checked."

"I do my own checkin' and double-checkin'."

"Give them a chance."

"Chance for what, Commander? I've seen guys like that butcher people. No reason. They like it. I was lucky to get away." His teeth glinted in the red light. "Now I'm lucky to get a chance to kill more of the bastards."

"Not on *Grayfish* you won't, Sergeant. They're American military personnel, same as you and me."

"Jap's a Jap. I'll watch my back."

"Just keep your sentiments to yourself, Sergeant. I'm the boss on *Grayfish*. Understood?"

"Aye-aye, sir."

20

"Let's go below." Hunley led Barton down through the forward hatch. The interior reeked of diesel fuel, hydraulic fluid, and mildew. They went aft to the vessel's tiny wardroom. Already there were Krag, Hara, and his men. Barton knew McGlynn was part of the mission, but he was surprised to see the same odd-looking old man he'd noticed at the afternoon briefing.

"Gentlemen, welcome aboard *Grayfish*," said Hunley. "All your gear stowed, Hara?"

"Ready to go."

"Hope you have gear for me and Barton," said Krag. "I feel naked."

"We've got everything you'll need."

"Got the Bren guns?"

"Two."

"Ammo?"

"Two thousand rounds, plus."

"Satisfied, Barton?" asked Hunley.

"Yessir. All we've got to do now is train somebody to use 'em."

"Later." Hunley looked around. "I apologize for the lighting. We're rigged for red because we'll be operating in the dark until we're out of Pearl. Crew and officers have to keep night vision adjusted. So, bear with us. I know Commander Krag and Sergeant Barton have shipped on a submarine before, but it's probably new to the rest of you, so let me tell you about the vessel.

"*Grayfish* is a patrol submarine. That means that in typical operations we hunt enemy vessels and sink them. But, of course, we're useful for other missions — picket work, pilot recovery, intelligence or whatever. This mission is a 'whatever.'

"Anyhow, *Grayfish* was built at Mare Island Navy Yard and commissioned eleven months ago. She has a new design of double-hull construction. We have an external attack center above the control room. She displaces 1,500 tons on the surface and 2,400 tons diving. She has 10 torpedo tubes of 21 inches each, six bow, four stern. Ordinarily we'd carry 24 torpedoes,

21

but this trip we're carrying none, which frees up a lot of cubic feet for the mission. You saw our deck gun. It's a three-incher. Originally, that gun was mounted abaft the conning tower. But we've moved it forward for this trip. We're carrying ammunition for it and for our four machine guns. That's the only defense we've got without our torpedoes.

"Usually, we carry an eighty-man crew, but we've cut that back to twenty-seven since we don't have to man the torpedo stations. The boys'll be busy. So, as much as you can, keep out of their way. Any questions so far?"

"How deep will she dive?" asked Endo.

"Designed for 250 feet, but she can get down a good bit more. We won't be running that deep unless we get in trouble. Okay? Let's go aft."

Hunley led the way to the engine room.

"Gentlemen, this is our engineering officer, Mr. Macklin. Mack, tell 'em what you've got here."

Macklin already was oil stained. "We have four Fairbanks-Morse diesels, each with 5,400 brake horsepower. Two diesels for each of the ship's two shafts. The diesels run the ship when we're on the surface and they also charge the batteries. When we're dived, the batteries run those two General Electric motors. Each can deliver about 2,800 horsepower to the shafts."

"Thanks, Mack," said Hunley. "Let's go forward."

"How fast do we go underwater?" asked Marumoto as they filed out of the engine room.

"Fast isn't the word, unfortunately. We make eight-point-seven knots, maximum. Contrary to popular opinion, submarines are mainly surface vessels. We can make twenty knots on top, but we usually cruise at about twelve. Saves wear and tear on the engines and us. We only dive when we're trying to keep out of sight, especially during an attack.

"If we get the chance, we'd rather hit a target with the deck gun. We never know when we'll need to dive, but we always know we've got a tight leash on our batteries. So we run mostly on the diesels and keep our batteries topped up."

They filed back through the holds to the forward torpedo room.

"And this," said Hunley, "is the dormitory. Even without the torpedoes and torpedo crews, it's going to be a tight fit and a long trip. We'll do the best we can."

Krag looked around. "This is downright palatial. Barton and I got the real cram course going to Midway."

"No private baths," Hunley grinned. "It can get real gamey after a week or so. But bear with us. We're going to cast off now. I'd appreciate your sitting tight until we're out of Pearl. 'Bout an hour. After that we'll have some chow, relax, and get acquainted. Commander Krag, would you join me topside?"

IV

From the conning tower Hunley and Krag watched the crew take stations for departure. Hunley issued commands crisply through a bullhorn. It was reassuring to Krag to see the young man as a competent professional. Life was short for amateurs in submarines.

"Cast off bow!. . .Cast off stern!. . .Right rudder 30 degrees! . . .Quarter ahead!. . .Midships!. . .Half ahead!. . ." Hunley put down his bullhorn and turned to Krag. "How's it feel going to sea after all that time in the jungle?"

"Strange. How many patrols have you run?"

"This is my second in command of *Grayfish*. We haven't been doing anything dramatic. Mostly picket and intelligence work at Midway. Picked some of our airmen out of the water."

"So this is your first real combat patrol into Japanese water?"

"That's right. And I guess we're going pretty deep into Japanese water if we're supposed to get you folks ashore."

"Just where is this place we're headed?"

"Don't know yet. We'll open the orders later. McGlynn's supposed to brief us."

"Who's the odd old duck?"

Hunley grinned. "Just one more hazard on a hazardous mission. A civilian. I was introduced to him, but I can't handle the

23

name. Borrow-something. Foreign." Hunley gestured toward the bow and the far-off channel out of Pearl Harbor. "There's the sea. We're on our way."

"Funny," said Krag. "I'm an old blue-water sailor, but I've done all my fighting on land."

"Whole different game. Like playing football when you've been practicing baseball."

"Sort of. But, odd as it sounds, there's something about the jungle that's like submarines."

"Really? What's that?"

"Living in the jungle's like being submerged. You're closed in. You can't see much. You navigate through it because there are no roads. You attack targets of opportunity. You avoid anything that could beat you. When you defend, you hunker down and hope the Japs don't see you in the bush. If they do, it's over."

"Yeah, I suppose a submariner is kind of a seagoing guerrilla. But jungle guerrilla war: nasty business."

"Nasty's not the word for it."

"Glad to be out of it?"

"Considering what's ahead I might be better off on Mindanao."

"Don't blame you."

"What do you suppose the chances are on a deal like this?"

"Better than you might think. We'll sure as hell have surprise on our side. We'll get you on the beach."

"Gettin' off the beach is what worries me."

"If we can get you on, we can get you off. And we'll stay 'til we do."

"Appreciate that, Hunley. But I'm skipper enough to know you'll do what's best for your ship."

"We'll need a lot of dumb luck." He laughed shortly. "Do you realize you'll be the first Americans to invade Japan from the sea?"

"That's an honor I'd rather share with the whole fleet. But, like the man said: ours not to reason . . ."

"There's one reason . . ." Hunley pointed toward a huge,

24

warped, and twisted crane-like structure etched black against the darkening sky.

"*Arizona?*"

"What's left of her."

"When they built her, no one dreamed that something as dinky and unreliable as an airplane could sink a battleship."

"With one bomb. I saw her go."

"Must have been some Sunday."

"It was some Sunday. Fortunately, *Grayfish* didn't get hit."

"My ship got hit a few days later."

"Hard?"

"She went down. Fast."

"Where was that?"

"Off Zamboanga. We were planting mines. Couple of Zeros strafed us. Hit the mines. Ship blew up."

"Lose many men?"

"All," Krag murmured. "All but me."

"Christ!"

"You could say I'm on borrowed time."

"What saved you?"

"Not sure. I was on the bridge. Because of the tropic heat out there, we'd taken down all the bridge siding. So, lucky for me, we were wide open. Blast tossed me a good hundred yards. All I got were burns."

"You were lucky."

"Luck? Yeah, but what kind? Either good or bad, take your choice." Krag shrugged. "When I came up out of the water, all I saw was debris coming down and one big ball of smoke. Grabbed a timber. Made it to shore."

"What then?"

"There was a small Regular Army garrison near Zamboanga. I joined them. We took to the hills with a platoon of Philippine Scouts. When the Japs landed on Mindanao, we began guerrilla operations. Wainright surrendered Corregidor five months later . . .ordered us to turn ourselves in to the Japanese."

"With a gun at his head."

"Probably. We said no dice. First time I ever deliberately disobeyed a direct order."

"Were you under Army or Navy command on Mindanao?"

"Well, we didn't go by the book much. Turned out I was ranking officer, so I took charge. The Army guys taught me infantry tactics, the Philippine Scouts taught me jungle fighting, and I taught them explosives."

"That where Barton joined you?"

"Max came in later. Escaped from a group of prisoners the Japs were going to ship up to Luzon."

"Lucky for him."

"Maybe. Maybe not."

"What do you mean?"

"Japs are mighty rough on prisoners. One thing they do is kill a couple for every guy that gets away. Deterrent to guys making a break."

"Didn't deter Barton."

"After Max made his break they used two of our boys for bayonet practice. Left the bodies tied up to trees to rot. Max came back after the Japs had left. Found 'em and buried 'em."

"Hell of a load, him knowing he caused the murder of two. . ."

"He doesn't see it that way. Max is a Marine. He figures his job is to fight the enemy, not make a deal *not* to fight. He puts the blame where it belongs. He blames the Japs, Hunley. They murdered the prisoners."

"Sure. Rules of War and all that." He hesitated. "Listen, Krag, Barton's got a bad attitude about Hara and his men. He sees them as the enemy."

"Barton's no philosopher, Hunley. He's got to learn for himself in his own way about Hara's people. They do their work, he'll come around. Meantime he sees what looks like people who murdered marines. Them dressing up in Imperial Navy uniforms doesn't help their image."

"Suppose he doesn't come around? That kind of crazy bigotry could jeopardize the mission, Krag."

"With Max the mission's first. He might be a little crazy.

26

So am I. But he's no bigot. He's spent most of his Marine time in the Orient. China. Japan. He knows how to speak some Japanese. Philippines. He has a Philippina wife on Luzon. Doesn't know if she's alive or dead. He's probably got more time in the Far East than all the rest of us put together, including Hara and his boys."

"Okay. But I run a tight ship, Krag. I won't have any hitches on this voyage. We go by the book."

"Look, Hunley, Barton's been fighting Japs and living off the jungle for more than six months. So have I. Maybe our attitude isn't Navy Regulation. Killing ruins your manners. But I guarantee that Barton'll do the job. He'll give his life, if that's what the job takes. I know *that* for a fact. I *don't* know that for a fact about anyone else on this ship."

2

At Sea, August, 1942

I

Later that night everyone but ship's crew was summoned to the wardroom. A projector had been set up. Hunley turned the meeting over to McGlynn.

"Gentlemen, the sealed material has been opened. There's a lot there, and we're not going into all of it tonight. We'll get through all of it before we get into Japanese waters. We'll work on briefings and plans every night at 2000 hours. During daylight, we'll work on ship and shore drill. But right now my job is to introduce the man who'll tell us precisely where we're going and why."

All eyes turned on the aging civilian, who was thumbing through some note cards. McGlynn went on. "I could read through a bunch of credentials, but I don't think they'd mean a whole lot to you. I'll just say that, professionally, he's one of the top men in the world on specialty steel. He is the architect of this mission."

"I knew it," Barton muttered to Krag.

"Meet Dr. Milov Borovitch."

"Yes." The old man pulled himself up from the wardroom bench with both hands. He sighed and looked around. "The name is pronounced Bo-ROW-vitch."

He was tall and stooped, but there was nothing feeble about

29

him. His hair was white and combed oddly to the front over his forehead. He wore thick horn-rimmed glasses. Though dressed in naval chinos, he had the rumpled, unmilitary look of a math teacher.

"Now we got a Russki," Barton whispered to Krag.

"Need all the help we can get," Krag muttered back.

Borovitch saw them whispering. "Perhaps I should explain where I come from...?" He looked questionly at McGlynn.

"Yes, that would help, Dr. Borovitch."

"Bo-ROW-vitch!"

"Sorry."

"Yes." He looked at them like a professor seeing a squad of the retarded at his lecture. "Before coming to U.S.A. ten months ago I was senior research and design engineer with the Swedish firm, Olson-Waldemann Limited. You probably don't know it, but this firm leads the world in the design of mills to make high-quality alloy steel."

He had a deep, sonorous voice. He spoke with an accent, but it didn't get in his way. "Sweden is famous for this. These alloys are called 'specialty' steels. They are special because they do exceptional jobs and they are very costly. You buy them by the pound, not by the ton. They are very different from the iron used for construction, ship-building, and so on. Lights, please..."

McGlynn switched off the light and started the projector. The slide was the same engine picture they had seen at the afternoon briefing. Borovitch continued:

"A major goal always is to make steel which can do better jobs at extreme high temperatures, but not melt. This is very important in such things as drilling and cutting tools. In guns. In engine design this is very important. The higher the temperature the steel can tolerate, the more efficient the design of the engine can be. Temperature is the limit even on conventional aircraft engines."

His hand swept through the projected picture, seeming to make it come alive. "In theory a ramjet engine like this could be the most efficient design of all. But an engine like this generates very, very high temperatures. That's especially true in the turbine parts and here, at the exhaust. These engines cannot be made to operate using existing conventional engine materials. That's why the jet has not been a practical engine. Next slide. . ."

Data was projected showing the amount of time required to make specialty steels measured against a comparable volume of structural steel.

"Specialty steel is very difficult to make. High-temperature alloys are the most difficult technical problem of all. They can be made only in very small batches under extreme control in a special environment. Keeping the process pure takes much time, as you see on this slide. This is very slow and very expensive. Obviously, this is not good for war-fighting type of production." Borovitch held up a finger in the projector beam. "Until now."

A new slide was projected. It showed a rugged seacoast and a small village.

"So," said Borovitch, "you ask, 'what's this?' To answer, I will tell you a story. While employed by the Swedish firm, I was a consulting engineer on the construction of a plant on the west coast of Honshu, Japan, near this town. This is the only picture I have of this place, a fishing village, called Ringo.

"That's the Japanese word for 'apple.' " Hara interjected.

"Yes," said Borovitch. "Quite right. Apples grow near there. Anyway, this Japanese plant near there has a unique design. More precisely, I should say that the *furnace* in the mill is unique. The building itself is much like any other steel plant. Of course, the Japanese took all my film. So the only picture of the town is the one you see, from a postcard. However, I remember enough of this furnace to draw a rough scheme."

The next slide was a somewhat complex diagram that could have been a ship's boiler or a liquor still.

"So, you ask, 'what's this?' " Borovitch hovered in front of the screen, inviting some kind of response from his problem pupils.

"I give up," said Krag. "What is it?"

31

"Gentlemen," said Borovitch, "meet the Argon Furnace."

"I still don't know what it is," said Krag.

"Very well," said Borovitch. "Technically, it is called an argon-oxygen decarburization furnace. But all you need remember is Argon Furnace." Borovitch warmed to his teaching role. "Argon is the magic of this furnace. It is a rather rare gas which is inert. That means it does not react in any way with any other element. So, it cannot make contaminating molecules. This is vital."

"I don't understand a goddamn word," Barton whispered to Krag.

"At least it ain't Mindanao."

"It is critically important," said Borovitch, "in making high-temperature alloys to have all the materials very, very pure. This is the most difficult problem of all. Most efforts fail. Ordinary air is useless in these processes. Why? Because air is made up of oxygen and nitrogen, which are active elements.

"They react with other elements to make oxides and nitrides that contaminate the alloy. But in the Argon Furnace the inert gas — argon — is pumped through the alloy under high pressure. It scrubs out the impurities. Because the argon does not react with elements in the alloy, the product is pure in a way that is absolutely impossible to attain any other way. Result: very high quality, very high temperature steel in very large batches. Fast. Cheap. There is no furnace like this anywhere else."

"So what's all this mean, exactly, Doctor Borovitch?" asked Krag.

"Bo-ROW-vitch," he said testily. "What it means exactly is that the Japanese can now make a practical high-performance jet aircraft engine. They will kill you with it."

"How much stuff does this kettle cook up?" asked Barton. "How many jet engines at the end of the line?"

"The Argon Furnace can make up to fifty *tons* of alloy in about four hours. In practical daily operations that means four, perhaps five, batches every 24 hours. Each batch is enough to make one hundred jet engines.

"The Japanese problem no longer is the supply of engine

material, but the manufacture of the engine itself. And that is not really a problem for them. They have the design, and they are excellent at manufacturing processes."

"If they get cranked up," McGlynn interjected, "they could be flying their first squadrons of jet-equipped Zippers by the end of the year."

Fujimura, the former steelworker, piped up. "Why doesn't the United States build one?"

"The U.S.A. doesn't have a practical design," said Borovitch.

"Hell, we can do anything," said Endo.

"Eventually, perhaps," said Borovitch. "But it is a far cry from theory to experimental proof. It is an even longer journey from the experiment that works to the machine that works. Execution is important, but design is everything. In this case, *I* don't know the exact design myself. The Japanese kept me away from the crucial details. However" — Borovitch held up a finger — "I know the general concept and I've worked on laboratory experiments. But there's a big difference between concept and execution. Even if the United States gets the secret, you could not have such a mill operating in less than one year."

"Doctor Borovitch, how long's this Japanese furnace been operating?" asked Hunley.

Borovitch looked pained. "Please. Pronounced Bo-ROW-vitch. The furnace may be starting just about now."

"How do you know?" asked Barton.

"When I left Japan last October to take a holiday in the States, it was not installed. The plan was to bring the furnace on stream in August of this year. Of course, the war started. I did not go back. But I assume the plan went ahead. So, after a test period, they should be in full production very soon. Perhaps they've already started."

McGlynn stood up. "Thank you, Dr. Borovitch . . ."

"*Bo-ROW-vitch!*"

"Sorry," said McGlynn. "I'll get that right before this voyage is over. Okay. Well, there it is. With steel from the Argon Furnace the Japanese can make jet engines . . . knock us out of

33

the sky."

"So," Krag said glumly, "we're going to hit that furnace."

"That's the mission," McGlynn said cheerily.

II

Barton poked a spoon at his black coffee. "Everybody's a college boy but me," he said.

"It's okay, Barton," said Endo. "We'll help you all we can. We call the first letter in the alphabet 'A'. Now. . ."

Barton allowed a grim smile. "You went to U.S.C., right?"

"Yep."

"Gonna be an engineer or a doctor?"

"Football first, then I'll think about the trivial stuff."

To Barton it figured that a halfback would be husky, but Mike Endo was built like a box of ammunition and not much taller. He carried a solid hundred and eighty pounds on a five-and-a-half-foot frame. He was twenty-two. "Any other sports?" asked Barton.

"Judo."

"Gee. Maybe you can teach me a trick."

"Didn't think you liked Jap stuff, Barton."

"Not really. But I'm *ni-don* in judo. Maybe we can play a little one of these days."

"Anytime."

Barton looked at Sakai. He was a tiny, wiry man about thirty years old with the somber reserve of an undertaker. "You, Shorty, what did you study?"

"I majored in physics."

"Physics?" Barton snorted. "That's something you take when you're constipated."

"Nice to find a man who understands the subject," Sakai muttered.

"What's your alma mater?"

"U.C.L.A."

"Another West Coast school." Barton feigned shock. "I think you boys are infiltrating. That's a Jap favorite. Get inside the other guy's camp and get him when he's asleep."

"So don't sleep, Barton," said Endo with a mean grin.

Barton winked at him. "But of course, there's the Perfesser here. Big man back east at Yale. They got lots of cute tootsies at Yale, Perfesser?"

"It's a men's school."

"Oooh. Lots of pretty boys, then. They hold hands?"

"About the same as in the Marine Corps."

Barton lifted an eyebrow. "You suggesting the marines are pretty boys, Perfesser?"

"I'm suggesting that the Marine Corps is all male — like Yale."

"Depends what you call 'male.' " Barton sipped his coffee. "Since you're the Japanese culture expert, Perfesser, you must know the martial arts."

"Sorry. Never had time for it."

"Too bad. We could go a couple of falls."

"Let him alone, Barton," Endo said testily. "I trained in kendo and judo, both. Be glad to work out with you."

"Calm down, Fireplug." Barton's smile suddenly turned friendly. "I know your type. You're too tough for me, kid. I need something Yale-size."

"Lay off, Barton," said Sakai.

"It's okay," said Marumoto. "Barton just can't stand civilians."

The marine grunted and nodded. "That's the size of it, Perfesser. Civilians make trouble. Like that old geezer we're shipping with. Borovitch."

"Pronounced Bo-ROW-vitch," said Sakai, faking the old man's accent.

"Yeah, a civilian. It's always some crazy civilian — a politician. Or a culture guy like you, Perfesser. Or a religious nut. Or a salesman. They all get us deep in the foo and they never know how to get us out."

35

3

I

At 1000 hours Hunley took *Grayfish* to the surface for a training session. No breeze stirred the tropical air, except the throbbing forward motion of the submarine. The sea was glassy calm. Once lookouts were posted, Hara's men and McGlynn gathered in a semicircle around Barton on the narrow foredeck of *Grayfish*. To Hunley and Krag, on the conning tower, it looked like a story hour at a boy's camp. On the afterdeck Borovitch sat in the shade of the conning tower, studying papers and books. Except for the lookouts, Hunley had ordered his own crew to stay below to keep out of the way of Barton's tutorial.

The sergeant, wearing a brace of ammunition pouches, fondled a light machine gun. "This here's a Bren gun. It looks and acts like a Japanese Type 99 light machine gun, better known as the Nambu. Any of you ever use one of these? No, didn't think so. Any of you trained on B.A.R.?"

"I had it in Army basic."

"Army!" Barton's contempt showed. "What's your name again?"

"Endo."

"You were the halfback at U.S.C., right?"

"Until I volunteered for Army intelligence."

"Anybody that volunteers for the Army deserves anything

37

he gets. Okay, Endo. I suppose Army basic is better than a kick in the ass. What they tell you about firing an automatic weapon?"

"You fire it in bursts of three."

"Why?"

"So you can keep your point of aim on target."

"Right! You must have had a Marine instructor, Endo. Army don't make lessons like that sink in."

In spite of himself, Endo liked the back-handed compliment. Barton held up a finger.

"First rule of firing a fully automatic weapon: keep a light trigger finger. Fire in bursts of three. Like the halfback said, it helps you maintain your point of aim. It also keeps the barrel from getting overheated."

Barton held the Bren gun out in front of him with one hand and pointed with the other.

"This here is a British Mark 4 Bren gun. It's a gas-operated, selective fire, clip-fed weapon. Each clip holds thirty rounds, but always underload your clip by a couple of rounds. It feeds better. This particular piece is chambered for the British caliber .303 cartridge. It's similar to our 30-06 ammo, but the rounds aren't interchangeable. Don't load U.S. ammo into this piece and don't load it with any of that Arisaka ammo you've got. Fortunately, we've got a few thousand rounds of the British stuff to practice with and use when we need it. Questions so far?"

"What's 'selective fire' mean?" asked Marumoto.

Barton gave him a pitying look. "Perfesser, selective fire means you can throw this switch here on the receiver" — he pointed — "and set this piece to fire only one shot for each squeeze of the trigger. Or set it to fire full automatic, which means the weapon fires as long as you keep squeezing the trigger and there's ammo in the clip. But don't never do that. Can Yale men count to three?"

Marumoto nodded.

"Wonderful! In Jap we say *ichi, ni, san*. Remember that?"

"What's that turkey weigh?" asked Sakai. The Bren gun

38

looked larger than him.

"Unloaded, it weighs 19 pounds. And your name again is. . .?"

"Sakai."

"Let's see, you're the Navy C.P.O."

"Right."

"Don't worry, Sakai. We'll get one of the bigger guys to lug it. But you might get to operate it." He looked around at their faces. "We'll all get a chance. Basically, you fire this piece from a prone position. If you have to fire while you're upright, fire from the hip. Cradle this piece, like so. Don't try to fire from the shoulder, you'll just spray the treetops."

Barton removed a loaded clip from his ammunition pouch. "To fire the Bren gun. . ."

Up on the conning tower Krag looked away from the gun class toward the horizon. "I just hope to hell our own planes or subs aren't around here."

Hunley, studying the sea through binoculars, asked why.

"They see Hara's boys and we've got a problem."

"No problem. Our subs have been sent out of the neighborhood. The closest U.S. planes are at Midway, way back. Out of range."

"What about Jap planes and subs?"

"This isn't their regular sub patrol area. And their planes are out of range, too. So, right now, we take our chances. Soon's the batteries are charged up, we go under until dark."

"Thought you didn't like running underneath."

"I think it's prudent from now on during daylight. It'll slow us down, but the closer we get to Japan, the dicier it gets."

"Can't argue that."

On the foredeck Barton threw an empty gallon can overboard. He waited until it drifted fifty yards abaft in the wake, then fired a burst of three from the hip. The shots knocked the can up in the air and pierced it.

"Okay," said Barton, "everybody gets a crack at this, only prone. Endo, show 'em how it's done."

"Knows his work," said Hunley.

"I hope the lessons stick. We might need those guns."

"Think so? I get the impression we're supposed to go skulking in, do the job, and get out."

"Guess we'll find out. Isn't that tonight's seminar?"

"So McGlynn says."

"What you make of him?"

"Like a lot of guys with no line experience, he thinks things work according to The Book and The Plan. Aside from that misperception, I guess he's okay."

The firing practice session underway, Barton swung up the conning tower ladder.

"You got to think like a Jap," he said.

"What?" said Hunley.

"I said you gotta think like a Jap. Look at those guys on the Bren gun. They'd fool anybody. They think Jap."

"I told you before, Barton. While you're on this vessel, keep your views to yourself."

"Relax, Hunley. In the jungle you learn to think the way they think. Then you keep a step ahead of 'em...or out of sight. Same thing here."

On the deck below, the Bren gun thudded four times.

"Three!" Barton bellowed. "Burst of three, dammit!"

II

After lunch in the wardroom, Marumoto brought out a ruled board and black and white stones for a game of go. "Who wants to play?" he invited.

"My game's football," said Endo. "But if anybody's interested in some friendly poker, I'm ready. We're setting up in the forward torpedo room."

"Hara?"

"No thanks, Professor, I never could figure that game out."

"I'll play," said Barton.

It surprised Marumoto. "You know how?"

"Yeah, I can manage a country version."

Marumoto extended his fists, a black stone in one, white in the other. "Choose."

"Right hand."

"Black."

"Story of my life."

The game proceeded at its usual crawl.

"This is like watching water evaporate," said Krag.

"So play poker with the boys in the back room," said Barton. "Go is for us zen fans."

"How come you know these things?" asked Marumoto.

"I did an embassy tour in Tokyo."

"Then you know Japan pretty well."

"Nobody knows Japan, Perfesser. Not even the Japanese."

Marumoto chuckled. "That just proves what I said: you know Japan well because you know what the Japanese know, namely, that nobody knows."

"That sounds about right." Barton slapped down a black stone.

Marumoto studied the board. Barton certainly was not a master of the game, but he was no novice, either.

"I hope you don't mind my saying so, Sergeant, but you seem to have absorbed a lot of Japanese culture despite your antipathy."

"Yeah? Is that what it is? What do you tell 'em at Yale about Japanese culture?"

Marumoto shrugged. "I suppose you'd say the usual things. I teach several courses. One centers on the social history of the country. Several language courses, beginner through more or less advanced..."

"Teach 'em about bayonetting prisoners?"

Marumoto sighed. "I thought we were past that, Barton."

"I'll never get past it, Perfesser. I guess that's the difference between Yale and the Marine Corps. Or maybe the difference between war and the Ivy League."

"Yes. There's a difference. There's always been a difference between the jungle and civilization. The tide goes back and

41

forth. Sometimes the jungle's ahead, sometimes civilization is on top."

"That's it, huh?"

"Sort of. Culture slides around between the two."

"You know something, Perfesser?"

"What?"

"I'm grateful to have been exposed to Japanese language and culture."

Marumoto was surprised. "Why?"

"It saved my life."

"How?"

"Because when I was ordered — *ordered*, mind you — to surrender, I was able to understand what was going to happen. I knew what the guards were saying, but I didn't let on that I knew."

"Probably the wise thing to do."

"They had a little group of us herded up on a trail." Barton slapped down another stone. "It was getting dark. I got close to a guard and called to him in Japanese. In the shadows he thinks I'm another guard, so he came over.

"I dealt him a little Japanese culture. I gave him this —" Barton chopped the air with the edge of his hand. "Broke his neck. Quick and clean. Textbook. Just like in the martial arts class." Barton slapped down another stone. "He didn't make a sound. I held him up like we were talking. Problem was the other marines were thirty feet from me and there were other guards between us. I couldn't get the word to them." Barton's expression turned bleak. "So I took the guard's rifle and lit out. They got off a couple of shots after me, but I was away in the dark." He shrugged. "After a couple of days in the jungle I made contact with Krag. Now I'm here."

"You were lucky."

"Yeah, but not the other guys."

Marumoto suspected the rest of the story, but he had to know. "What happened to them?"

"The Japs bayonetted them, Perfesser. Over and over."

42

Marumoto thought he detected a tear in Barton's eye. "Culture, Perfesser. It helps you get through, right?"

III

It was a six-hand game joined by *Grayfish* crewmen. They had spread a blanket across a row of ammunition boxes. They used washers for chips.

"What's your game, Slim?" asked Endo.

"Seven-card, nothing wild. Two winners. Ante up."

"You're singin' my song," said Fujimura.

"That's it, kid. Run up the pot so daddy can have an extra payday."

"In a pig's keester."

"You played ball for U.S.C., didn't you?" Slim asked Endo.

"One varsity season before Pearl Harbor."

"Ace bets. Is it true they pay off the players over there with cars and girls?"

"Raise it a quarter. If they do, my name must have fallen off the list. That kind of propaganda comes out of U.C.L.A. They're all fags over there."

"Think you'll go back to playing when this crap is over?"

"Maybe. You betting, Fuj, or are you going to sit there with your finger up your ass?"

"I'm thinkin', I'm thinkin'."

"Man wants to go home rich," said another crewman. "That ain't fair."

"I'm just a poor little steelworker from Seattle and I need food for the table. I'll kick it a quarter."

"Listen to that shit. I see right through you," said Slim. "I got X-ray eyes like Superman. You're bluffing."

"You talkin' or bettin'?" Fujimura grinned.

"I'm in a nest of thieves. I'll call."

Krag came in. "Who's winning?"

"Riverboat Endo, who else? How's the go bowl going?"

43

"They're still in the ritual warm-up. That'll take another eight or ten hours, then they'll move into the fast action with a play every twenty minutes or so."

"Never could get with that game," Sakai muttered. He tossed some washers on the blanket. "Up yours, Fuj."

"Back at you, buddy." More washers bounced.

Krag smiled to himself. Good poker made a good team.

IV

At 2000 hours the group assembled in the wardroom.

"Time to brief you on the next phase and talk geography," said McGlynn. He went to a covered object at the end of the table and shoved it to the middle. He pulled off the cover. They saw a three-dimensional diorama of a town, its harbor, and surrounding hills.

"Ringo. This gives you a birds-eye view of the town, the coast, the terrain around it, the roads, and over here, a couple of miles away on the road out of town, Steel Mill One." He tapped a little block representing the mill. He pointed to lines representing railroad tracks. "The mill's where it is because of this rail line. The railroad parallels the coast and leads north to Niigata. That's where they ship in the raw iron from Manchuria. But that's outside of our mission."

Krag studied the diorama. "Rugged country."

"Like Mindanao," Barton added.

"Pine forest instead of jungle," said McGlynn. "Not much to hide in."

"Better cover in woods and hills than in grass and plains," said Krag.

"Garrisons?" asked Barton.

"You'll have to be alert for some kind of police or military presence," said McGlynn. "Patrols. Probably not much. Anything's possible, but in practical terms, it's unlikely. There's no army or navy base in the region. The town's not a commercial port. Just a fishing village. That means there's no reason for them to mine the harbor."

The word "mine" sent a chill up Hunley's spine. "But you don't know," he said.

"No. But we think it's safe." McGlynn unrolled a large chart. "According to this chart the waters leading into the harbor are around fifty fathoms up to within two hundred yards of shore."

"Whose chart?" asked Hunley.

"Old Japanese chart. We think it's reliable."

Hunley stood and leaned over the chart. "May I look?"

"Sure." McGlynn fingered the contour lines. "Anyway, on arrival Hunley'll take *Grayfish* into the harbor. . ."

Hunley interrupted. "How old's this chart?"

"Well, matter of fact," said McGlynn, "it's Russo-Japanese War vintage, around 1905. But there's no reason to think there's been any material change in the. . ."

Hunley was aghast. "You want me to take a submarine — *my* submarine — into *this* harbor using a forty-year-old chart?"

"It's the best we could get."

"The hell you say!" growled Hunley. "Look at that bottom! Looks like a hacksaw. What with earthquakes, wrecks, and God knows what else, it could have changed totally in thirty, forty years. They don't need mines."

McGlynn lifted an eyebrow. "What's the bottom got to do with it?"

"Look at it, for Christ's sake! It's treacherous. Why a submerged boat. . ."

"Who said submerged?" McGlynn asked innocently.

Krag smelled a rat. "Surfaced?"

"Right."

"*Surfaced?*" Hunley gasped. "You telling me an American sub is going to cruise into a Japanese harbor on the surface?"

McGlynn looked smug. "Exactly! Right up to the pier."

"It's nuts!" said Hunley.

"No," said McGlynn, "it's the best way."

Hunley looked at Krag. "Remember what I said about line

experience?"

"Yeah." Krag tapped his temple with his forefinger.

"It'll work, Hunley," said McGlynn.

"Convince me."

"This is how we'll do it." McGlynn pulled a large three-ring binder from his briefcase and opened it up to line drawings of two submarines. "The lines of *Grayfish* are nearly identical to the Japanese K-5 class boat. See, Hunley? The K-5 has its deck gun forward of the conning tower. That's why we moved your deck gun forward, to make it look more like a K-5."

"That explains that part of it, anyhow," said Hunley.

"Actually," McGlynn went on, "the K-5s are a little smaller, 950 tons surface displacement against our 1,500 tons. . ."

"A *little* smaller," Hunley said sarcastically. "The Jap boat's a good third smaller."

"In the water they look the same. Believe me. We studied these lines side-by-side. The look is identical to *Grayfish*. Of course, we have to do some more disguising."

"What we need," said Krag, "is the Power To Cloud Men's Minds, like The Shadow."

McGlynn ignored him. "Intelligence has given us identifying codes and markings for the conning tower and deck. That's why we stowed all that paint, Hunley, in case you were wondering. Japanese navy ensign, numbers, some kanji characters, and we'll go right through."

Hunley shook his head. "Their patrol boats have identity kits. If they're doing their job, they'll check out our I.D. and markings."

"We've covered that," McGlynn said smoothly. "We'll use the identity of a Nip sub that we nailed off New Guinea about three weeks ago, the RO-76. To them it's overdue. They don't know it's down."

"Yeah?" Hunley said skeptically.

"What about recognition signals?" asked Krag.

McGlynn smiled. "Submarines coming back from patrol don't use 'em. They're almost always on radio silence. Am I right,

Hunley?"

"That's right, but by the time we get there, they might wonder how come their ship's coming in so late."

"The Jap sub was based in Rabaul. Not likely the home islands would have any word on it. Do you think one of our overdue subs gets reported to Naval Operations in Washington before a lot of the year's gone by. Hell no!"

"They do look alike," said Hara, studying the diagrams.

"Only an experienced submarine man looking for spooks could tell *Grayfish* isn't the real thing," said McGlynn.

"Why didn't you tell me earlier?" Hunley asked. "We could have done all this painting at Pearl Harbor."

"Security. That's why you're only learning about it now. We don't know who the hell's watching Pearl. They see a U.S. sub being rigged out as a Jap K-5 and we tip our hand. Too risky. Besides, there's too much threat from our own units. Hell, they see Japanese markings and they shoot."

Hunley looked grim. "Okay. So we sail along merrily looking like a Jap K-5. What about dealing with patrol craft if they hail us?"

McGlynn nodded toward Hara. "That's your department."

"Whenever we're surfaced in Japanese waters, I'll be on the conning tower. My boys and I've got a routine worked out."

"Suppose they want to board?" asked Krag.

"No dice," said Hara. "My boys'll be on the deck gun. We've trained on guns like it. If they make a stink, we shoot it out right there."

"Jap eats Jap," said Barton.

"None of that, Barton!" Hunley snapped. "We've got enough problems dealing with this half-assed plan."

"It's not half-assed. This mission wasn't dreamed up by fools, Hunley," said McGlynn.

"Yeah?"

The intelligence officer stared coldly, then said, "I think we should get to work on the disguise. Now."

Grayfish broached under a star-filled tropic sky. There was only a hangnail moon, but it and the reflected light of the Pacific sky were enough to work by. Hunley's crew assisted Hara's squad in painting prominent Rising Sun flags on both sides of the conning tower and on the foredeck. McGlynn supervised from an instruction manual prepared by the Office of Naval Intelligence. Hara and former Professor Marumoto made sure the Japanese kanji characters were correct. The work proceeded without incident. It took them less than three hours. The paint was a quick-drying type. It wouldn't withstand regular naval service but would be more than adequate for the job at hand. When it was done, Hunley, Hara, Krag, and McGlynn walked around to inspect the work.

"Ironic," said Hunley. "I raise hell to get my own sub command to sink Jap flags and..." He laughed and waved his hand at the Rising Sun decorating the conning tower.

"What do those characters say, Hara?" asked Krag.

"Well, those big characters are the ship's designation. The little ones are the name."

"Interesting," said Hunley. "And what's the Japanese name *Grayfish* is wearing?"

"The *Sacred Blossom.*"

"Blossom? My ship's a flower?"

"Sorry," said Hara.

"Had to stick to the script," said McGlynn. "It was the name of the K-5 we got in New Guinea."

"They'll never win the war naming their ships for flowers," said Hunley.

V

The landing party was clustered around the diorama of Ringo. "Getting ashore might be the easiest part of the whole trip," Krag said. He pointed to the town's long pier. "Doc Borovitch says this is a heavy-duty pier designed for trawlers, but the chart indicates the water's not deep enough for the draft of this submarine at low tide. We don't have tide information on the harbor.

So while it's still daylight — approximately 1800 hours — Hunley's going to run *Grayfish* up as close as possible without getting stuck on the bottom."

Krag grinned at them. "Then, with balls of purest brass, we eagerly put our inflatable landing boats over the side. These are the kind you have to paddle. The inflatables with the little motors come later. We stow all our gear, our guns, and the explosives. As you know, the explosives are packed in four carts, each carrying a hundred and twenty-five pounds of blocks, plus our fuzes and primacord. Once we get all that cargo in the boats, we make for the dock."

"Will Hunley's men cover us going in?"

"No. Can't risk having American faces on the guns. Hunley will be on the bridge to bring the sub in and to watch as we go in, but we're going to disguise him a little — dark glasses, Jap hat."

"What happens if they start shooting?" asked Endo.

"Back-paddle like hell, Halfback! Hope to hell you can get below without getting hit. But don't count on it. Hunley, McGlynn, and I have agreed that the whole mission depends on deception.

"If they're on to us going in, we might as well go home. So everybody's got to play his role like Lionel Barrymore, not like John Wayne. This ain't a suicide mission. Understood?"

The others murmured assent.

"Okay, once ashore, we find the local police station or whatever guard house they've got. Hara's got plenty of fake papers testifying who he and the rest of us are. In the case of me and Barton, that's fake Army Air Corps I.D., some maps of China, and so on.

"Once we've made contact with the local authorities, Hara will requisition a vehicle or two — a truck, we hope — that supposedly is to transport me and Barton to Yokosuka for grilling by Japanese Naval Intelligence. It's a plausible yarn. We all work to make 'em buy it. That means, if you have to, you slap, kick, or punch me or Barton. If someone else, especially one of them does it, let 'em alone." Krag lifted his eyebrows. "Within reason, of course. We can't help if our bones are broken."

"What if the authorities refuse the vehicles? Or they don't have any?" Endo asked.

Hara answered. "If they have the vehicles, it's unlikely they'll refuse, assuming they buy our yarn. As long as my papers look okay and I sign all kinds of receipts, they'll cooperate. Right, Professor?"

"That's right," said Marumoto. "Procedure — bureaucracy — is everything. If we can make them believe the cover story, the rest is paperwork. Once Hara's signed and sealed his immortal soul away on the right paper, it'll be okay."

"Gotta think like a Jap," Barton muttered.

"Lay off that 'Jap' stuff, Barton," Hara snapped.

"Ask the Perfesser," Barton protested. "Am I right?"

Marumoto glared and nodded. "You've got to think Japanese."

"Okay, okay." Krag resumed. "In the event there are no vehicles, then we just have to tell the locals that we're going to hike east to the railroad — which is where we want to go anyway — and flag a train. That problem was anticipated by McGlynn and the other intelligence guys. That's why we've got those handy demo carts. Nobody has to carry five hundred pounds of TNT."

"Bless you, Naval Intelligence, for being so intelligent," said Toda.

"You mean for being so out-of-character," said Hara.

"Pay attention," said Krag. "Now, either by vehicle or by foot, we make the couple of miles to Plant One. By now it's getting dark. We wait until full darkness and then make our approach via the main gate. We don't know what the guard situation will be. It could be nobody. It could be civilian security. It could be army. Whoever's there, we don't look for more than one or two. We'll cover the entry process when we get there.

"We'll work later on the details of the job we have to do inside. But, for now, we assume we get that done the way we're supposed to. Once the charges are set, we have to get the hell out and

50

back to shore before she blows."

"Is *Grayfish* going to stay parked offshore from Ringo?" asked Endo.

"No," Krag replied. "As far as the townspeople are concerned, *Grayfish* is going back to sea. Actually, she's going out, lie low, then come back to get us later at another place."

"Why that way?" asked Fujimura.

McGlynn explained. "Part of our scam — if it works — is to leave the Japanese wondering how the hell it happened. Ideally, they'll not link Krag, Barton, Hara, and you boys to the explosions. At least not until there's some kind of detailed investigation."

"Why bother, once we get the target?" asked Barton.

"Because if it clicks," said McGlynn, "we might want to try it again sometime, somehow. Of course, at some point the realization will dawn on them that they've been infiltrated cleverly by people who look and talk and act Japanese as well as they do. Only they're enemies."

"Damn scary for them," Marumoto added.

"Why's that, Perfesser?" asked Barton.

"Goes deep into Japanese cultural psychology. Most of them, especially the young ones who've grown up during the rule of the militarists, are inculcated with the idea that they're unique. There's a powerful and nurtured sense of superiority and national pride — *Yamato minzoku*. All other peoples are inferiors. Implicit in this idea, if you're a native-born Japanese today, is the notion that there could be no such thing as a counterfeit Japanese — they believe they'd recognize one right away as a fake. So if we counterfeits go in there and fool them, we upset that idea. Once their own investigation smokes out what's really happened, they have to start looking for spooks in a way they never did before. Ever."

"So what?" said Hunley.

Marumoto smiled sardonically. "If you turn over one of their basic ideas, you'd give 'em a very, very bad shock. The effect would be better than a couple of Doolittle raids."

"Sounds far-fetched," said Krag.

"Of course it does to us Americans," said Marumoto. "We haven't been living in a closed island society for two thousand years. Our parents or grandparents or whatever all came from somewhere else. We take it as a matter of course that none of us is anything special by birth. Just lucky."

Krag laughed. "Lucky? Us?"

"The ones back home."

"Meanwhile," said Marumoto, "it's a good idea to leave 'em confused and wondering. It cramps their style."

Krag nodded. "Thanks, Perfesser. That's a little extra incentive to make this thing work."

"Staying alive's the biggest," said Marumoto.

"Right. And that brings me to the getaway. We're not going out the way we came. Instead, we drive — if we have a vehicle — back to the coast on this trail." Krag pointed out a route along the coast north of Ringo. "Without a vehicle, we'll have to jog. I hope you guys are in shape. At this cove" — he indicated a sharp notch in the coastline — "we meet McGlynn on the beach where Hunley will have parked him. He'll have the remaining inflatable boats. The ones with the motors. He fires a signal flare. *Grayfish* surfaces, picks us up. Then we go home. The proverbial piece of cake — a believable plan."

Krag looked around at them. He didn't see a flicker of belief.

VI

Grayfish idled on an empty sea while the landing party practiced hauling two of the rubber boats up on the narrow deck and loading them. It was no easy task. Though the sea was calm under a sky full of thunderheads, there was a light, persistent, and troublesome swell. The round sides of the vessel weren't designed for surface work. The trick for the Nisei was to keep from sliding feet first into the sea. The explosives carts were awkward and had to be manipulated with lines. They used submarine scrap for weight rather than risk their supply of TNT.

They agreed that it took too much time to take both boats out the forward hatch. So when the landing was made, they'd take one boat through the conning tower hatch and the other through the forward hatch.

Neither Krag nor Barton could assist. As "prisoners" their hands would be bound during the actual landing. So they laughed and jibed at the occasional splash into the sea by one or another of the landing group. Despite that, the group soon mastered some tricks for loading the bobbing boats, such as lashing them tightly with lines fore and aft while the loading went ahead, learning how to board and how to sit.

Practicing a boarding maneuver, Hara went into the sea. Krag tossed him a line and hauled him up on the deck.

"Don't worry. Intelligence says it'll be easier in Ringo harbor. Barring a typhoon — which is highly unlikely — there won't be any swells or waves."

Hara shook himself like a dog. "Let's hope intelligence knows what it's talking about. Damn! That water's cold! I thought we're in the tropics."

"Not exactly. We're well north of the equator by now. Probably running through a cold spot."

"You're telling me."

"Calm or not, I want more lines over the side when we land. That round hull's treacherous."

"Agreed. And I think it might be smart to take a coil of line ashore with us, just in case."

"Good idea." Krag grinned. "If the deal goes sour, I can hang myself."

"Not to worry," said Hara. "They'll do it for you."

VII

"Where do you come from, sailor?" Marumoto asked sharply in Japanese.

"Yamaguchi *ken*," Sakai answered.

"Oh? I am from Yamaguchi myself. Where do you live?"

"My family has left there. They live in Osaka now."

"Yes, but where is your family *from?*"

Sakai looked blank.

Marumoto sighed. "Make up a place," he said in English.

"Agano," said Sakai.

Marumoto switched back to Japanese. "Never heard of it."

"Of course not. It is such a small place that there was not room for me. So I joined the navy."

"Excellent!" Marumoto beamed. "A joke's a good touch. All of you: keep the conversation bantering. Smile like hell. Even if you're tight as a drum, look relaxed, but don't look 'American' relaxed. Nod your head a lot when you talk. Know what I mean? You've all seen your folks doing it. Now, Sakai, if you can work on that San Fernando Valley accent, you might get by."

"You think they might grill us that hard, Professor?" asked Fujimura.

"Don't let yourself be grilled. Turn it around. Get *them* talking. Ask to see pictures, that kind of stuff. And those accents" — he shook his head — "they stand out like spotlights to me." He looked over at Barton, who was sipping coffee and watching from a corner of the wardroom. "Do they hit you that way, Sergeant?"

Barton shrugged. "Not solo, but when you get a chorus of guys standing around who all talk the same way, it might make somebody curious. Especially an officer."

"Why not a cover story?" asked Hara. "We could say our crew was all recruited in southern Honshu. Special volunteers."

"Good idea," said Marumoto.

"Makes sense," said Barton. "But the main thing is don't get in that kind of a box. If they catch you, they'll cut off your balls and stuff 'em in your mouths no matter what kind of accent you got."

VIII

It was Barton's turn to lecture.

"Demolitions," he said. "I know you've had the course, but

54

we're going to repeat the basics. After that we'll repeat 'em again. But first" — he held up a miner's helmet with a lamp attached — "Perfesser, what do you think this is?"

"Miner's helmet."

"Very good, Perfesser. Mr. Toda, why do you think I am showing you a miner's helmet?"

"To cast some light on the subject?"

Everybody laughed.

"Mr. Toda aspires to the Fred Allen Show. Unfortunately, he doesn't know what's going on. Halfback Endo, tell 'em the news."

Endo shook his head. "You got me, Sarge."

Barton looked around balefully. "This hat is the symbol of an important fact we all have to deal with. Darkness. The fact is that it will be dark inside the mill. You can't do your work and hold a flashlight at the same time. Each man will get one of these sombreros with this neat little string attached to keep it from falling off your big, fat heads. You'll also have a flashlight. If you want to, you can hold it in your buck teeth." He reached into a carton and passed out the helmets. "Everybody got a party hat? Great." He switched on his lamp and put his helmet on. "Okay, Sakai, douse the lights."

At first there was only Barton's beam in the blackness, then others appeared.

"You guys learn fast. Amazing."

In the crossing beams, Barton piled dozens of dummy demolition blocks and fuze on the wardroom table. "Okay, this is the way we're going to practice our demo work because this is the way we're going to have to do it."

IX

Twelve hours later they were running two hundred feet below the surface. At that depth there was no sensation of being at sea, or even of motion. The electric motors hummed in near silence, a welcome relief from the throb of diesels. The air inside

55

was chilled and clammy, responding to the abyss around them, one of cold and eternal night. In the tiny chart room Krag and Hara huddled around Hunley and McGlynn.

Crawford, the *Grayfish* navigation officer, presided at the chart table. They studied the anatomy of the coastal waters of southern Japan.

"My sailing instructions are to cruise west until McGlynn's secret orders say otherwise," said Hunley.

"Unfortunately, those orders have given us only the vaguest directions for getting around Honshu and up the west side into Ringo. I'm new to this particular part of the world, so I'm open to suggestions."

"If we hold our present course, we'll enter the Inland Sea about here," said Crawford. "This is the Bungo Strait between Shikoku here to the northeast and Kyushu to the southwest." He pointed with his calipers.

"Exit in the west is past their Inland Sea naval bases, here, through Shimonoseki Strait. That takes us into Tsushima Strait. It runs south-to-north between Tsushima Island and Honshu. Then up the slot to here" — he indicated a point on the Honshu west coast — "between Cape Suzu, north of Kanazawa, and Cape Kyoga, south of Wakasa Bay. Ringo is here. On paper, the Inland Sea route is the shortest way."

"McGlynn, you're the intelligence boss," said Krag. "What's the skinny on going through the Inland Sea?"

"They sent me some stuff before we sailed." McGlynn rummaged in his briefcase and found a file. He handed it to Hunley, who riffled through sheets bearing the red TOP SECRET stamp until he found one that had the information. He studied it for a minute, then looked up.

"I won't read all this crap to you, but the essence of it is that the Inland Sea has a number of active naval installations, it might have some mine fields, though there weren't any as of last November. It carries heavy local traffic, and it's shallow.

"Also, there's a lot of small craft in there — local fishing boats, patrol craft, aircraft, occasional major warship. Strikes me that there's a lot people there that could spot something out of the ordinary."

"But we look like a Japanese sub," said McGlynn. "Who's going to know the difference. That's the whole idea."

"I don't like it," said Hunley. "On the surface, the more eyes, the more gets seen. Nor do we want to risk a run through there submerged all the time."

"Why?" asked McGlynn.

"Nine months is plenty of time to get mine fields laid, for one thing," said Hunley.

"For another reason, navigation. Our inertial navigation system is good enough at sea," Crawford interjected, "but we can't really rely on it in tricky waters like the Inland Sea. No room for error. Coast is too rugged, and the bottom's too rough."

"I buy that," said Krag. "But what's the option?"

They all studied the chart a moment.

"Let's do the opposite," said Hara. "Instead of the short way, take the long way around." He brushed the chart. "Go south around Kyushu."

"That'd take us through the Van Diemen Strait between Kyushu and Tanega Island," said Crawford. "I have charts for that water. It's an old shipping lane."

Hunley pointed locations on the main chart. "Okay, that takes us by Kyushu and Kagoshima Bay on the south into the China Sea."

"Right," said Crawford, "then we could cut north, run up the west side of Kyushu and on into the Tsushima Strait."

"Looks good to me," said Hunley. "How much extra time is that?"

Crawford shrugged. "If we can make surface time, I'd say an extra forty-eight to fifty-two hours. Underwater, longer."

McGlynn shook his head. "It adds too much time to the trip."

"Getting sunk would add a lot more days to the trip," said Hunley.

"Every hour we add is one hour closer they get to building a jet engine," McGlynn observed.

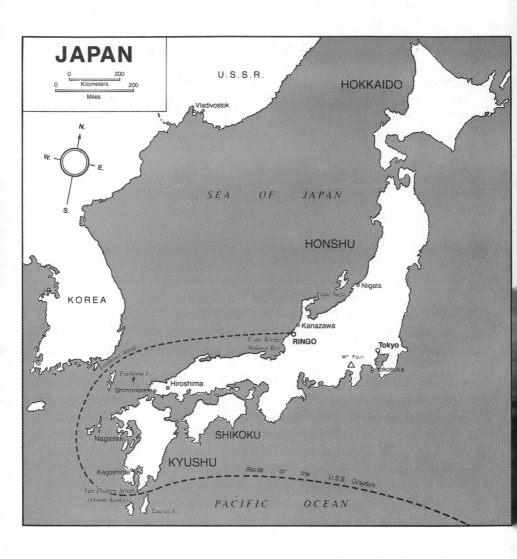

58

"More important to get there whole than to get there fast," said Krag. "I think maybe Hara's got the right idea. McGlynn, what do your intelligence notes have on the Tsushima Strait?"

The intelligence officer found a data sheet with a chart stapled to it. He read it quickly. "Looks pretty good. Lot of commercial traffic, but that should help cover us. Also, this time of year they get a lot of fog in there."

"All the better for us," said Hunley.

"May I see the chart?" asked Crawford. McGlynn handed it back to him. He squinted at it closely. "Good deep channel, Skipper. No problems with the water."

"But the time, dammit, the time!" McGlynn exclaimed.

"We're talking an extra fifty, fifty-five hours at most," said Hunley. "Taking the Kyushu route we can run on the surface more. Going through the Inland Sea we'd have to be traveling underneath and less than half as fast."

"He's right, McGlynn," said Krag. "You're outvoted."

"Okay." McGlynn smiled ruefully. "I'm outvoted. Navy's getting democratic. Just when I can't use it."

"Okay," said Hunley. "Now that we've got that settled, I think it's time to go on the air." He switched on the speaker system. "Now hear this! This is the Captain. About now we're getting into Japanese water. That means that every time we surface, only Commander Hara's men will go topside. They will man the lookouts, dressed in appropriate Japanese naval gear.

"*Grayfish* crew will go topside only on direct order from me or the executive officer and then only at night. Ship's officers and other officers, except myself and Commander Hara, will restrict themselves to the bridge. That's all." He looked at Crawford. "What's our approximate location now?"

"Five hundred and ten miles east of Shikoku and closing."

"Very well."

X

After dark Hunley surfaced to give his crew some fresh air. Krag and Barton went to the stern. They were in warm seas here.

and Barton went to the stern. They were in warm seas here. The wake tumbled and glowed with phosphorescence.

"What do you think of our team?" Krag asked.

"I think they can make the scam work okay. If it comes to fighting, I don't know."

"What's the problem?"

"No problem. Just some little nags. And we won't know until we get on the job whether they're problems or not."

"Give me an example."

"Take the Perfesser. Smart guy and all that, but I don't know about his guts."

"You think he might take a dive?"

"No, he'll do the demo work. But if it comes to a showdown, I don't know whether he has the brass for killing. Some people don't. Simple as that."

"We can watch him. How about the others?"

"Sakai's too little. Gutsy enough, but Christ he's only four feet high."

"He's bigger than that."

"Not much."

"He can pull a trigger, Max. What's the real nag?"

"You know the nag. In the jungle we never left anyone behind, not even the dead, right?"

"Yeah."

"So if we have casualties and Sakai has to carry — see what I mean? He's not even big enough for the Bren gun."

Krag nodded. "We have to work around it. How about the others?"

"Hara's good. Endo would make a hell of a marine. Strong, tough kid. Toda's okay. Fujimura's maybe a little slow on the uptake. But he can cut it."

"How about you and me, Max?" He stretched out his hand and stared at it. "Nervous in the service?"

"At least I know you'll carry me if it comes to that."

"Not willingly. You're one heavy son of a bitch."

"Yeah, but you'd do it. It's like them movies: Krag and Barton,

60

together again."

"More like Laurel and Hardy. 'Well this is a fine mess you've gotten us into, Stanley,' " Krag mimicked.

Barton laughed. "Jesus, couldn't they make a great little movie out of this fandango?"

"Don't count us out, Max. The possibilities are endless."

4

The Van Diemen Strait, September 3, 1942

I

At 600 hours Hunley swung the periscope all the way around, studying the gray horizon. The sky was overcast. The ceiling was low, but visibility was good. In the near distance were some small Japanese fishing craft with their huge rear oars and high prows.

"Down periscope." He switched on the microphone. "Now hear this! Commander Hara and his men prepare for surface. Repeat. Commander Hara and his men prepare for surface. Commander Hara report to the control room when ready." He switched off the microphone and waited. Less than two minutes later Hara appeared in his Imperial Navy uniform. It was still startling to Hunley to see him appear through the hatch looking all too much like the enemy.

"Ready when you are, Skipper."

"Very well." He looked around at the bemused crewmen and his executive officer. "Here we go." He gave the orders to surface.

They came up in tropical heat that denied the wintry, leaden sky. A few large, soft drops fell. Hara and Hunley went to the bridge. Two of Hara's men scrambled awkwardly into the lookout positions. The rest of the squad gathered around the deck gun to practice.

"Enemy eyes are watching," Hara said. 'Better wear this." He handed Hunley a Japanese officer's duty cap. It was a dark blue peaked hat with a tapered crown like an army forage hat.

"It's too small," Hunley complained.

"One size fits all. Fiddle with those laces in back."

"I feel like a damn fool."

"Some periscope might be looking. They can't make out your face, but a U.S. officer's hat is nothing like theirs. Why chance it?"

"So, okay," Hunley grinned. "I'll wear the damn thing. I just hope none of the crew catches my act."

The sea was calm with a light swell.

"Could almost be a tour cruise. Painting class. Deck sports. Bren gun skeet," said Hara.

"You been to Japan?"

"Once. When I was thirteen."

"Touring?"

"The family was making noises about sending me to school over there. That wasn't on my personal agenda. So I spent a summer with relatives in Hiroshima."

"Where's that?"

"It's a seaport in southern Honshu."

"Oh yeah. I remember it from the chart. On the Inland Sea. Like it there?"

"It was fun in a kind of low-key way, but Japan wasn't for me. I managed to convince Mom and Pop that I'd be an embarrassment to the family in Japan. That was the end of that."

"Is there as much to this cultural difference between you and your guys and Japanese people as Marumoto says."

"Oh sure. He's not blowing smoke. Suppose, for example, during the Civil War you were an Alabama man trying to infiltrate a Boston regiment. Even if you got your accent polished just right, there'd be lots of other things — an expression, a phrase. You'd be useless without the right kind of coaching."

"That makes a lot of sense. I guess pale faces like mine figure anyone with parents like yours is an instant authority on Japan."

"That's why I wound up in O.N.I. The Navy figured my parents had taught me everything there was to know about Japan, along with the language."

"How do they feel about you being U.S. Navy?"

"Proud, I guess." Hara looked grim. "At the moment I'm sure they're more than a little bit confused."

"Where they living?"

"A place called Manzanar."

"Where's that."

"California."

"Nice town?"

"It's a concentration camp."

"Small towns are like that," Hunley laughed. "Come from one myself."

"No. I mean it really *is* a concentration camp."

"What're you talking about?"

"Don't you know what happened on the West Coast?"

"I haven't been stateside since the war started. What happened?"

"On the West Coast all the people of Japanese ancestry were rounded up and shipped to concentration camps. President Franklin Delano Roosevelt personally signed the order without batting an eye."

"You're kidding!"

"No. Wish I was kidding."

"They're citizens, aren't they?"

"It didn't make any difference. Citizen or not, everybody went."

"Everybody?"

"Everybody."

"That's nuts!"

"You're telling me."

"They didn't do it in Hawaii!" Hunley said. "Hell, half the people rebuilding our fleet at Pearl have Japanese parents or something."

Hara shrugged. "Maybe they just haven't gotten around to them yet."

"If they ship them out, the war'll stop." Hunley shook his head.

"Why?"

"Why what?"

"Why concentration camps?"

"Why? Because..." Hara shrugged again.

"Was there trouble of some kind?"

"No trouble at all. Even J. Edgar Hoover said there wasn't any spy activity in the Japanese-American communities. Made no difference. Off they went to the cages. Barbed wire, armed guards, the whole thing."

"Makes no sense."

"Your government and mine wants it that way, Hunley. They're very wise. There's an agenda someplace. Keep the Japanese-Americans working hard at Pearl Harbor on the frontline, but lock 'em up stateside, two thousand miles away from the action. You've got to roll with the plan."

"Yeah, or have it roll over you."

"Hell, look at me!" Hara laughed bitterly. "I'm off on a top-secret mission against Japan because I'm an American citizen who looks and talks Japanese. Meanwhile, my parents are behind barbed wire and bayonets for the same reason."

"Christ! And I'm commanding a submarine wearing the Rising Sun on my conning tower and flying the Japanese naval jack at the stern. Talk about irony. Iron men and irony."

"*Aircraft!*" Murray Sakai shouted. "Port side! Ten o'clock!"

"Fat's in the fire! Everybody stand to!" Hunley ordered.

"Now we find out how good we are," said Hara.

"Look sharp on those guns, Sakai!" Hunley turned to the bridge microphone. "Hear this! This is the Captain. A Japanese patrol plane is approaching. We should be able to fake 'em out. Sergeant Barton stand by in the radio room for contacts from the plane. That is all."

"Better get down, Hunley," said Hara. "They might be using glasses. They could make out your face."

"Right. Here, take mine."

"Ahoy, on deck!" Hara shouted. "Japanese aircraft coming!

66

Wave like hell!"

"Aye, aye, sir!" Toda called back.

Hunley squatted on his haunches, hidden behind the bridge bulkhead.

"Do they see us?"

"Sure do. And here she comes."

"What is it?"

"Single-engine float plane." Hara refocused the binoculars. "I think we've got a 'Jake' — an Aichi E-13."

The plane wore a sea camouflage pattern that virtually hid it against the leaden sky. It droned steadily toward them. The speaker rasped from below. "Barton to bridge."

"Bridge. This is Hara."

"Plane made contact. Acknowledged we're on radio silence."

"Very well." Hara switched off the mike. "That's a break," he said to Hunley.

"Yeah, I heard. Thank God for tiny favors."

The plane roared closer, then zoomed directly overhead at a hundred feet. It gained altitude, banked, then came around for another pass.

"Give 'em a *banzai*, dammit!" Hara shouted at his men.

Marumoto gave them the signal. As the plane approached, the Nisei men raised their arms overhead enthusiastically.

"*Bullshit!*" they yelled, raising their arms in the classic *banzai* gesture.

The plane zoomed closer, off the bow. They could see the pilot waving.

"*Bullshit!*" the crew shouted, arms flung overhead again. "*Bullshit!*"

The plane waggled its wings, then turned and disappeared over the horizon.

Hunley was choking with laughter and relief. "I hope to hell that son of a bitch can't read lips."

Hara was laughing, too. "I think we conned him. He was loaded for bear. If he hadn't bought the story, he'd have dumped an egg on us on the second pass."

Hunley pulled himself to his feet. "Only the first of many."
He picked up the bridge bullhorn. "Well done! Thanks!"

II

Tak Toda went below to retrieve a Bren gun for practice. Barton
was in the forward torpedo room dormitory playing solitaire.
"What kind of plane was it?" he asked, not looking up.
"Float plane. Single engine."
"Yeah, one of the little ones. They've got some big multi-engine
jobs, too."
"Guess it went okay. He was armed, but no attack."
"Yeah, on the radio the observer behind the pilot gave us the
big *ohayo go zai masu.*"
'For a guy who hates Japs, how come you know the lingo?"
"I had two years of embassy guard duty in Tokyo. I picked
up a little. Can't read it or write it, though."
Toda took the Bren gun from its case and two hundred rounds
of ammunition in bandoliers. "How'd you like Tokyo?"
"Liked it. Good duty. We were tailed by *kempeitai* agents all
the time, but no problems. And no war either. That was before
I went to China. Before the Philippines. Long time ago."
"So how come the vitriol about 'Japs' and me and the other
guys? The war?"
Barton looked up at him. He wore a half-smile that belied his
eyes. "You're an officer, right?"
"That's right. Ensign."
"Naval Academy?"
"No. Naval ROTC. University of Washington. That's in Seattle,
where I grew up."
"Many Japs live there?"
"A large community of Japanese-Americans. We don't call
ourselves 'Japs' and we don't like anybody else to do it either."
"Same thing."
"No, Sergeant. It's not."

"Okay." Barton laughed coldly. "Got a question for you?"

"Go ahead."

"When I was in Japan I thought, these are nice people. That's why I bothered to learn some of their language. Then I'm sent to China and I see the other side of the coin, the slaughter."

"What's the question?"

"What's in the Jap make-up that turns you into mad-dog rapists and butchers when you put on a uniform? Why do you insist on starving and torturing your prisoners? Killing babies? Burning villages for the hell of it? Do you learn that along with origami? Is butchery like making sashimi?"

Barton spoke softly, but the venom in his voice froze Toda.

"No answer, Mister Toda?" he pressed.

"I suppose there are lots of answers, Sergeant Barton. I'm not an expert on Japanese psychology. Why should I be? I'm not Japanese. But I'll tell you something. All the people on this submarine are Americans. All of us. Even Doc Borovitch. He volunteered. We didn't have to be asked. We didn't wait to be drafted. Whatever the behavior of the Imperial Army, Navy, or Marines is, that's not us any more than it's you or the U.S. Marine Corps. It's *them*. The enemy. If they get in our way, we'll cut 'em down. We'll cut 'em down just as fast as I'll cut you down if you get in my way on this mission."

"You will, huh?"

"And don't call me 'Jap' while I'm holding a Bren gun and ammo."

Barton stared hard at him, then suddenly laughed. "Son of a bitch."

"What's funny?"

"I like your style. You just might survive this thing." He tossed his head. "You better get topside with that gun before it rusts."

III

During machine gun drill, Hunley ran *Grayfish* on the surface.

69

By 1400 hours the overcast had burned away under a bright sun. Numerous small craft and trawlers were fishing the strait as if there were no war anywhere.

And, mused Hunley, why not? Except for Doolittle's Tokyo raid months before, the American enemy was no closer than a sand bar called Midway, two thousand miles to the east.

Once another patrol plane passed in the distance. Either it didn't see them or it ignored them. The world was at peace here. It worried Hunley. He called below.

"Bridge for McGlynn."

McGlynn came on the speaker. "McGlynn. What's up?"

"Why don't we have our mission briefing now instead of at 2000 hours? I'd prefer to run underneath in daylight and go up top after dark. How about it?"

"Okay with me."

"Very well." On the bullhorn he ordered Hara's men to go below. When they were all down and the hatches sealed, he and Hara descended into the control room, sealing the bridge hatch behind them. "Take her down, Exec."

"Yessir."

The orders were issued. *Grayfish* slid easily below the surface. "Hold her at a hundred feet and maintain course." Hunley turned to Hara. "We'll be through the corridor in an hour and then it's easy cruising into the China Sea. We'll turn north after dark and run on the surface."

He and Hara made their way to the wardroom. The others already were there. On the table Doctor Borovitch had set up a small scale model of the interior features of a steel mill and furnace.

McGlynn presided, as usual.

"The lesson today," he said, "is the anatomy of a steel mill. More to the point, the anatomy of our steel mill. Doctor. . ." Borovitch drew himself up sternly as if this were the first time he was lecturing this particular group of freshmen.

"Anatomy is a very good analogy." He bobbed his head. The overhead lamps cast tiny pools of white light through his thick spectacles. "Why is it a good analogy? Because the Argon Furnace is like a man. It has a body, a heart, arms, hands...and a brain."

He used a pointer and spoke with a subdued intensity that underlined every word.

"The torso is the furnace — this big kettle where the steel is made.

"The heart is the power supply. These are large electrical transformers that get outside power. At times banks of diesel engines in the same powerhouse are used for auxiliary power. Brain? Here, the control room." He tapped a cubicle next to the furnace. "It tells everyone and every machine what to do and when.

"Arms and hands are the two cranes, the cables, and the motors that move things around. The Argon Furnace cannot feed its body without its arms and hands. And it has a great appetite. It eats from a giant ladle that is manipulated by one of the cranes. Both cranes can go from end to end of the mill swiftly. They run on overhead tracks.

"The food is raw molten scrap steel supplied from these electric arc furnaces — here. It is seasoned with important, expensive metals — cobalt, molybdenum, manganese.

"And finally, the blood — argon. The furnace needs its supply of argon like a man needs oxygen. Without it, the product is nothing but low-grade tool steel. Impure. Useless for jet engines.

"Yes" — Borovitch nodded — "the Argon Furnace in many ways is like a man.

"But" — he held up his pointer like an exclamation mark — "in other ways the Argon Furnace is very different from a man. If you kill the brain or heart of a man, he dies. But the Argon Furnace doesn't die. It only sleeps until the part is fixed or replaced.

"So, gentlemen" — Borovitch looked around at each face — "in order to kill the Argon Furnace, you must destroy each and every part. Even then, the whole monster could eventually be replaced. But that would take a great amount of time. A year.

Maybe more. That year is what your enemy cannot spare."

He handed the pointer back to McGlynn.

"So," the intelligence officer said, "the job is to attack each piece of the mill and the furnace in a coordinated way. Kill the whole sucker. Barton, you're an explosives man. What are the special problems here?"

"Depends. In demo work an ounce of TNT in the right spot is worth a ton in the wrong one. I'd like to hear Doc tell us where we put our ounces. These furnaces, cranes, and that kind of stuff are big and heavy. Looks tough."

"Yes, that's right," said Borovitch. "If this job is attempted without science, effort could be wasted. Perhaps I can counsel you on that by telling you what is the most delicate and what is the strongest."

"Exactly," said Barton.

"Very well, write down this list. I start with the most delicate." He tapped a spot on the model. "Control panel in the control room: the most fragile part of the whole system. All kinds of wires, connections, meters, and so on. A few pounds of explosives would wreck it forever."

"Easy enough," said Barton.

Borovitch's forehead knotted. "Next easiest, I think, is the supply of argon. It would be stored in this part of the building" — he tapped a place — "where it can be retrieved and connected readily to the tubes that channel the gas through the molten alloy. It is stored away from the heat of the furnace because it is kept under very high pressure in large, very long tanks."

"How many tanks?" asked Krag.

"I don't know for sure, but in full operation there would have to be an inventory of a dozen to twenty to serve the furnace on a round-the-clock basis. Of course, you could get rid of the gas merely by opening the valves, but it would take a long time for the gas to escape. On the other hand, if you can rupture the tank with explosives, the gas will escape rapidly."

Krag scratched thoughtfully. "We'll hit it, but if the gas is shippable in tanks like that, they'd have a new supply fast."

"I doubt that," said Borovitch. "One of the problems facing production from this furnace is getting a steady supply of argon gas. It cannot be obtained easily. It's a relatively rare gas. It would take them weeks to rebuild their whole inventory."

"Maybe we ought to skip it," said Hara, "and save our explosives for the stuff that takes months to replace."

"How much pressure is that gas under, Doc?" asked Barton.

"Fourteen thousand pounds per square inch."

"Tanks like that are no problem," said Barton. "Two demo blocks — half pound each — would rupture 'em easy. Gas under that kind of pressure will do the rest. Split 'em wide open. We're talking a few minutes' work."

"Okay, argon tanks are on the list," said Krag. "What's next?"

"The furnace itself," said Borovitch.

"Blow a hole in it," said Endo.

"No," said Borovitch, "the furnace is a system that includes hydraulic tubing, inlet pipes for argon gas, mechanical gearing, heavy control cables and pulleys, electrical motors, and so on. I will tell you exactly what must be damaged. This is an intricate furnace, but even so, I think it will take a lot of your explosives."

"Why?" asked Barton.

"Because the system is built to withstand very extreme temperatures, high pressures, and great weights."

"Okay, we have more work to do on that. Probably take the bulk of our explosives. What next?"

"The cranes," said Borovitch. "If you destroy the cranes, you make the job of rebuilding almost impossible. But this is a very difficult problem." He pointed at the model. The cranes were carried on tracks on top of what looked like a three-dimensional parallelogram. "See? There are two cranes. The control cabs and beams ride on these tracks high above the mill floor. The tracks are exceptionally heavy girders, as are the crane beams themselves."

"I-beams?" asked Barton.

"Yes."

"How large?"

"I believe twenty inches," said Borovitch. "They must handle more than fifty tons at a time. They have to haul the ladle of molten steel rapidly up and down the length of the mill to carry melted raw material from the arc furnaces to the Argon Furnace. When the Argon Furnace has done its job, it returns the product back into the ladle. Then the cranes have to haul the ladle back down to the far end of the mill and pour the steel into ingot molds. When these have cooled for forty-eight hours or so, they are shipped to rolling mills in Nagoya."

"I see why they're important," said Krag.

"I worked in a steel mill," said Fujimura. "Take it from me, when the crane stops, everything stops. Like Doc said, it's the thing that feeds the furnace."

"What do you think, Max?" Krag asked Barton.

"They use cranes like that in shipyards. Heavy steel. They run on big, thick I-beams. But demo blocks can cut I-beams easy."

"How much stuff?"

Barton shrugged. "The rule's one quarter-pound demo block for every square inch of iron cross section. Let's be safe and add a little more. Beam that size would probably have one-inch plate in the vertical part of the 'I'.

"In other words, you got a twenty-inch beam, you cut it with twenty demo blocks in line on the upright, plus enough to cut the top and bottom horizontal parts of the 'I'. Say another two dozen blocks. Okay, we're talking, um, forty-four blocks to cut the beam. That's eleven pounds. Add a pound for luck. Twelve pounds. Hell, we've got five *hundred* pounds."

"Enough to do the job a couple of times over," said Krag. "And we'll use it all. No point in carrying the groceries back to the store."

Barton turned to Hara. "How deep did your training go into demo work?"

"We know how to set the fuzes and timers we're using."

"Get to practice with live explosives?"

"One day."

"Did you practice on I-beams, that kind of stuff?"

"Not really. Little stuff, mostly. Nothing like we're getting into at Mill One."

"Right," said Endo, "we need some briefing on how much stuff to lay on and where — like Barton was saying about the I-beams."

"We'll do that with Doc's help," said Krag. "Which brings up another point. It's time to organize our demo teams and assign targets based on Doc's list."

"Fair enough," said Hara. "Let's organize the teams and get to it."

The meeting wore on. The task became clearer. Borovitch sketched the elements of the furnace which were the critical targets. Barton described the most effective arrangement of demolition blocks to cut steel. They agreed that every charge could be doubled and there would still be TNT to spare.

McGlynn sprang one small surprise: a camera. He insisted that photographs be taken of the mill elements for Borovitch to study and for later study by intelligence at Pearl Harbor. The team agreed that photography was no problem.

Hours later each man knew what he was to do: On entry all would aid in rounding up workers and herding them into the mill's tool cage. After that, Toda and Fujimura would stand guard with the Bren guns. Endo and Marumoto on the cranes. Barton and Hara on the control room and furnace. Krag on the powerhouse. Sakai, the smallest man, was made the photographer and the killer of the argon supply.

At the end of it Krag looked into their faces. "I'll be honest. When I first heard about this deal, I thought it was nuts. A week ago I began thinking it was possible, but improbable. But right now I'm telling you, it'll work. No bullshit.

"It'll work because I believe now what I wasn't sure of before. We've got a good plan. More important, to make a good plan work, you need good people. We've got 'em. I don't think there are any better anywhere. Okay, let's call it a day."

As they filed toward their torpedo room bunks, Marumoto asked Barton, "You think it'll work, Sergeant?"

"Depends on you, Perfesser. Can you act like a Jap?"

"You said I was one."

Barton snorted. "Like it or not, my life's in your hands. Krag likes the plan. That's good enough for me. We'll just have to see how it works out."

5

Tsushima Strait, September 4, 1942

I

Krag dreamed of Mindanao. In his vision shards of sunlight cut through the high, dark canopy of the rain forest. Orchids gleamed like vigil lamps in the foliage. It was a kind of special peace because the trees stood in rows of columns, like the pillars of some gothic cathedral growing from the soft, black humus of the forest floor. It was devoid of any other growth. And yet, he sensed, this beauty is ominous, for there is no concealment except among the trunks of trees. And the enemy is seaching. . .

A rough hand jarred him awake and back into the red-lit world of the forward torpedo room.

"Huh? What's up?"

It was Hunley. "We're going through the Tsushima Strait," he whispered. "I'd like you, Hara, and his crew topside."

"Topside?"

"We're surfacing to charge batteries. If a patrol boat comes by, we'll need Hara to talk. Couple of his boys on the lookout guns. Report to me when you're ready."

"Right." Krag rubbed the sleep out of his eyes and put on his shirt. It stank of old sweat. After many days at sea, no laundry, and limited bathing, his clothes — everybody's clothes — smelled like old cheese. He went to Hara's bunk.

"Rise and shine, kiddo."

77

"Wha...?"

"It's showtime. Put on your imperial duds and break a leg."

"Nuts! They were just bringing on the Tahitian dancers."

"War is hell."

Krag went down the line of bunks waking the others.

II

It was still dark when *Grayfish* surfaced, though dawn tinged the eastern sky. There was a skim of fog at water level, but the air above was clear and warm. The Morning Star gleamed like a beacon. Even the throbbing diesels couldn't overcome the clean smell of morning. Endo and Sakai took the lookout posts on the conning tower and mounted machine guns. Hara joined Krag and Hunley on the bridge. The other Nisei hovered around the deck gun. They seemed at ease, but a shell had been chambered. They could aim and fire in seconds.

"Beautiful morning," said Krag.

Hunley fiddled with his Japanese officer's cap. "I'd feel better if it stayed dark."

"Nobody'll see you in the hat." Krag grinned.

"I was thinking of the ship, Commander. This isn't exactly San Diego, you know."

"We in the straits now?" Hara asked.

"Yeah," Hunley replied. "See that coastline? Korea. We're taking the route north between Korea and Tsushima Island. That's the coastline just east of us. Honshu's farther east."

Hara turned his head as if looking for some other landmark. "This is where the Japanese Navy wiped out the Russian fleet in 1905," he said.

"What a nourishing thought," Krag muttered.

"My father was in it."

"Is that so, Hara?" said Hunley. "Officer?"

"No. Able seaman. Lucky for me."

"Why?"

"If he'd been an officer, he'd have stayed in Japan. I'd have been raised in an Imperial Navy family. But there was no future in his being a seaman. So, when his service was finished, he came to the States."

"And now you're back here on the other side," said Krag.

"Full circle."

"*Patrol boat!*" Endo shouted. "Starboard! Bearing 30 degrees!"

"Uh-oh!" Hunley studied the distant craft through his binoculars."

"What've we got?" asked Krag.

"Looks like a Skoshi Class patrol boat. Not much firepower. But they've got a radio that can call in the tough guys."

"Think they've seen us?"

"Hell yes!" said Hunley. "Here's the bullhorn, Hara. How do you intend to handle this?"

"Before that PB gets too close, you and Krag go below."

"I can't leave the bridge," said Hunley.

"Then hunker down out of sight. Krag, when you get below, tell Barton to stand by the radio."

"Got it."

"They're turning our way," said Hunley. "Fast."

"Okay!" Hara signaled the crew on the deck through the bullhorn. "Here we go!"

Hunley handed his binoculars to Hara and slid down behind the bulkhead. "You've got the con, Tomi."

"First time for everything."

"You never handled a ship?"

"Hell, I'm an intelligence officer, remember? Since when does intelligence know how to do anything?"

"Christ!"

Toda shouted up from the deck. "What's the deal?"

"Patrol boat. You and Fujimura get on that deck gun! Quick! Don't aim at 'em, but be ready to go!" He leaned down. "Lend me your hat, Hunley. Hey, Marumoto, up on the bridge! You're an officer!"

Marumoto scrambled up the outside ladder to the bridge.

"What do I do?"

"Look imperial. I might need you to deal with them if there's too much culture clash."

"How close are they?" asked Hunley.

"Two thousand yards. Closing."

Barton called from the radio room. "They tried to raise us on radio."

"They sound excited?" Hara asked.

"Sounded routine to me. I didn't acknowledge."

"Hang on there."

The enemy craft came on steadily, its bow wave catching the first red rays of the sun.

III

On board the speeding patrol boat a petty officer studied *Grayfish* through binoculars.

"Ours, Captain. I think K-4 or K-5 Class. Designation RO-76." The young ensign commanding the patrol boat thumbed through his thick ship's identity book. "Ah! Here it is. Good work, Petty Officer, it is a K-5. Um. RO-76, the *Sacred Blossom*. Very well. Helmsman, take us in!"

"Aye, sir!"

The boat's engines gunned. In short order it was within a hundred meters of the submarine. The crewmen of RO-76 seemed obviously unconcerned.

"Throttle down, Helm, and bring her about."

"Aye, sir."

Engines idling, the patrol boat turned abreast *Grayfish*. The ensign triggered his bullhorn. "Good morning! We tried to raise you on radio!"

"Good morning!" said Hara through his own bullhorn. "We're running on strict radio silence. I'm very sorry for the trouble."

"No matter. Are you going out on patrol or coming in?"

"I'm not allowed to tell you, Captain. But the hunting was

very good anyway." Hara beamed broadly. On deck Hara's men grinned and waved.

"In that case we won't detain you from shore leave." The ensign smiled at the way the submarine commander stuck to his orders but at the same time told him they were returning from patrol.

"Many thanks, Captain. Good hunting yourself."

"Thank you," said the ensign. "But our ship is for very small fish, I am afraid."

"Any fish are better than none. Make Yankee sashimi."

"So true. *Sayonara*, then."

"*Sayonara*."

The ensign turned to his work. "Take a 180 degree heading, Helm. Patrol speed."

On *Grayfish* Hunley heard the patrol boat engines gunning away. "What they want?"

"Routine check. We didn't answer their radio signal. I told them we're on radio silence."

"We are. They just don't know how silent we're trying to be. Think they bought it?"

"Sure. Why not? Radio silence is routine for subs. Besides, suppose you saw a submarine chugging into Pearl Harbor with a blond crew and the U.S. flag flying, would you make 'em heave to?"

"Probably not. Maybe that's something we ought to start worrying about. You're the intelligence officer. Do they have any blond crews?"

"No, but there's always hair bleach and dark glasses."

"I'll feel better when we get underneath again."

"How long before we get to Ringo?"

"About sunset, running underneath." He took the ship's microphone. "Bridge to engine room."

There was a crackle of static. "Engine room."·

"How're the batteries doing, Mac?"

"Topped off. Ready to go."

"Very well."

Hara looked at the brightening sky. A rind of sun was nudging at the horizon. "It'll be a long day."

"And night," said Hunley. "Five more minutes of daylight, Hara, then we duck for the cellar. With a little luck, this time tomorrow we'll be heading home."

"A little luck," Hara murmured. "Just a little luck."

IV

The ship ran deep and silent through the Tsushima Strait on a course that took it nearly straight north. At midafternoon, Hunley changed course east-northeast on a line toward Wakasa Bay. Later, still another course change brought *Grayfish* close to shore in early evening.

"Now hear this!" Hunley said into the P.A. system. "Doctor Borovitch and commanders Krag and Hara report to the control room."

Two minutes later the three edged into the cramped control area, brushing past crewmen manning the diving controls.

"Gentlemen," said Hunley, "according to our usually reliable ship's inertial navigation system, we are about a mile off shore from the town of Ringo, Japan." He turned to his crew and ordered the submarine up to periscope depth.

Hara and Krag looked at each other silently. Each thought the other looked amazingly calm. Each knew himself to be in the early stages of a truly cold sweat.

"Up periscope!" said Hunley. He hung on the focus arms and swung a full 360 degrees. Except for some fishing boats and a distant freighter, there was little going on at sea. Shoreward at the edge of a half-circle harbor there was a small, low village. Each house wore a classic profile of tiled roof curling upward at the eaves. A few wispy fingers of smoke pointed skyward. A long pier built on a stone jetty reached toward the sea.

"Anything?" asked Krag.

"Take a look."

Krag peered into the periscope and focused. "That's a town,

all right." He swung around, looking west. "The sky's a cliché."

"What?" asked Hunley.

"Setting sun looks just like the Jap flag." He swung around again. "Nobody on shore. At least nothing that looks like artillery. Town looks quiet. Don't see any patrol boat . . ."

"Doctor Borovitch, take a look please," said Hunley.

"Yes, of course," the old man murmured. He took the scope and studied the shore.

"Ringo?" asked Hunley.

"Yes, Ringo."

"You're sure?"

"Positive," said Borovitch, still looking. "I see the characteristic pier. I see Mount Gima in the distance, just where it should be. I even see the house on the shore where I once lived." Borovitch relinquished the periscope. "To return to Ringo this way. . ." He shook his head.

"Welcome home," said Krag.

"Down periscope!" Hunley ordered. He searched their faces. The arrival seemed almost anticlimax. "Well, here we are," he said lamely.

Krag nodded. "Now for step two."

Hunley sighed. "Step two. Right now, or do you want to wait until dark?"

"Now," said Krag. "Better to get our gear ashore while there's some light."

"Very well." Hunley got on the P.A. "Landing party prepare for shore." He turned to Hara and Krag. "I'll maneuver in at a crawl until we scrape. When you're ready, report to me."

They nodded, then went forward to join the others. It didn't take long. The preparations had been made long before, checked, rechecked, and rechecked again. The inflatable boats were in place by the forward and bridge hatches. Krag told Hunley they were ready. There was only one order to give.

"Surface!"

6

Ringo, September 4, 1942

I

Hara wore Japanese Navy deck blues, a sword, and a pistol belt. The other Nisei wore fatigue whites and ammunition belts. As soon as *Grayfish* was up, they raced to unload the landing boats and inflate them quickly from tanks of compressed air. Krag and Barton wore conventional U.S. Army Air Force chinos and leather flying jackets. Their hands were bound behind them. Both had let a couple of days' growth of beard accumulate to give them the disheveled appearance of prisoners. For the benefit of any watchers on shore, they stood silent and grim while the four heavy carts of explosives, Bren guns, rifles, and ammunition were stowed expertly in the boats. Fortunately, the harbor was glassy calm. The water line on the pier indicated dead low.

"Neap tide 1800," Hara called in a hoarse whisper up to Hunley on the bridge. "Write it down."

Hunley, wearing dark glasses and his too-small Japanese naval officer's cap, nodded but said nothing. Voices carried over water. He had the feeling that English words would carry the farthest of all.

The Nisei worked silently and efficiently. They'd practiced this dozens of times and in rougher water. When the gear was stowed, Endo and Fujimura muscled Krag and Barton roughly into separate boats. That, too, was part of the scenario.

The crew climbed aboard and, last, Hara. He gave the thumbs-up sign to Hunley. In Japanese he ordered the boats to shove off.

Without hurry they paddled toward the pier, fifty yards away. Halfway there they heard the submarine's hatches clank and seal. The idling diesels throbbed louder. Hunley backed *Grayfish* toward open water. There was no looking back.

"Remember!" said Marumoto in Japanese. "Watch your accents!"

"Watch your ass, too!" Endo muttered.

Hara saw two people, mouths agape, at the shore end of the long pier. Soon others appeared.

"Don't look at them!" he told the others. "Relax! So far no army, no navy, no police. Just people. Here come some more."

"An audience is a good omen," said Marumoto. "If they thought we were the enemy, they'd be heading the other way."

"Something to that," Hara conceded. "We'll soon find out. Steady as she goes. We're just a squad of nice Japanese boys coming home."

They reached the pier without incident and tied up the boats. As quickly as they had stowed the gear, they unloaded it. They looked seaward. *Grayfish* was a half-mile out now.

"There she goes," said Sakai.

The submarine slipped beneath the surface, leaving nothing but a fading wake. Each man ashore felt in his own way abandoned and alone.

"*Haiaku!* Let's go!" said Hara. "We don't have time to wave bye-bye."

They organized in a line, each of the four Nisei crewmen on a cart handle. Each had his Arisaka slung crossways across his back. The Bren guns rode on two of the carts, their bundles of ammunition pouches rode on the other two. Toda, as a Japanese petty officer, took a supervising position at the rear. Hara took the van. Krag and Barton, trying to look properly hangdog, were in the middle of the line.

"Forward . . ." Hara shouted, " 'harch!"

Toda counted cadence. "*Ichi! Ni! San! Shi . . . !*"

They marched down the pier toward the growing cluster of townspeople. The little crowd parted silently to let them through.

Looking neither right nor left, Hara led them up the main street in the direction Borovitch had said led to the town hall. But the streets were crooked. A hundred yards into the village, Hara realized he didn't know where he was going.

"Detail! Halt!"

Everything stopped. He looked around. The crowd of curious townspeople, following at a discreet distance, stopped too. If this weren't so dangerous, he thought, it'd be embarrassing. Hara thought of an old question: Am I leading a parade or fleeing a mob?

He spotted a young woman standing in the gateway of a walled yard. She was dressed in a plain gray kimono with a silvery colored obi. Despite his bizarre situation, Hara was struck by her classic features. An American slang word fit her perfectly: classy. And quite beautiful.

He saluted her. "Excuse me. Is there any army or navy garrison here? Or a police office?"

"Yes." She bowed. "A small one. Army."

"Will you lead us to it, please?"

"Yes" — she bowed even lower — "of course." She straightened and hesitated, staring at Krag and Barton.

"Well...?" Hara prompted.

"Forgive my stare," she said. "I haven't seen foreigners before."

"They're prisoners."

"Are they Americans?"

"Yes. American pilots. We captured them."

"That was very brave of you."

He liked the way she looked at him. He smiled. "Their plane crashed in the sea near our vessel."

"Oh my." She smiled back.

"They were helpless." I must look like a goof, he thought. I don't know if I'm in a tragedy or a comedy.

She bowed again. "Follow me, please." She led the parade around a corner and down a side street to what had been a small schoolhouse. A guard with a rifle leaned against the wall.

"That is the army post," the woman said. She bowed once more.

"Thank you very much," said Hara. "You are very helpful."

"No bother. Goodbye."

Reluctantly, Hara said goodbye and turned to face the army post. He marched his group to it and halted in front of the door.

The startled guard snapped to attention. "Captain Kamasaki!" he shouted.

A moment later an Imperial Army officer in summer field dress burst out the door, buckling on his pistol belt and sword.

"Why are you shout...?"

He stopped short when he saw the contingent of naval troops and two *gaijin*. He was a small, thin man with a pencil moustache. He wore odd gold-rimmed glasses that gave him the look of a petulant clerk. "What is the meaning of this?"

Hara saluted briskly. "Good evening, Captain. I am Lieutenant Hara, Imperial Navy Submarine Service. We have two American prisoners."

"Why wasn't I notified?"

"We are notifying you now."

"Ah?" He stared curiously at Krag and Barton, then at the squad of Nisei who stood at rigid attention. "Where did you come from? How did you get here?"

"My vessel came into the harbor a few minutes ago, and we came ashore. There was" — he said snidely — "no guard. My papers..."

"Of course there was no guard," said Kamasaki, grabbing the papers. "We post a sentry there only after dark." He glanced at Hara's sheaf of papers. They had the dense, oppressive quality of the real thing. He handed them back. "Where did these Americans come from?"

"Our ship was returning from patrol," Hara recited. "Not far from here. We saw an aircraft in the distance. Flying low. Coming from the China coast. There was smoke. The craft was in trouble. Then it hit the water. So, we went to assist. Imagine our surprise when we discovered that the floating wreckage was an American reconnaissance plane! Only these two survived. Ringo was the handiest port, so we've landed them here. Our vessel is back out at sea."

Hara watched the Japanese officer carefully. The little captain's reaction seemed appropriate. If Kamasaki doubted at all that he was dealing with a Japanese naval landing party, there was no sign. Hara knew there would have been, had the officer been even a little bit skeptical. In fact, the man seemed irked solely by the fact that his routine had been upset.

"This is very irregular," he said.

"War has surprises," Hara replied.

Kamasaki looked curiously at the explosives carts. "What are these?"

"Submarine utility carts." Hara smiled in spite of himself. "We're using them to carry our clothing and equipment until we return to our vessel."

"Very well," said Kamasaki. "We'll take charge of the prisoners."

"My orders are to requisition a truck immediately and take the prisoners to Naval Headquarters in Yokosuka for interrogation. Here is my. . ."

Kamasaki's jaw dropped in amazement. He waved the papers aside officiously. "Hah! Requisition? By the Navy? Impossible!"

Hara knew from both intelligence reports and published accounts that there was a long-simmering antipathy between the Imperial Army and the Navy that bordered on hostility. He drew himself up and glared down at Kamasaki.

"Captain, this is no time for pettiness. I. . ."

"Hah! You're in Army jurisdiction, lieutenant. We'll find out what *Army* headquarters wants to do."

"I must protest," said Hara.

"You are not in command here!" Kamasaki snapped. He put his hands on his hips and jutted his jaw. He had to look up at Hara, who was a good five inches taller. "I am in charge until Major Sumida returns." He circled the contingent slowly, inspecting. Hara's men were models of military form, backs straight, eyes straight ahead. Kamasaki leaned over casually and poked at one of the Bren guns. "What model is this?"

"Those are British Bren guns. We captured them in Hong Kong."

"Ah? They look much like our Type 99."

"Very similar."

"The British copy everything."

"They're thieves."

"We will keep your prisoners under guard until the Major returns. You and your men may wait here until he comes back."

"Very well. We have no choice. How long will that be?"

"I don't know. Meanwhile, keep out of the way."

"But these prisoners have important information," Hara complained. "We must get them to Naval Intelligence as soon as possible!"

"You have my decision, Lieutenant."

Kamasaki swaggered up to Krag and Barton, who both towered over him. In garbled English he yelled, "You! Yankee! Bow! Bad person! I say you bow down!" He slapped Krag hard. "Bow down!"

"Captain!" snapped Hara.

"They must learn." Three armed soldiers had turned out after Kamasaki. "Take the prisoners inside," he told them.

Hara, tight-lipped, motioned his own men aside so the soldiers could grab Krag and Barton and manhandle them into the guard house. "Stand at ease," he told them. "I'll call you, if needed." He gave them a meaningful look, then followed the others inside.

The former school classroom had been turned into an army orderly room. There were two rough wooden desks, chairs, and several file cabinets. A corner of the room had been partitioned off, obviously an office for the absent Major Sumida.

Kamasaki ordered his men to tie Krag and Barton into two of the chairs.

"I think we will interrogate them here," said Kamasaki, now able to look down at the prisoners.

"That is for intelligence officers," said Hara. "You don't know enough English."

Kamasaki bristled. "All Army officers are instructed in English." Turning on Krag, he shouted, "You! Yankee head! What you mission?"

"Krag. Major, U.S. Army Air Corps. Serial number. . ."

Kamasaki struck him again. Blood beaded on Krag's lip. "Fool! What you mission?"

"Brutality will get nothing, Captain," Hara protested.

"We shall see. . ."

II

Outside, the Nisei heard the shouts and slaps.

"What the hell's going on in there?" Toda asked.

Endo went to the window and peeked in. "That Army captain's working over Krag."

"How long do we let this crap go on?" Fujimura asked the others.

"We give him two more slaps," said Endo, "then. . ."

"Don't get excited!" said Toda. "Tomi will give us the high sign."

"Better be soon," said Endo. "I don't like this."

Toda saw a staff car in the distance, approaching the post. Two small flags fluttered from the front fenders. "Uh-oh, here comes the power!"

"Okay, boys!" said Endo. "Don't let the navy down! Look sharp!"

"And watch those goddamn accents!" snapped Marumoto. "You're talking pure California!"

The car pulled up. As senior rank present, Toda called the squad to attention. A driver leaped from the car and pulled open a rear door. A burly officer, a major, edged out slowly, dragging a stiff leg.

His boots were polished to a mirror sheen, and his brass gleamed. He wore white gloves. He held his sword firmly with his left hand and carried a stout cane in the other. He

91

straightened up and limped toward them.

Toda saluted smartly. "Chief Petty Officer Toda reporting, sir!"

The Japanese officer inspected Toda with a practiced eye. The Major was middle-aged with iron-gray hair. He had the weathered look of an outdoorsman. From his insignia and ribbons it was obvious that he was an infantry veteran seasoned by many campaigns.

He returned Toda's salute. "Navy? Here?"

"Our commander is inside. We have brought two American prisoners ashore, sir."

"Oh?" He seemed faintly amused. "Well, we must see about this." He turned and moved up the steps, trailing his stiff leg.

III

Krag and Barton distracted themselves between slaps by trying to comprehend Kamasaki's questions in mangled English.

"You there!" he shouted at Barton. "Yankee person no good! Bad ears. You speak at me or I spit your head."

"Barton. Sergeant. U.S. Army Air Corps. Serial..."

Kamasaki struck again. Barton was grateful the captain was a small man. A few more pounds behind the slaps and he'd be spitting teeth. Hara, standing angry and tense at one side of the room, saw the Japanese major move quietly into the room. Kamasaki and his men were looking at their prisoners and didn't notice.

"Again!" shouted Kamasaki in his mangled English. "Say you speak! Spit head or speaking!"

"Barton. Sergeant. U.S...."

Wap! "What you mission?"

"Captain!" The major had a parade-ground voice that jolted the others. The enlisted men faced him and braced.

Kamasaki bowed stiffly.

"Ah? Major." He spoke without straightening. "I did not see you. I am sorry."

92

"Alertness is not your strong point, Captain." The major turned to Hara. "Who are you?"

"Hara. Lieutenant. Imperial Navy Submarine Service." He bowed quickly and straightened. "My papers."

"I am Major Sumida, in command of this unfortunate backwater." He accepted the papers and looked at them cursorily. They appeared in order.

"Where did you get these prisoners?"

Hara went into his script. "They are American pilots. As I explained to Captain Kamasaki, our crew witnessed the crash at sea of their plane. We picked them up. My orders are to take them to Naval Intelligence in Yokosuka as quickly as possible." Hara pulled more documents from his shoulder pouch and passed them to Sumida. "We need a truck or some other vehicles that can carry all of us. Here are the cable orders and papers of authorization from my commander."

Sumida flipped through them quickly. The cabled instructions were signed "Kondo, Captain, for Yamamoto, Admiral Commanding." The name Yamamoto was one that transcended any interservice rivalries. "These look in order. Please stand at ease." He scrutinized Hara. Obviously, this was an officer of family. He was tall and handsome, but a man, not a flower. Sumida read character in his face. "Are you willing to sign a receipt and risk a statement of charges?"

"Of course, sir."

"How many days will you need the truck?"

"Only as many as it takes to get to Yokosuka round trip. Two. Three at most. Yokosuka is not that far. I promise that the Navy will return it to you promptly."

"I see." Sumida thought about it for a minute. He glanced at Krag and Barton. "Yes, these are important prisoners. Very well. Then we can arrange for the vehicle." He turned. "Captain Kamasaki, please order the truck to be brought around."

"But, Major," the little captain said, "our Army intelligence officers will want to interrogate these prisoners while they are in our custody."

93

"Captain," Sumida said icily, "war has no room for bureaucrats. When you are in command here, you may make such decisions. But, as I understand it, the Imperial Navy is on our side in this conflict. Until we are advised otherwise, please follow orders."

Kamasaki snapped to attention. "Yessir! But. . ."

"Well?" Sumida's tone turned even colder.

Kamasaki clearly was suffering, to Krag and Barton's delight. He stammered, then blurted out, "The truck is elsewhere."

"What?"

"Sir, you ordered me to send a patrol along the south coast."

"That was this morning! The truck should have been back hours ago!'"

"Yessir!" He bobbed up and down in short nervous bows. "The, uh, departure was delayed. It started at noon. The patrol is due back any time now."

"Delayed?" Sumida eyed the top of Kamasaki's bobbing head.

"Yessir!"

"We shall speak of this later."

"Yessir!"

Sumida turned back to Hara. "I apologize, Lieutenant. If orders were followed promptly, we would have the truck here for you. As it is, we must wait."

"Of course, sir." Hara began to breathe a bit easier. "I understand. We are most appreciative of your cooperation."

"Do you need to use my telephone?" Sumida asked.

"Arrangements have been made by radio," Hara lied. "In fact, you should have had notice by radio of our arrival by now."

"We have no radio here. This is a backwater. Only telephone. And it doesn't work that well. So, we have no word about you. But I am not surprised." He laughed brusquely. "At high levels, the Navy finds it very difficult to talk to the Army."

Hara laughed, too. "I am sure it works both ways at high levels." He looked Sumida in the eye. "But not on the front line."

Sumida nodded. "You are a combat man." He cast a scornful glance in Kamasaki's direction. "You understand. While we

94

wait perhaps you would care to join me for supper?"

Becoming a dinner guest was not in any scenario that Hara and the others had worked out. But there could be no refusal under the circumstances.

"How kind of you," Hara murmured. He bowed. "I am honored."

"Captain!" Sumida barked. "See that Lieutenant Hara's men are fed. And for God's sake, make them welcome! They aren't the enemy!"

"What about the prisoners?"

"Give them some rice. Americans don't eat fish."

"I mean, who should guard them?"

"They are Lieutenant Hara's prisoners. His men can guard them."

"Yessir!" Kamasaki seemed relieved to be out of it.

"This way, please, Lieutenant." Sumida led him outside.

The Nisei came to attention.

"Toda," said Hara, "you and the others guard the prisoners. Major Sumida very kindly has arranged for you to be fed. And the prisoners. He also has very kindly invited me to his home while we wait for the truck to arrive."

"Yessir! How shall we notify you when the truck comes?"

Sumida answered. "One of my men will notify me. I want to inspect the patrol when they return. Also, petrol will have to be put in the truck for your trip."

"Yessir! Thank you, sir."

"Carry on," said Hara. As he passed them following Sumida, he winked.

"Accent!" Marumoto whispered.

Hara nodded and wondered if he could make it through dinner without making some cultural gaffe that would give him away.

7

I

It wasn't far to Sumida's house. It was the one with the wall and gate where Hara had enlisted the young woman's help. Indeed, she was at the gate to greet them.

"Lieutenant," Sumida said, "this is my daughter. Her name is Chiyo. Chiyo this is Lieutenant Hara of the Navy."

She bowed gracefully. "An honor to meet you formally, Lieutenant Hara."

"And I am honored, too," said Hara, also bowing. He was all too aware that his bowing technique needed work. It was one of those little cultural giveaways that Marumoto harped on. He straightened. To Sumida he said, "We met informally when I landed with the prisoners."

"Oh?"

"Your daughter very kindly showed us to your headquarters."

"Captain Kamasaki was unkind to the prisoners," said Chiyo. She must have been watching them from the sidelines, thought Hara.

"He has a lot to learn," said Sumida. "He's really not a bad soldier, Lieutenant, but his character needs development. A few days of combat will fix that."

Chiyo slid open the door to Sumida's house. Hara slipped off his shoes and stood aside. Chiyo produced a bootjack and helped

97

her father. Sumida grimaced silently as the boot came off his stiff leg.

"May I help?" Hara volunteered.

"Thank you, no," said Sumida. "Chiyo knows just how to make this bearable."

"His leg improves every day," she said.

Sumida snorted. "But not fast enough! Lieutenant, please, enter our little house."

They went in.

II

Krag and Barton sat leaning against the wall of the orderly room, staring at the floor. Their arms had been unbound to let them eat the rice rations that were due. Several Japanese soldiers stood by out of curiosity, preventing any conversation in English between the Americans.

"Where you from, sailor?" one of the soldiers asked Toda.

"I am a chief petty officer, not a sailor."

"I apologize. I don't know Navy ranks. But I think I know your accent."

"I am from Hiroshima."

"Of course! I knew that accent. Me too. What neighborhood?"

"I choose to forget. Home is the Navy."

The soldier ignored the snub. "Ah! You are very serious. A career man."

"I wish I knew English," said one of the other soldiers. "I'd like to talk to these barbarians."

"Not allowed," said Toda. "Naval Intelligence will take care of them."

"Will they be executed?" asked the first soldier.

"Why would they be executed?" Marumoto asked.

"Why not?" said the other soldier. "They are enemy pilots. They are the kind of people who attacked our homeland last spring. Some of those were caught and executed. These should be, too." He managed to catch the eye of Krag. He made a head-chopping gesture and laughed.

Barton's eyes met Marumoto's briefly. He wore a faint I-told-you-so smile on bloody lips.

III

Hara was grateful for one small blessing explained by Sumida: "Because my damned leg doesn't fold as it should, we've turned our hibachi pit into a hole where I can hang the thing in comfort. Chiyo cooks in that other room."

"Very clever," said Hara. "And comfortable for me, too. On the submarine we operate Western style. No sitting on the deck. So my legs have become unaccustomed to tatami.

Chiyo produced bottles of sake which had been warming for her father's meal. Sumida poured some into Hara's tiny cup, then his own. He raised his cup in a toast.

"Welcome to my house."

Hara thanked him effusively and added, "A great future for Army and Navy cooperation and solidarity."

"Hah! We need much more sake for that." Sumida poured two more cups, and they downed them.

The last thing Hara wanted to do was to get into a round of toasts and a convivial binge with Sumida. There was work to be done, and God knew how long it would be before the truck reappeared from its patrol. He changed the subject.

"I note your ribbons, Major. You have seen a lot of action."

"Yes." Sumida was matter-of-fact. "First in China. Two campaigns. Then the Malay campaign to Singapore. Then in the Philippines. I went there with the staff of the great General Homma."

"You fought directly against the Americans, then?"

"Yes, in staff duties. I was in the fighting on Bataan Peninsula against the Americans. Very hard going there. That's where I got this leg."

99

"For a staff officer you must have gotten close to the action."

Sumida smiled. "Paperwork was never my goal. Every chance I got I made an excuse to go to the front." He slapped his leg. "Unfortunately, American artillery was at the front, too."

"Not too bad, I hope."

"Bad enough. But it's healing. I'll be going back to my line regiment soon."

IV

Toda offered a cigarette to one of the soldiers.

"Go ahead. We took these from the Americans."

The soldier looked furtively out the door. "All right. But the Captain could be anywhere."

"What is it that you guard here?"

"Nothing really. Mostly we patrol the coast and occasionally along the railroad." He pointed. "Over there about five or six kilometers. Lately, two or three men have been assigned from time to time at the gate of some mill."

"A mill? What does it make?"

"I don't know. I haven't drawn that duty yet." He pulled on the cigarette. "Ah. Very good."

"One thing the Yankees know how to do."

The man motioned toward Krag and Barton. "What do you think they were after?"

"Reconnaissance mission. The interesting thing is they were flying from China."

"I thought we owned China."

"China is very big."

"True."

Toda was about to press the soldier for more details when they heard the truck approaching. There was a shriek of clashing gears. Toda and the other Americans winced. The engine gunned futilely as the driver battled to master the clutch. He managed it and, shortly, the truck approached. Toda stepped outside with the soldiers. The truck careened down the street. It seemed to lean at an odd angle. Toda saw why. Its left front tire not only was flat, it was shredded. The patrol must have driven on it for miles. The vehicle virtually limped up to the orderly room and stopped. Five fully equipped soldiers piled out of the back. A sergeant ordered them to fall in.

Kamasaki, who must have heard the truck noise, appeared out of the shadows. The sergeant called his men to attention and saluted.

"Sir, Sergeant Wakataki and detail report completion of patrol."

Kamasaki was livid. "What happened to that wheel?"

"Sir. The tire went flat just as we reached the end of the patrol route."

"Why didn't you fix it?"

The sergeant looked startled. "We had no spare, sir."

"Fool! Don't you know the spare is stowed underneath?" He stabbed a finger at the truck bed. "Look there, you idiot!"

The sergeant leaned over. Toda felt sorry for him. The spare tire was not only stowed out of the way, but out of sight for anyone who didn't know it was there. The sergeant straightened up, looking ill.

"Sir, it is all my fault. I am an infantryman. I know nothing about trucks, sir, except to ride in them."

"Obviously. Well, don't just stand there! Change the wheel!"

"Sir!" The sergeant saluted smartly, then stood frozen.

"Well?"

"How?"

Toda could barely contain himself. Kamasaki was close to apoplexy.

"Sir," said Toda.

"What do you want?"

"My men are used to this kind of equipment. We can change the wheel quickly. We would be pleased to assist, since we are supposed to use the truck for the prisoners."

Kamasaki was on the verge of rejecting the offer. Instead he stopped to think about it.

"How come Navy men know about trucks?"

Toda made up a plausible answer. "Many trucks are used at navy bases to carry heavy parts and ammunition. Most personnel are trained to deal with trucks."

Saying that, Toda wondered how Kamasaki would cope with the reality that most American men learned how to drive — and change tires — as part of growing up.

Kamasaki stared at Toda. His anger subsided. "Very well. You are right. You are going to use the truck, so you can change the wheel."

"Yessir! And may I inform Lieutenant Hara that the truck is back."

"No," Kamasaki said hastily. "When the wheel is changed, I will send an orderly to Major Sumida's house. You may get started whenever you like."

"Yessir. And will your men guard the prisoners?"

"Of course."

"Thank you, sir." Toda went to the orderly room. The others had overheard the conversation and were standing by. Barton caught Toda's eye and gave him a wink.

V

Chiyo slid into the room, expertly balancing a tray with some deliciously fragrant stew in small lacquered bowls. Hara took it to be a variation on *suki yaki,* but it had a character of its own and no sugar — a bow, he supposed, to the war effort.

"I wish my father never had to go back to war," she said.

"That's unpatriotic!" Sumidia snapped. "I'm a soldier! It's my life!"

"Of course," said Hara. "But a daughter's concern for her father is understandable, too."

"Women!" Sumida grumbled. "What do they know?"

"They know their heart," she said.

Hara liked her style. She wasn't afraid of her formidable father.
"Sentimentalism!" said Sumida. Then he smiled at her. "But
this woman is a good person, Lieutenant. Too outspoken
sometimes. But of good character."

"That is easy to see," said Hara.

"Since my wife died five years ago, she has devoted herself
to this old soldier, when I have been home. And I am not easy
to deal with."

"Father!" She looked down. "Please! You embarrass me."

"I speak truth. You will make a fine wife and mother."

She bowed lower at the compliment.

"But you must learn to control your tongue."

"What did you think of the Americans?" Hara asked.

"They fought very well, considering their disadvantages and
ignorance. They performed better than the British, which surprised us."

"Yes. I would think the British should be better fighters."

"The Americans inflicted a great many casualties — including
me." He patted his stiff leg.

"But they surrendered," said Hara. "Obviously, their character
is weak if they do not choose to fight to the death."

"Perhaps," Sumida agreed. "But they were starving and running out of ammunition. Who knows? I was wounded. So I wasn't
there for that part."

Chiyo went to the room where she was cooking. Sumida leaned
over and whispered confidentially to Hara.

"It is one of the goals of my life to find a suitable husband
for Chiyo. This is much on my mind. As a soldier with a war
on, this becomes a burden."

"Why is that? Obviously, she is a woman of good family. I can
tell she has a good character."

"And not ugly, either!" said Sumida.

Hara smiled with sincerity. "Sir, I must say you are to be com-
plimented for having produced such a beautiful and charming
daughter."

"Thank you." Sumida bowed, thought for a moment, then

asked, "Ummm. Are you married, Lieutenant?"

"No, sir."

"Umm. Anything. . .arranged?"

"No, sir."

"Ahhh. . ." He said no more as Chiyo returned with another tray of food.

"Tell us about submarines, Lieutenant," she said. "It must be very exciting to voyage under the sea."

"Yes!" Sumida said enthusiastically. "Can you see out? Can you see the fish?"

"Oh no. We're closed in completely. But we come to the surface often to recharge our batteries. So we get fresh air and sun."

"Have you encountered enemy vessels?" asked Sumida.

"Oh yes," Hara lied. He described a mythical encounter in the Coral Sea.

Sumida was fascinated. "What a way to do battle! I am afraid old-fashioned soldiers like me are not prepared for such mechanical miracles as periscopes and torpedoes. I have enough trouble with simple mortars."

"In their place, they are vital," said Hara.

"True enough. There is no way to shoot a torpedo in the jungles." He laughed, then frowned thoughtfully. "I suppose you know that the enemy is counter-attacking in New Guinea."

"Yes," said Hara. "And also in the Solomon Islands."

"I have not heard that. Where are those islands?"

Hara realized he might be talking too much. "They are near Australia. The enemy has been repulsed, of course."

"Yes, it's hopeless for them." Sumida said it with conviction. "Were you in the naval battles of June?"

"No. My vessel stayed in New Guinea waters."

Sumida dropped his voice. "I understand the sea battles were not as successful as planned. We have not yet captured Hawaii. Is that correct?"

"Yes. But it is only a matter of time."

"Hawaii must be very beautiful," said Chiyo. "I would love to visit."

"Yes, it is magnificent," said Hara. As soon as he said it, he realized he almost gave himself away.

"You have been there?" she asked.

He smiled lamely. "I speak only from hearsay. Some of our officers have been there."

Sumida nodded. "I was. . ." Hammering at the door interrupted him. "Who's there?"

"Orderly Hakatori, sir!" a voice shouted. "Excuse me, Major. The truck has returned."

"Very well. I will come after my supper."

"But, Major, there is a problem."

"Problem?" Sumida's aura of mellowness evaporated.

"Sir, the tire is very flat and there is a problem about the spare tire. Requisition papers must be signed. Captain Kamasaki requests your presence, sir."

"Bah! Kamasaki should work for some city hall." He looked morosely at his food and sake, then sighed. "Well, I suppose I must go. Please excuse me, Lieutenant."

"Of course," said Hara, suddenly tense. The truck was important. "Is there any way I can assist?"

Sumida nodded vigorously. "Assist by eating my daughter's delicious dinner." It seemed a happy idea. He smiled. "Relax. Get to know each other. I should be back soon." Painfully he hauled himself to the entry and pulled on his boots. Then he was gone.

Hara looked at Chiyo. She turned her gaze on the table.

"This seems to be a very quiet town," he said.

"Yes."

"Are there no military bases nearby?"

"No. Only father's small unit. He is only here until he recuperates."

"How many men does he have?" Hara asked casually.

"I think ten. And himself and Captain Kamasaki. There is not much here to protect."

"No factories? No railroad?"

"No. Not in Ringo."

"Nothing?"

She thought a moment. "There is a railroad about five kilometers from here by road. There are some factories there."

"What do they make?"

"I don't know. Metal, I think. Perhaps steel."

Hara sipped some sake and looked into her face. She averted her eyes.

"It must be very lonely for you here."

"It is a beautiful place." She smiled at him. "Father likes to fish, and I go with him. The seacoast is very dramatic."

"Yes, we saw it as we came into the harbor."

"Please, more sake."

"No thank you. I must keep my head clear. We have to get the prisoners to Yokosuka."

"Do you like voyaging under the sea?"

"It is not always amusing."

"Once I read a book, by a French person I think, about voyaging under the sea. It was very exciting."

"Yes, I have read a book like that. The book's title in English is *Twenty Thousand Leagues Under the Sea*. By Jules Verne. One of my favorites."

"I liked it very much. Is your life like that?"

"No. But a submarine is interesting duty. A little crowded, but better, I think, than surface duty. Our voyages are much shorter for one thing. So we get back often."

"I think I would like to fly in an airplane. Have you done that?"

"Oh yes."

"Is it frightening? Would I like it as much as I think?"

"You would love it. The world is spread out below you."

"I think it would be like seeing everything from the top of Mount Fuji."

"Even higher."

"Imagine! More rice?"

"No thank you. You are a very good cook."

"Thank you. I get lots of practice. Father likes to eat."

"You are a nice person, Chiyo."

She blushed. "Thank you, Lieutenant."

"Call me Tomi."

"That would be forward."

"Please. Wartime requires us to put aside such formalities."

"All right." Her eyes met his. "Tomi."

"Where did you come from originally?"

"Mito. In Saitama Prefecture."

"Oh. Doesn't the Emperor have a summer palace there?"

"Yes." She looked at him more boldly. "I know where you come from, Tomi. May I tell you?"

"Of course," Hara said uncomfortably. "Where do you think I come from?"

"Hiroshima."

He was relieved. "How did you guess that?"

"You have a Hiroshima-*ken* accent."

"That is very clever! And here I thought the Imperial Naval Academy had taught me to speak perfectly."

She was pleased. "I like your accent, Tomi."

"I am glad."

She averted her eyes again and said softly, "You are a nice person, too."

"Thank you. Sometimes it is difficult."

She was about to say something more, but the door slid open and Sumida returned. "I am plagued with fools, Lieutenant. A simple problem with a truck tire becomes a mountain of irritation. Would you believe that those soldiers drove for eight kilometers on a flat tire? They didn't know there was a spare underneath. Your men had to show those simpletons how to change the wheel. Bah! We should send all such fools to the American Army. It would guarantee our victory."

"I am afraid my arrival and the situation with the prisoners has aggravated your problem."

"Not at all! Your men were most helpful. Excellent attitude. Good spirit. I would like to have such men. You can be proud of them."

"Thank you. If the truck is ready, perhaps we should be on our way."

"Yes, of course."

"Major, I want to thank you and your daughter for your great kindness and hospitality. Your daughter is a fine manager and I know that reflects her parent."

"Thank you, Lieutenant. Let's go then."

Hara looked at her. "Chiyo, I hope we meet again."

She bowed deeply. "That is my hope, too."

"Mine too." Sumida chuckled, pleased with this little venture. As they left the house, he asked, "By the way, Lieutenant, are you stationed far away from here?"

"Too far. I wish it were otherwise. I wish many things were otherwise." Hara looked back. She kneeled, watching them, framed by the doorway. Soft light from the house etched her into a balmy night punctuated by fireflies in the garden. She, he thought, is what I want. But it can't be.

IV

Kamasaki ordered Krag and Barton taken outside and put under the care of Toda and Endo. They all stood by while the other Nisei and several Japanese soldiers loaded the truck. Other soldiers trundled five-gallon cans of petrol from a supply behind the orderly room and filled the truck's tank.

Kamasaki addressed Toda. "Petty Officer!"

Toda came to attention. "Sir!"

"I have sent for Major Sumida. He will be here shortly. When he arrives, inform him that I have gone in the car to inspect the guard posts."

"Understood, sir!" Toda saluted.

"Carry on." Kamasaki returned the salute and went around the back of the old schoolhouse. A few moments later the post's sedan veered around the corner with a driver at the wheel, Kamasaki looking self-important in the back.

"He doesn't want to face Major Sumida," the Japanese patrol sergeant said to Toda. "He leaves it on my shoulders."

"You mean about the truck wheel?"

He looked morose. "Yes."

"Is the Major bad-tempered?"

"He is a combat man. He can't stand it here, so he takes it out on us. We have to work and drill like regular infantry." The sergeant laughed and waved his arm. "As if there will ever be any fighting in this little place."

"You are lucky. This is a quiet place."

"Too quiet for me. I am from Tokyo. I like some excitement."

"Better this kind of quiet than the excitement of battle."

"Have you been in battles?"

"Yes." Toda knew the set script. "Around New Guinea."

"I don't even know where that is."

"I hope for your sake you never get there."

"I suppose not. The war will be over soon. The Americans cannot last much longer."

"Any day now."

At the truck Krag and Barton had their arms retied. They were pushed into positions just behind the cab. Equipment was loaded behind them. One of the soldiers helped Sakai lift a cart into the back of the truck.

"These things are heavy. What do you have in there?"

"Canned rations, mostly. We never know where we'll wind up."

"Any to spare?" asked another soldier.

"We'd better keep what we've got." He took out a pack of Camels. But how about these?"

"Ah, cigarettes."

"American cigarettes. We took them from the prisoners."

"Oh?" The first soldier accepted one and bobbed his head in gratitude. "I will save this for off duty. Major Sumida will be along soon, and he gets angry if he sees us smoking on duty." He looked curiously at the cigarette. "It's lucky it didn't get wet in the sea."

"*Attention!*" shouted the patrol sergeant.

Sumida limped forward, Hara just behind him. "Report!"

The sergeant saluted. "The truck is loaded, sir, and the petrol tank has been filled."

"Very good. Where is Captain Kamasaki?"

"Sir!" said Toda. "Captain Kamasaki asked me to tell you he has gone to inspect the guard posts, sir."

Sumida looked grim. "I suppose he took the car?"

"Yessir," said the sergeant.

"Damn!" Sumida banged his cane against the ground. "Well, no matter!" He turned to Hara. "If the car were here, Lieutenant, I would accompany you to the main highway to Yokosuka."

Hara was glad Kamasaki had made off with the car. Sumida would have been a problem to have been solved cruelly. He would not have liked that. "Is the highway difficult to find?"

"No. Follow this road out of town." Sumida pointed with his cane. "It is the only one. After about five kilometers you cross a railroad track by a factory. Then the road widens and is paved. Keep on that road for ten more kilometers and you will intersect the main highway going east. It will take you straight toward Tokyo and Yokosuka."

Hara nodded as if he were memorizing the directions. When Sumida stopped speaking, he suddenly realized that he and the others had succeeded in the most difficult task they had — deception. He turned from the road and looked into Sumida's eyes. "Major Sumida, I must thank you once again for your courtesy, for your hospitality, and for your cooperation. I promise to include these things in my report to headquarters. I will send you a private copy of my report."

"That is generous." To Hara the man seemed genuinely touched. Perhaps it was the sake.

Hara spoke more softly. "And please thank your beautiful daughter for me. It is a burden to have to feed surprise visitors — especially Navy officers."

Sumida smiled appreciatively. "That is thoughtful, Lieutenant." He took Hara confidentially by the elbow and spoke almost in a whisper. "Perhaps you can arrange to come visit us again. The fishing is good here."

"You flatter me, Major. I love to fish."

"You do? Wonderful!" His voice went even softer. Hara strained to hear over the hubbub in the background. "I think my daughter especially would enjoy such a visit."

"On that basis alone I think such a visit would be very nice. I will turn my thoughts to it."

"Goodbye, then." Sumida saluted.

Hara returned the salute and turned to his men. "Mount up! *Haiaku!*" He climbed into the truck cab. Marumoto was at the wheel. "Until we meet again," he shouted at Sumida.

"Good trip."

Marumoto rolled the truck down the main street out of town. "Stay on this road," said Hara. "Mind your speed. We don't want to jostle five hundred pounds of TNT into a pothole."

"It's never off my mind, Tomi."

Krag spoke through the canvas lacings at the back of the cab. "What was that bullshit all about back there?"

"Major Sumida was playing genial host."

"Took long enough."

"I sure as hell didn't want to insult him, so I played along."

"My Japanese ain't very good, but I heard something about a daughter. Is that what took you so goddamn long, Hara?"

Hara smiled wistfully. "He has a daughter he's hoping to marry off. He has me spotted as a prospect."

"She's probably a dog."

"Right!" In fact, Hara muttered to himself, she is gorgeous.

"Should have brought her along," said Krag.

"Should have." They were out of town now. He turned and looked back at the others. "Sumida and his daughter were so damn nice to me I was almost tempted to turn you guys in and call off the war."

"That ain't funny, Hara," Barton growled.

"Wasn't meant to be."

The Target, September 4, 1942

I

The route was just as Sumida had described it. Marumoto held the truck in second gear most of the way to avoid shocks from the rutted road. But even at that crawling pace it was only a matter of minutes before the route led to a pass out of the hills into a narrow flat valley squared like a checkboard with rice paddies and an occasional farm compound. The railroad tracks were easily visible despite the dark. A large, seemingly quiet building, partially illuminated by low-wattage pole lamps, was located not far from the junction of the road and the tracks. Surrounded by a high chain-link fence, it was offset by about a hundred yards from each of the arteries. Sidings ran into it, but they were empty. About a mile farther north was a similar building. Its sidings seemed to be filled with freight cars. Smoke and steam plumed from numerous chimneys and outlets.

Marumoto took the truck well off the highway and stopped. The team got out, and they all worked to conceal the truck under branches. Then they moved forward through the pines to a vantage point overlooking the valley. Krag checked his map by flashlight. "Is that it?"

Hara scanned the site with binoculars. "There's the rail line. There's the road crossing. Just like the model. Just where Borovitch said it would be." He looked at Krag. "Must be it."

Krag took the binoculars. "What's that factory down the line that's all lit up?"

"Not on our map," said Hara.

"Borovitch didn't say anything about another factory," said Barton.

"This one in front of us looks like the target," said Hara. "Barton, what do you think?"

"Let me have those." He took Hara's glasses. He looked for a long time, then shrugged. "Squares with what Borovitch said. Looks pretty damn quiet."

Krag took the binoculars and studied the building. "It's dead."

"But that place down the line's going all out," said Barton. "Suppose this one's a decoy? A setup? Is there a battalion hiding in there?"

"Why?" asked Hara. "We got in clean. I don't think they're on to us. Why bother with lending us the truck? Hell, Sumida couldn't have faked all that goodwill."

"Yeah? Well, Japs like to smile a lot. Even when they kill you."

"Barton," Hara muttered, "someday you're going to say 'Jap' to me and I'll put a bayonet up your kazoo."

"Nothin' personal, Commander."

"We'd better sniff around a little," said Krag. "Tomi, send two of your guys down to check out that sentry hut."

"Endo! Marumoto! You heard him. Take a quick look. Keep out of sight. Don't make trouble. Leave your rifles and belts here. Do a drunken sailor routine if somebody stops you. Get in, look, and get out. If there's someone there, watch your accents."

"Right," said Endo. "We're off." As they jogged down the road, he said to Marumoto, "He must think we talk funny."

"You do. You've got a Southern Cal accent a mile wide. Fortunately, that's the Hiroshima accent. But me, the professor. Hell, it's an insult."

II

As they moved down to the flat ground, the tree cover became more scarce. They moved along the side of the banked road beside a rice paddy until they reached the chain-link fence. The mill site was elevated a few feet above the surrounding wet paddy land. They stopped and peered over the embankment into the mill grounds.

"Wish to hell I wasn't wearing a white sailor suit," Endo whispered.

"You'd think we'd be in navy blue for this."

"See anything?"

"Looks like nobody's home." He pointed at the dim post lamps around the perimeter. "Even the lights are turned low."

"Let's check that entrance hut."

Staying low behind the mill embankment, they made their way toward the lane leading from the main road to the plant. The lane led to a large gate chained shut and locked. An entrance hut flanked the gate. They worked their way closer, then waited to see if there was any sign of life inside.

Finally, Endo ran to the hut and looked in a window. He waved Marumoto forward.

"Empty," he said. "Dusty."

Marumoto tried a side door. "Not locked." he went inside. "Dust on the telephone. Hell, it's not even connected."

"No one's been using this place. See anything by the mill?"

Marumoto brushed grime from a window facing the mill. "The place is closed. Looks like some construction equipment."

"Kind of spooky. Let's get back."

III

Krag watched through binoculars. "They got to the gatehouse."

"Any reaction?" asked Hara.

"Nothing." He scanned the railroad and highway for any sign of an army patrol. "Everything's quiet." He saw the two figures in white jogging back. "Next time, Hara, the uniform of the day's going to be blues. I don't give a damn what Imperial Navy regs say."

"You're so right. You can see 'em a mile."

They waited until Endo and Marumoto moved in, gasping.

"What's the story?" asked Krag.

"Quiet as a tomb," Endo puffed. "Sentry post was empty and dusty. Place looks like they're still working on it."

"That fits what Borovitch said," said Hara.

"Yeah," said Barton. "The place just hasn't started production yet. Or they quit."

Krag didn't like it. "You'd expect a little more activity though, wouldn't you?" He studied the mill grounds through his binoculars for another minute. "What the hell! Makes it easier for us if she's empty. Okay. Let's get to it. You know the drill, but I'll say again: we go in with the truck. Marumoto drives. Toda, you and Fujimura set up the Bren guns. See that ditch near the gate? There. Cover the road. If Kamasaki or Sumida shows, cut 'em down quick as you can. We don't want gunplay if we can avoid it."

"I don't think we have to worry about Sumida," said Hara. "He was heading home to the sake jug when I saw him last."

"That's a break. Anyway," Krag continued, "the rest of us go inside and get to work. It's now 2235. Remember: set your timers on 2400 hours. When all charges are planted, we take off the way we came in. Drive to the beach for pickup. If there's a hitch — shooting, arrival of the marines, anything like that — set your charges on double fifteen-second fuze. Get the hell out the best way you can. But make sure those charges are primed right. Understood?"

Everyone nodded silently.

"If we have to run cross country," Krag went on, "we rendezvous on the beach no later than midnight. If you're late, sorry: you're stuck. Questions? No? That's good, because I don't have answers. Let's do it."

IV

It took less than four minutes for Marumoto to move the truck down the road, turn down the lane, and drive toward the silent

116

mill. Krag rode in the cab with him.

"Barrel right through that gate, Bob, and stop inside."

The chain was no match for the truck. The gate flew open with a clang. Toda and Fujimura leaped out the back and set up their guns. The truck lurched on forward. The huge main doors of the mill weren't barred. Krag slid them open. The truck moved inside, and Krag pulled the doors closed behind. The others climbed out of the truck and looked around. The only illumination was from widely spaced security lamps.

"All clear this side!" said Barton.

"Nobody, Skipper!" said Endo.

"Let's not stand around, then!" Krag told them. "Let's get that crap off the truck."

It didn't take long. Each man took his quota of explosives from the cart. The demolition blocks were packed in canvas pouches with straps, ten pounds to a pack. Friction tape, timers, and fuzes were packed in belts, like ammunition bandoliers. Each man slung one coil of fuze and two of primacord around him. They donned their miners' helmets. In addition there was a squat, square work lamp with a strap for each of them and a small flashlight for backup. Krag quickly inspected each man. They were ready.

"When you use up your quota, come back to the carts for more. Don't spare the blocks. Questions?"

No one had any. They were ready.

"Good. Let's get at it: Barton, you and Hara on the furnace and control. Endo! Marumoto! On the crane! Sakai get your pictures. Find the argon gas supply. Then join me in the powerhouse. Remember: set your charges for 2400 hours. Go!"

The teams jogged off to their assignments.

At the furnace Hara looked up. The cauldron bellied out above him, huge, ugly, ominous — and silent. Workmen's tools were stowed randomly about. Power-supply cables trailed this way and that. Hydraulic lines weren't connected.

"This thing looks like it's a long way from completion," he said.

"Who the hell cares?" Barton muttered. "I don't build 'em, I

117

just blow 'em up. Hey, Sakai! Get shots of this sucker!"

"Get the hell out of the picture, Barton. I want the furnace, not your fat ass."

"Don't smart-mouth me, kid. I gotta set these charges."

Hara suddenly shivered. "This place's cold. . .Listen, you work here. I'm going up to set charges in the control room."

"Yeah. Hand me that coil of primacord."

Sakai took some more photographs of the exposed innards of the unfinished furnace. He liked his assignment. It was the only time when his being the smallest of the group had paid off. Not that he was penalized for being small, but he felt there might be some resentment that he hadn't been put on a Bren gun or sent up on the cranes lugging heavy satchels of explosive. He followed Hara up the ladder to the control room.

"Get some shots of this before I charge it," said Hara.

"Looks like they're still working on it."

"Seems so." Parts of the control panel itself were disassembled, exposing a hydra of cable underneath. Toolboxes and power tools were stowed by walls made of firebrick. Thick tempered glass windows overlooked the top of the Argon Furnace itself. An operator sitting at the control panel could manipulate the huge cauldron back and forth on its pinions while, at the same time, monitoring the critical temperature and behavior of the alloy inside. Hara looked down. He could see Barton expertly weaving demolition blocks together with primacord. He did it in a way that would turn the furnace and all its appendages to twisted scrap.

Sakai popped a flashbulb and then another. "Okay, Tomi. Done."

"Thanks, see you around the campus."

"Right."

Sakai scrambled back down the ladder and trotted toward a large, walled-off area. Borovitch said it would be the part of the mill housing administrative offices, tool and heavy equipment rooms, and a large open storage area. Sakai pushed open a heavy sliding door. The offices and equipment areas were just where

Borovitch had promised — but empty and silent. He went to the window wall of the offices, knocked out some panes, and took a photograph of the vacant interior. Then he did the same at the equipment storage areas. They, at least, housed such things as small tractors, compressors, jackhammers, heavy tools, and the like. He turned from the tool area to the storage area. Empty. Not a sign of an argon tank or anything that looked like one.

"Very strange," he muttered aloud. "Maybe outside."

He flashed a shot of the empty area, then located an exit door in the far wall. Warily, he opened the door and peeped out on the exterior storage area. It was the one on the other side of the mill from where they had entered. Except for some odds and ends of heavy equipment, it, too, was vacant. No argon tanks. Well, he thought, if they're not there, I can't set charges on them.

He trotted back through the mill to the cranes. High above he saw Endo and Marumoto taping charges to the heavy I beams of the crane arms. The lights on their helmets were like fireflies. Their work lamps glowed in a way that made him think of the paper Japanese lanterns he'd seen as a boy. Quickly, he snapped his photographs, then went to join Krag in the powerhouse.

It was set apart from the main mill building by a narrow alley. Krag was busy attaching charges to the cylinder blocks of the big auxiliary diesels.

"Smile, Commander!" said Sakai.

Krag snorted.

"You get shots of the cranes? Furnace?"

"Yessir. Plenty. Ugly son of a bitch. It's bigger than what Borovitch said. Lot bigger."

"How do you know it's bigger? Ever seen a fifty-ton furnace before?"

"No," Sakai conceded. "But it still looks bigger."

"Maybe it's because you're standing underneath looking up." He set the timer on the charge. "You find the argon tanks?"

"Nossir! Saw nothing anywhere like Borovitch described. Nothing even close."

"Nuts!" Krag looked around glumly. "'Course this place obviously isn't finished. Figures they wouldn't stock up on their supplies yet." He unwound more primacord and linked it to charges already in place on a bank of huge electrical generators. "You're sure they're not around some corner?"

"Positive. Did the whole perimeter. Looked every likely place, Commander. Even looked outside. Doc said they're big sons of bitches, so they couldn't hide 'em."

"Right." Krag sighed. "Wish we had 'em, though. Doc says argon's hard to come by. Since we've come this far, I'd like to get the whole mushroom. But..."

"What do you want me to do?"

"Give me a hand with these charges. Tape down that primacord."

V

Work proceeded on the cranes. Marumoto even forgot that he was working nearly forty feet above the mill floor with nothing but air between him and the cement. He completed taping demo blocks in a double rank on the vertical section of the crane beam. He strung primacord between them and another double rank nearer to the base. He set his timers. He played his lamp over the work. Done. Satisfied, he crawled down the crane track to help Endo.

"Tape on enough of those demo blocks to cut that track beam."

"Got it."

"Gimme the tape." The muscular Endo was perspiring profusely. Sweat dribbled in steady droplets from his nose to the mill floor. While it was cool and damp down there, up near the corrugated steel roof of the mill the day's heat had been trapped. It radiated like an oven.

Marumoto attached charges to narrow rails. These were the tracks that would carry the rolling cranes up and down the mill. He was sweating heavily himself now. He wiped his brow and looked below. In the gloom he saw the helmets and work lamps of the others moving like lethargic embers around some slow fire.

"Boy, I'm glad nobody's around."

"Yeah, this work's tough enough without a bunch of citizens in the background."

"But if there were people — you know, guards and that kind of thing — we'd have to deal with 'em."

"So?"

"Now that we're on the scene, I don't know if I've got the stomach to kill a man."

"Hell of a time to get nerves, Professor."

"I don't call it nerves. I call it morality."

"Whatever it is, it's got nothing to do with our job."

"Been on my mind for days. . ."

"What brought that on?"

"Barton, crazy as it sounds."

"That bastard? What'd he say?"

"At the briefing back at Pearl. He asked me if I knew how to use a bayonet. Said 'Japs like to use the pigsticker.' "

"Forget it!" Endo strapped his last blocks in place and leaned more or less at ease on the broad crane beam. "He had a hard time in the Philippines. He's getting over it." Endo laughed. "He might even be thinking we're Americans."

"It's not that." Marumoto looked at his grimy hands. "It's the bayonet. I don't think I could do it. . ."

Endo looked at him sympathetically. "Forget it! At the rate we're going, we'll be out of here and on our way home in a couple of hours. You can use your bayonet to open the congratulatory mail."

Marumoto smiled wanly. "Sure."

"Okay," said Endo, "I think that does it." He rummaged a sheet of paper from his pocket. "Check me out."

"Go ahead."

Endo read from the sheet. "Two twenty-pound cutting charges on crane main cross-beam. . ."

Marumoto looked and counted quickly. "Check!"

121

"Four ten-pound cutting charges in four places on crane track."
"One. Two. Three. Four. Check!"
"Primacord connecting all charges."
"Check."

VI

It was just past 2300 hours by Krag's watch when the teams assembled once again by the truck. The carts, empty of their cargoes, looked like scooters abandoned by some children who'd run off somewhere else to play.

Krag looked around at them. Their faces were begrimed by the dirt, grease, and soot of the mill. What had been sailor's whites now were black-and-grays.

"All here? Report!"

Hara was first. "Charges planted in the control room. Double-primed and timed for 2400 hours."

"Furnace," said Barton, "double-primed and timed. 2400."

"Crane double-primed and timed," said Endo. "2400."

"Same here," said Marumoto.

"And," said Krag, "power transformers and auxiliary diesels double-primed and timed. 2400. Sakai, tell 'em about the gas."

"No argon gas supply located. Seventy-one photographs taken. One to go."

"What's that?"

"You guys. Stand by the furnace."

"Oh Jesus!"

"Okay, I just fiddle with this timer. . ." Sakai propped the camera on one of the explosive carts and ran to get into the picture. "Look into the lens." An instant later the flashbulb blinked. "Got it!"

"Let's go!" barked Krag. "Load those carts."

The carts were light without their loads of explosives and ammunition. They were tossed clattering into the truck, and the squad piled in behind. Marumoto gunned the engine while Krag slid open the main door.

Seconds later they were rolling out the way they had entered. Past the broken gate, Krag shouted at Toda and Fujimura, "On the truck! Bren guns at the tailgate. Let's go!"

The Cove, September 4, 1942

I

The truck ride was faster this time. No one had to worry about demolition blocks. Marumoto retraced the route to within a kilometer of Ringo. There, as Borovitch had said, there was a narrow dirt lane. It branched off and wound through boulder-strewn, pine-laced terrain to a cove just north of where the old man's house had been. Marumoto drove very slowly now, using the truck's parking lights to pick out the lane from the rocks. He and Krag had worked out a crude timetable that gave them roughly ten minutes to reach the cove, if they averaged eight kilometers per hour.

"Time," said Krag.

"Okay. When I find a likely spot, I'll pull this thing in."

"How about there?" Krag pointed to a gap between two huge boulders.

"Looks good." Marumoto steered through the gap and pulled the truck into a thicket of brush and pine saplings and stopped. Everyone got out quickly. Working in the light of their helmet lamps, they piled brush around the truck.

"Good enough," said Krag. "By the time they find the truck, Japanese intelligence will have figured out the scam anyway."

"And we'll be back in Pearl, baby!" Endo enthused...

"Not unless we get down to that beach," said Krag. "Leave

125

everything in the truck you don't need. Let's go. Lights out!"

Barton, wise in the ways of dark, alien forests, took the lead. The others followed him single file. Their eyes soon became accustomed to the variations of shadow. It was a moonless night, but a brilliant star-lit sky helped them along. The lane was only a hundred yards from the edge of the rocky scarp above the cove.

"Wait!" said Barton. "I'll take a look-see."

He got down and crawled on elbows and knees to the cliff. Using binoculars as a light enhancer, he scanned the terrain around the cove for nearly five minutes. Then he crawled back.

"All clear. McGlynn's down there on the sea side of a big rock."

"Glad to hear it," Krag murmured. "At least we know Hunley hasn't run off or got sunk."

"Or both," said Hara.

"Follow me." Barton moved back toward the cliff. "The way down's a little tricky. Keep a handhold."

It didn't take long. While studying the cove, Barton had picked out the best path. Silently, he led them straight to McGlynn's boulder. "Come out, come out, wherever you are!" he called quietly.

McGlynn stepped out of the shadows. He was dressed in blues. He had blackened his face with diesel soot and wore a dark blue watch cap over his blond hair. He carried a Thomson sub-machine gun.

"How'd you know where I was?"

"You stood out like a beacon," said Barton. "You might as well have worn landing lights." It wasn't true, but Barton couldn't resist the jibe.

McGlynn ignored him. "Well, you're right on time. Any problems?"

"Later!" Krag snapped. "Let's get out of here! Those charges are set for 2400."

"Okay," said McGlynn. "The boats are this way. Hunley's watching for us." He took a stubby flare gun from his pocket. "Stand back." He banged the base of the gun against a boulder. The cartridge popped and a bright red ball of phosphor gleamed briefly, then, because he had intentionally pointed it at a low angle, it hissed out in the sea. It was enough. Over the soft wash of surf they could hear the regurgitating sound of the submarine's tanks blowing. In less than a minute the sub had broached, black against the flickering dark water of the cove, framed in a film of white wake that faded away like a ghost.

By that time they were pushing the boats out. These were smaller than the landing boats, presumably still tied up at the Ringo pier. There was nothing to carry back but the shore party. Each boat had a small, powerful, specially muffled outboard motor. The two-hundred-yard trip to *Grayfish* went quickly. At the submarine, Hunley's own men were on deck in blues and blackface to aid the boarding.

"Stow those boats!" Hunley croaked in a voice between a whisper and a bellow. "Lively!" He swung down from the bridge and personally gave Krag a hand up. "How'd it go?"

"Too damn easy."

"Any patrols on shore?"

"Small garrison in town. Hara handled that. Otherwise not a damn thing."

"Good. Let's go below. I've got some bourbon that'll make the trip seem worthwhile."

"The New Navy," said Hara. "I'm for that."

"Hold it!" Krag barked. He looked at his watch, then held up his hands, fingers extended. "Six! Five! Four! Three! Two! One! 2400!"

They all turned and stood transfixed, watching the rugged horizon to the east. Then, like something from a summer storm, flashes studded the sky. Seconds later came the sounds of a series of dull, almost unobtrusive thuds.

"I thought it'd be bigger," said Endo.

"Me too," somebody else said in the dark.

"It did the job," said Krag. "Let's go get that drink."

II

Sumida sat bolt upright. "What was that?" He listened intently, but there was nothing more. He felt cold sweat around his mouth. A war dream? Thunder?

Chiyo came in from her own chamber. "Was it an earthquake?"

Sumida was relieved to know he wasn't in the grip of a childish nightmare. "I don't know. Listen!"

There were no more sounds, but Sumida was uneasy. He was awake now anyway. "I better go find out. It seemed like explosions, but I was asleep."

Sumida slipped into his uniform. As he was buckling on his pistol belt there was a pounding at the door.

"Major!" It was the voice of his orderly. "There has been an explosion."

"I know! I'm on my way. Get Captain Kamasaki."

"What do you think it is?" asked Chiyo, helping him maneuver toward the door of the house.

"Probably an accident on the railroad. They're always banging their cars together."

"Shall I make tea to bring to you?"

"No. Go back to sleep. It is nothing."

Outside, Sumida stopped to look up at the brilliant heavens. Not a sign of a thunderhead. So what he heard must have been something other than distant thunder.

He limped as quickly as he could to the orderly room. Inside, Kamasaki was on the telephone. His face had the stunned look of a bureaucrat confronting a dead mouse in his in-basket. He bowed to the telephone as if the other party were present. "Yes! Yes! I understand." He hung up and turned to Sumida, eyes wide with dismay. "Major, there has been an explosion at one of the steel mills."

"Calm down, Captain. What steel mill?"

"The one near the highway."

"The empty one?"

"Correct, sir."

"We had no sentries there. Where did the report come from?"

"From the company guards at the other plant."

"Are they all right?"

"All quiet there."

"Good." Sumida breathed more easily. "It's probably some stupid accident. But take the men out there and stand by until we find out what's going on. Good experience for them."

Kamasaki looked even more perplexed. "But we lent the truck to the naval officer."

"Truck?" Sumida felt his temper rising. He suppressed it. Anger would gain nothing. After a pause he asked, "You're an infantry officer, are you not, Kamasaki?"

"Yessir."

"By tradition, you know how to march?"

"Of course, sir."

"So, *march!*"

For an instant, Kamasaki didn't quite comprehend. Then it was all clear. He snapped at attention. "Yessir! Where will you be?"

"I am going ahead in the car. I will meet you there."

III

They gathered in the wardroom. Borovitch was waiting for them. Hunley went for his bottle of bourbon. They looked at each other with near disbelief.

Barton suddenly chuckled. "Son a bitch! We pulled it off. We out-Japped the Jap."

"I feel too good even to get mad at you, you bastard," Endo laughed.

"I got your pictures, Doc," said Sakai, holding up the camera bag. His usual funereal expression had given way to a kind of somber grin.

"Excellent," said Borovitch. "We must process them immediately. Please assist me."

Sakai frowned. "Boy, I could use some shut-eye."

"Do what he says," said Hara. "You can sleep all the way home."

Hunley returned with a fifth of sour mash. He put it in the middle of the wardroom table, took off the cap and put it into his pocket. A crewman followed with a tray full of coffee cups.

Barton dealt the cups around the table, took one himself, and splashed bourbon.

"When do we shove off, Hunley?" asked Barton.

"We sit tight until McGlynn debriefs you. Borovitch wants to see the pictures first."

"Why? You think we faked it, McGlynn?"

The intelligence officer shrugged. "You blew up something, Barton. I just want Borovitch to see what you got."

Hunley helped himself to some of the bourbon. "We'll sit on the bottom until he's satisfied. Then home."

IV

It was one in the morning when Sumida's driver took the sedan through the main gate of the mill. Sumida noted immediately that the heavy iron mesh gates were hanging askew. They had been knocked off their hinges, twisted out of shape. Some other vehicles already were there. A small group of civilians had pushed open the big sliding door and were peering inside.

A small fire cast them in an orange glow. Except for paneless windows everywhere, the building itself seemed undamaged.

Sumida directed his driver to take him to the group and stop. The driver held the door as Sumida climbed out. The civilians turned to him in amazement. Sumida saluted.

"Good evening. I am Major Sumida, commander of the army garrison in Ringo. What has happened?"

The civilians approached and bowed.

"I am Nakashita, manager of Steel Mill One." He pointed vaguely north. "Down the tracks."

"You reported the incident?"

"Our civilian guards reported it. I was called from home, as were my colleagues." He introduced them. Each wore pale gray coveralls. They looked alike, even to their worried expressions. Sumida catalogued them as Managers One, Two and Three.

"Shall we go inside?"

Nakashita looked more worried. "It may not be safe. We don't know what else could explode."

"The fire seems to be dying down," said Sumida. "Do you have any idea how this happened?"

"We can only guess," said Nakashita. "It might have been paint. Or possibly fuel oil. Gasoline in some equipment, perhaps."

"Oh?" Sumida lifted an eyebrow. "The explosions seemed quite formidable. They awakened me and my daughter. By any chance were workers dealing with explosives here?"

"I am not directly involved with this plant," said Nakashita. "But, I cannot think why they would be using explosives. I understood this plant is only a few weeks away from completion. No need for blasting or anything like that."

"But I definitely heard explosions," Sumida persisted.

"I heard them," said Manager One.

"They woke me, also," said Manager Two.

"Why don't we go inside and see," Sumida prompted. He led the way. The fire had spent itself on some wooden partitions. Except for the embers, it was dark. However, each of the managers had a large flashlight. Their beams crisscrossed in sweeps around the interior.

"Look!" exclaimed Manager Two. "The cranes have collapsed!"

"And the furnace!"

"No paint-can explosion did that," said Sumida. "Those girders have been twisted by high explosives." He felt his pulse quickening. "This was no accident!"

"It might have been a bomber," Nakashita said excitedly. "They attacked Tokyo, you know."

"Aerial bombing?" Sumida snorted. "Here? At night? That would be very difficult." He walked closer to inspect the wreckage. "Besides, this isn't bomb damage."

"How do you know?" asked Manager Three.

"There are no craters. No fragment marks. Bombs make big pits. Even a two-hundred-kilo bomb will make a pit fifty feet across and thirty feet deep. Fragments would make the walls of this place a sieve. I see no such evidence."

"Perhaps the enemy dropped saboteurs from airplanes," said Manager Two. "On parachutes. I've read about such things."

"That's a possibility," Sumida agreed. "But why *this* place? It was not even completed. You said so."

"I am sorry, Major." Nakashita bowed apologetically. "We're forbidden to talk about our work."

"Oh come, now! What foolishness!"

"I am sorry." Nakashita bowed more deeply. "It is a strict rule. As an officer, you understand..."

Sumida sighed. "Yes, of course." He looked around at the wreckage. "But this isn't an airplane factory. It's some kind of mill that makes steel, isn't it? Can you tell me that?"

"Yes, of course," said Manager One. "That's correct."

"And there are many steel mills in Japan. Is that correct?"

"Yes, of course," said Nakashita impatiently. "Dozens of them."

"Most of them much bigger than this?"

"Bigger," said Manager Three. "Yes."

"Yet," Sumida wondered, "the enemy — somebody — comes here...?

"Possibly they came by ship," said Manager Two.

"Not possible," said Manager One. "Our navy would have intercepted them."

"But why here?" Sumida persisted. "Didn't anybody hear or see anything besides explosions?"

"We had no reason to be on guard or suspect anything here," said Nakashita. "After all, this mill is weeks away from completion. We have enough work to do to keep Mill Number One working. It's brand-new, you know. There are still kinks in the machinery."

"I know nothing of steel mills," said Sumida. "All I know is that *this* place was damaged by explosives. By sabotage."

132

"Could there be" — Manager Two whispered the word — "Traitors?"

"Traitors?"

"Impossible!" Manager One chided.

"It must have been the Americans," said Manager Two.

"If it was an American force," said Manager Three, "they should be easy to track down. Where can they go with their American faces?"

"They would head for the coast probably," Sumida murmured. "A boat could slip in, or a submarine." He thought of Hara and how easily that young man and his entourage had landed in Ringo. Of course, they were the Imperial Japanese Navy and had every right to be there. "But" — he shook his head — "no airplane could land and pick up saboteurs without being seen. Where would it land?"

"Maybe they were Chinese," Nakashita ventured. "They look like us. . ."

Sumida nodded. "That makes more sense. But" — he held up a cautioning finger — "they would have to know our Japanese language and manners to get away with it."

"That would be most difficult for Chinese people," said Manager One.

"They could never fool us for long," said Manager Three.

"But, perhaps, long enough," said Sumida, waving at the damage. "But why?"

"We should notify the navy immediately," said Manager Three.

Again Sumida thought of Hara. "Damn!" he grumbled. "I had dinner just tonight with a naval officer. He could have helped us."

"Why don't you call the Navy directly?"

"Hah! It is not that easy. First, I must report to my own commander. Then he must notify his commander. It goes like that until some commander has authority to speak directly to the navy. If it were a little thing — like lending a truck — I could do it."

"You may use my office, of course," said Nakashita.

"They will want to know how bad the damage is here."

"It's complete," said Manager Two, kicking ineffectually at a twisted crane beam.

"It doesn't look that serious — except that crane," said Sumida.

"Not to you," said Nakashita. "But to an engineer it is clear that this job was done by professionals." He pointed at the scattered, warped wreckage of the furnace. "This equipment is irreparable. It will have to be replaced. But we have no replacements."

"They knew exactly what to destroy," said Manager Three. "Look at the furnace! The controls. . ." He played his flashlight on the control room. Its windows were gone. Huge holes gaped in the walls. Fragments of cable and glass were everywhere.

"Fortunately," said Manager Two, "they didn't attack Mill Number One. That would have stopped our production, and we might never get it going with damage like this."

"I will post my men around it until the mystery is resolved," said Sumida.

"The enemy has fled by now, surely," said Nakashita.

"Who knows?"

V

Grayfish rested on the bottom a mile off shore and a hundred and fifty feet below the surface. Krag led the debriefing. Hunley's executive officer and Crawford, the navigation officer, transcribed the proceedings. Only Borovitch and Sakai were absent. They were in the galley, where a temporary darkroom had been set up.

"The landing followed the script," said Krag. "The only variation was that the local authorities aren't in the town hall, but in a little schoolhouse. It's an army post. Tomi, why don't you pick it up here?"

"Sure." He went to the map of Ringo. "The schoolhouse is here. The army garrison is only a dozen men, commanded by a Major

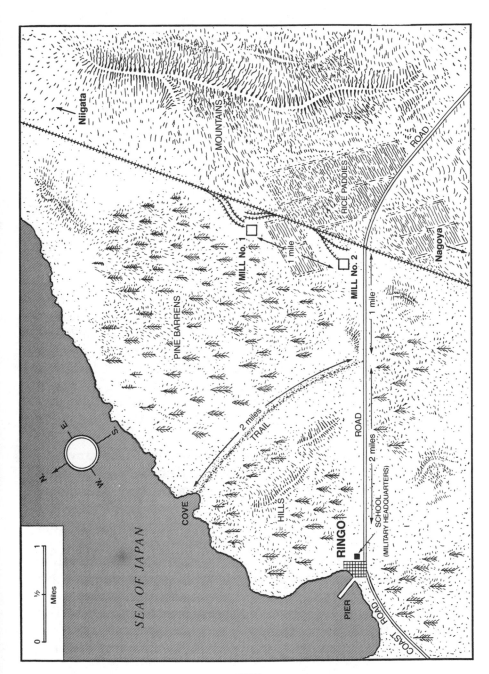

Sumida. Second in command is a Captain Kamasaki. Sumida is a combat veteran, wounded on Bataan. He's got this assignment while he's recuperating."

"The other guy's a little rat," said Barton.

"Also a little stupid," Hara went on. "He's a petty bureaucrat. But Sumida's no fool. Tough."

"Tell 'em about the daughter," Endo prompted.

Hara blushed. The others laughed. For the record, Hara described the delay, because of the truck, and his dinner at Sumida's home.

"And he had no inkling that you weren't a Japanese officer?" McGlynn asked.

"He'd have done something about it," said Hara. "He's the direct-action type. He wouldn't be subtle. I'd be dead."

"Incredible."

"But that's what we expected," said Marumoto. "Put yourself in his shoes. Then on top of that add what I told you before about Japanese attitudes. Did he question your accent, Tomi?"

"No, but his daughter pinned it right to Hiroshima."

"What's so important about accents?" asked McGlynn.

"Most of the Japanese immigrants — our parents — came to the United States from the prefectures of southern Honshu, Hiroshima and Yamaguchi."

"So what?"

"So it labels us. The trick was to make sure that if anybody asked, we were to say that's where we came from. If we said we came from Tokyo or Kyushu or somewhere else, they'd wonder about it.

"Anyway," Hara went on, "the truck finally got back with a flat tire, which our able seamen changed. Krag. . ."

"Well, once Tomi got us into the truck, everything went like clockwork. We got to the mill, but it wasn't operating. No guards."

"No people at all?" asked McGlynn, scribbling notes. "Tell us about the equipment."

"The equipment looked just about like Doc described it, only it was obvious the project wasn't finished. No sign of operations. No argon supply. We set our charges by the book and got the hell out. You know the rest. You heard it go up."

"Anything else unusual about the mill?" McGlynn looked around at them. "Anything in the neighborhood we should get intelligence to look into?"

"One thing," said Barton. "There's a whole other factory of some kind about a mile down the railroad. All lit up. Isn't on our map."

"What kind of factory?"

"On the outside the building looks just like Mill One. There was a freight siding with a lot of cars. Obviously, a busy place."

"Some kind of war plant?"

"Probably," said Krag. "But Doc didn't mention any other factory being there."

Just then Borovitch came through the bulkhead door behind him. "I didn't mention it, my friend, because it wasn't there a year ago when I left. Nor was it spoken of around me."

"What do you think it is, Doc?"

Borovitch looked very old and tired. "I fear that it is something that has complicated our lives."

10

The Cove, September 5, 1942

I

Quite clearly something was very wrong. They all stared at Borovitch. McGlynn broke the silence. "What do you mean?"

The old man made a futile gesture with his hand. "Blame it on Sakai. As we began to work in the darkroom, he happened to mention that there is a second plant," Borovitch said. "This was news to me."

"What's so remarkable about that?" asked Krag.

"Sakai gave me details." Borovitch smiled morosely. "And I smelled trouble."

Krag's eyes narrowed. "What trouble?"

"Sakai is a very good photographer. His photographs confirm this. So, let's look at the pictures. . ."

Borovitch spread a dozen damp glossies out on the wardroom table. He pointed at one. "There. This exterior picture."

"So?" asked McGlynn.

"This unquestionably is what *I* know as Mill *One,*" Borovitch said. "But notice that sign."

They all looked. The sign was written in Japanese kanji.

"Means nothin' to me," said Endo. The others muttered agreement.

"Lieutenant Hara, can you read it?" asked Borovitch.

"Sure. It says, Special Steel Mill Number Two. Restricted to authorized..."

"Stop!" Borovitch snapped. He looked around. "Reactions to what Hara just read?"

"Nothin' to me," said Barton.

Marumoto frowned at the kanji in concentration. "Special Steel Mill Number..." His mouth fell open in surprise. "Of course, number *two*."

"Exactly!" said Borovitch.

Most of the others looked puzzled. "So it's called Mill Two instead of Mill One," said Barton. "So what?"

"Opinions?" asked McGlynn.

"I'm afraid I know the problem," Marumoto murmured.

"Let's hear it," said Krag.

"The Japanese have a tradition of numbering things according to when they begin — chronologically."

"What's so odd about that?"

"Think about it," Marumoto continued. "Americans almost always number things as part of an established sequence. For example, say you've got a housing development. Each address reflects a location in a sequence. The house at address *one* might get finished a year after the house at address *nine*. But its address is still *one*."

"So?" said Hunley.

"In Japan the first house completed gets number one," Marumoto explained. "The next house completed might be a mile away, but it gets number two." He smiled ruefully. "Raises hell with their postal service."

"What's that got to do with the Argon Furnace?" Krag asked suspiciously.

"Simply this," said Borovitch. "For reasons I will explain, the Japanese elected to complete *another* mill before they finished the one you attacked — the building I worked on — the one I described to you."

"What're you leading up to?" Krag persisted.

"I believe the Japanese engineers have installed the *first* Argon Furnace in the other building you saw instead of in the

140

building we all call Mill One."

"And," said Marumoto, "following Japanese practice, *that* building became Mill One. Our building became Mill Two."

"So what the hell was that junk we blew up, Doc?" Barton asked angrily.

"That's right, Doc," said Endo. "It sure looked like the furnace you described."

"It did, indeed," said Borovitch. "It *was* an Argon Furnace. In fact, a much *larger* Argon Furnace. But it was incomplete. Unfinished. Here: this picture...see? Lines not connected. In this one: pipes not connected. Here: the head is off a diesel engine. I'm afraid, gentlemen, you killed only the unborn child of the first Argon Furnace. The monster lives. But it lives in another house."

"Godammit!" Barton exploded.

"So near and yet so far," said Hara.

"Sakai and his damned camera," Endo muttered.

"My doing," said McGlynn. "We had to have pictures for Doc to analyze."

"Anyway, we got something," said Barton. He looked glum.

"You did what you could," Hunley told them. "How could you know? We got you in; we got you out. You did your job. You may only have killed the baby, but that brat would have grown up. It's not a waste."

"The bastards fooled us after all," said McGlynn.

"They didn't plan it that way," said Fujimura. "They were lucky."

"I thought it went too easy," said Toda.

The silence was a pall. Finally, Hunley said, "Well. Only thing to do now is pull out." He started for the control room.

"Wait a minute!" Krag said suddenly. It startled them. "Let's talk this thing through."

"Talk what through?" asked McGlynn.

"We might not be finished."

"Hell, you've used up all your explosives, fuze..."

"I know that, dammit!" Krag shouted. He brought his voice

141

down. "But we have to talk it through."

They all stared at him. "So talk!" said Hunley.

"All right," said Krag. "We've used up all of our explosives. Does Sumida's army post have any?"

"Doubt it very much," said Hara. "He was complaining what a backwater it is. They didn't even have a radio hookup."

"I agree," said Barton. "I saw rifles and ammo. That's the heaviest thing around."

"I didn't see anything either," said Krag. "But we outgun them. Barton — in the mill — could we work something explosive out of gasoline? Fuel oil?"

"They make low-yield explosives. Deflagrating, not detonating."

"What's that mean?" asked Fujimura.

"No good for demo work. For cutting steel, blowing bridges, that kind of thing you need high-yield explosives like RDX, TNT, Nitro. Of course, fuels would burn and that'd do something."

"Could we take ammo apart?"

"You have the same problem with cartridge powders," Barton told them. "They don't detonate. Besides, taking ammo apart is very tricky. Don't recommend it." Then he had an idea. "But we could use deck gun shells as is. . ."

"I won't disarm this vessel, Krag, to support some. . ."

"We're just talking it through, Hunley."

Barton shook his head. "Actually, there ain't much TNT in a three-inch shell. . .only a couple pounds. Wouldn't do much. Fire would be your best bet. But that wouldn't do much to the cranes or furnace."

"But you have to hit all those pieces — control room, furnace, crane," said Hara. "The whole bag of goods. Could fire do that?"

"He's right," said Borovitch. "You must kill each of the creature's parts. They must be beyond repair." He shook his head. "But I question the value of fire in, say, destroying the crane. Obviously, your shells might do it, if you could get them in place."

Hunley had been standing, fuming.

142

Krag called on him. "Get it off your chest, Hunley."

"Listen! I will not risk this ship and crew on a half-assed pick-up scheme against an enemy that's got to be up and running by now. We could have Jap destroyers down on us from now on. The risk gets bigger every hour."

"There's another thing," McGlynn interjected. "We may only have gotten half a loaf on shore, but we sure as hell got something else. We got exact information. We have to get that information to Intelligence. They've got to know there's another plant and that it's operating. Right now that information is the most important part of this mission."

Krag looked around. "Doc?"

"The information is important, of course. But, meanwhile, the Argon Furnace is making enough alloy even while we talk to put a squadron of jet-engined fighters in the air. It will keep doing that every day from now on."

"So what do you propose, Doc?" Krag asked.

The old man looked down, poking at the photographs. Finally he said, "Attack again."

"With what?"

The old man shook his head bitterly. "I don't know."

Hunley slapped the table. "We can't go charging in like King Kong. What the hell damage could we do? The price is too high."

McGlynn nodded vigorous agreement. "I say, let Naval Intelligence work it out for another mission! We've shot our wad. The information is what counts now."

"Is intelligence more important than reality?" asked Borovitch.

"Under these conditions," said McGlynn, "I believe so, yes."

"But with luck," said Krag, looking around at their faces, "we could stop this Argon Furnace and, perhaps, save our fleet. Even shorten the war."

"You're blowing smoke. We can't bank on luck," said Hunley. "Besides, we've used up our quota already. I think we've been damn lucky to get this far."

"Any more ideas?" Krag prodded.

"Well," said Barton, "we probably could knock out the control panel with a fuel oil fire. We'd have to dismantle it. Three-inch shells might do the furnace. But some of that other stuff, I don't know. Tricky. I don't think we could fix up shells to cut those crane beams. Besides, what do we use for fuze and timers?"

"Looks like you're running out of options, Krag," said Hunley.

"You can't cut steel with fire," said McGlynn.

"Yes you can," Fujimura said quietly.

They all looked at him.

"Oh yeah?" said Barton.

"I been thinking." Fujimura spoke like a man reluctant to say what he had to say. "I know a way."

"Spit it out, kid!" Krag snapped.

"I worked in a steel mill," Fujimura said. "One thing they got lots of in a steel mill is acetylene torches."

"They do?" asked McGlynn. "Why?"

"They use 'em for scarfing, for cutting, for tapping, all kinds of stuff."

"What's 'scarfing'?" asked Hara.

"Well, say you've got an ingot of high-alloy steel like the stuff these mills make. When the ingot is cooling, it gets little cracks on the surface. When they flatten it out in the rolling mills, the little cracks turn into big problems."

"So?"

"So to beat that problem there are guys with acetylene torches who sweep the surface of each ingot, back and forth. Melting the surface a little gets rid of the tiny cracks. They call it scarfing. That takes lots of guys and lots of torches. So the torch is a basic tool. You can melt anything with a torch. Melting's as good as exploding."

"I think he's got something," said Krag.

"Good boy, Fuj!" Barton exclaimed.

"He's right!" Borovitch was excited by the idea. "You could cut down the cranes with a torch, cut the cables, melt the control panels, short the electric transformers — almost anything you can do with explosives."

"Hell," said Barton, "I know how to use a torch. Learned it in shipwright training. Fujimura and me can teach the rest of you."

Krag looked around. "Comments?"

"It's the least bad thing on a list of bad options," said Hara.

"If we go, that's the way to go, Skipper," said Endo. Others nodded reluctant agreement.

"Take an awful long time, wouldn't it?" asked Hunley.

"What about the time, Fuj?" Krag asked.

"Yeah. It would take a lot of time. Couple hours to do it right. Depends how many torches you've got."

"Another thing," said McGlynn. "You can't walk away from this job like you can do with explosives. You have to sit there and burn it. It'd take forever. We don't have the time."

"If we can get back, we can make the time," said Krag.

McGlynn protested. "We can't risk losing this intelligence just to take another questionable crack at the Argon Furnace. That mill is operating. It'll be swarming with workers, guards. Hell, they might have a regiment of guards in there by now."

"Maybe," Krag shrugged. "But I doubt it. I think they're still tryin' to figure out what the hell happened."

"Dammit!" Hunley banged the table. "I will not risk this boat!"

"Siddown, Hunley," said Krag. He didn't raise his voice, but the tone of command was unmistakable.

Hunley wavered. "I'm the skipper of *Grayfish*, Krag. . ."

"And I'm commander of this mission! Read your orders. Your job is to put us on the beach and to take us off the beach. It doesn't say once. It doesn't say twice. It says as many times as I decide."

"It's suicide."

"We have a mission. You damn well know that *Grayfish* and every one of us is expendable. Totally. That's not the way I want it. But that's sure as hell the way it is."

Hunley took some deep breaths. "Okay." He put out his hand to Krag. "You're right. I think you're nuts. But you're mission commander. So command."

"Thank you." Krag took his hand and shook it.

"Besides, when it comes to the heavy breathing, we have small torches on board that you can borrow," said Hunley. "But I can't lend crewmen. We're working in our jockstraps now."

"Fair enough."

Krag looked at their faces. There was resignation and a little sadness — recognition that a second try would be on a level of danger far greater than the first. Only Barton wore a half-smile.

"What's it going to be, Krag?" asked McGlynn.

Krag looked at the table. He couldn't bear to look them in the eyes. "We go back," he said softly, staring at his hands. "Nobody's sorrier than me."

II

Kamasaki had marched all the troops to the damaged mill. Sumida ordered him to post a guard around the working plant. Then he continued his inspection of the wrecked machinery with the mill managers. It was nearly dawn when Sumida's driver delivered all of them back at the guardhouse by the main gate of the operating mill.

"Kamasaki! Are your guards stationed?"

"Yessir. But we're spread thin. Five on duty, five in reserve."

"I'm going to ask for reinforcements. We cannot conduct our patrols and guard this place at the same time. But this takes priority for the time being."

"Very good, sir."

Sumida shook his head in puzzlement. "But why attack this place in the middle of nowhere?"

"The enemy?"

"Of course the enemy!"

Kamasaki thought about it. "The enemy is as foolish as he is insolent. They make attacks frivolously."

"It's insane. Or," he mused, "a mistake."

"A mistake," Kamasaki parroted. "What fools!"

"But why come all the way to Honshu to attack a little steel mill that's not even working?"

"They are very stupid," said Kamasaki.

"Or," said Sumida, "very wise in a way we don't understand."

"I cannot believe the enemy is wise."

"Anyway, we must be vigilant."

"Yessir!"

III

Fujimura found himself playing the unlikely role of teacher to a class that included Professor Marumoto, not to mention assorted officers and enlisted men. He had an easel to draw on. He used a ship's torch for his show-and-tell. Barton and a ship's mechanic's mate used the vessel's other torch as a visual prop.

"I'm not going to light this thing," said Fujimura. "The air's bad enough in here. But let me make a couple of points about using a torch."

He drew a picture of a flame. "You don't want a puffy yellow flame. The main thing is to set the nozzle so you've got the hottest possible flame. You want a flame that's almost invisible. Pale blue or lavender. Acetylene burns at around 5,500 to 6,000 degrees Fahrenheit. The hotter that flame, the better she cuts. I compare it to a saw. A dull saw takes longer to cut something than a sharp saw. So, to help the cutting, when we get into the mill, me and Barton are going to try to come up with the best nozzle tips they've got to make sure you'll get the right flame for cutting."

"How long's it take to cut one of those crane beams?" asked Marumoto.

"Getting to that." Fujimura drew an end-on picture of an I beam. "When you're cutting the beam, start at the top of the upright part."

"The vertical section?" prompted Borovitch.

147

"Yeah, this part. Focus the tip of your flame there and let it melt a hole all the way through the beam. Got it? All the way through. The melted steel will flow down, away from you. Got it?"

"How do you know you've cut all the way through the beam without being able to see both sides of it?" asked Endo. "It's pretty dicey up on those beams."

"Easy. You'll see the sparks of melted steel falling down from the other side. When you see sparks coming down, you start moving the tip of your flame very slowly down the beam. If the sparks stop falling, it means you're going too fast, not cutting all the way through. So slow down until they start again, then go ahead."

"How long's this take?" Marumoto asked again.

"Probably take you ten, fifteen minutes to go the distance. If there's a lot of weight on that beam, iron in the ladle or something like that, it might break off early."

"Be sure to watch out for that," Barton cautioned. "Like sawing a limb off a tree. When she goes, she can surprise you. Backlash."

"Just cutting the vertical part of the 'I' should do the job," Fujimura went on. "If not, start chopping the top flat part of the 'I' like you did the upright part."

"The control room shouldn't be any problem," said Hara, "but the furnace itself looks tough, especially if it's full of molten alloy."

Fujimura nodded. "Cutting up the furnace would be tough. Not really enough time to do it, either. But you don't have to. You can weld all those pinions and gears. Once you melt all those wheels together, they're useless. If they can't work the machinery, they can't get the steel out of the furnace. It'll go solid on 'em. Then they got a real problem. One big fifty-ton blob of iron. After you do the machinery, then you can chop up the hydraulic and gas lines."

Hara nodded. "Right."

"Any ideas on the powerhouse?" asked Krag.

Fujimura shook his head. "Don't know enough about it."

Barton spoke up. "Best bet's to shut down the diesels and weld their crankshafts and bearings to the housing. Same for the electrical motors. On the diesels, weld the cylinder head to the block. They'll have to yank out the whole damn thing and replace it."

"Argon tanks?" asked Sakai.

Borovitch spoke. "You must be very careful there," he said. "The gas is under extreme pressure. If you weaken the wall of the cylinder with heat, it could explode and kill you."

"So what do I do, Doc?"

Borovitch tugged his chin. "I think, perhaps, the best thing to do is to melt the nozzles. That will weld them to the steel collar of the tank. It would be virtually impossible then to get the argon gas out of the tank."

"It won't blow up if I do that?" Sakai asked apprehensively.

"Probably not, but do the work from one side. That way, if a nozzle blows off, it won't hit you. The gas, of course, will dissipate. But be very, very careful about the sides of the tank."

"Count on it."

IV

With Kamasaki, Sumida inspected the perimeter of the working mill.

"An enemy would have a hard time with this fence," said Kamasaki, plucking at the chain links.

"Bah! It wouldn't stop a goat. A few snips with wire cutters and they are through. But it is not the fence that concerns me."

"No?"

"Look!" Sumida waved at the pine trees and shrubs that came within yards of the fence. In the spare light of the predawn the foliage was like dark green ink smeared against the horizon. "Concealment, Kamasaki! An enemy force could get within feet of this place and we would never know it. They could be watching

149

us now."

Kamasaki's hand tightened on the hilt of his sword. "How many do you think there might be?"

"Who knows?" Sumida shrugged. "But in view of the limits of the attack I would guess it was a small force — a dozen, perhaps fewer."

Kamasaki was acutely aware that they were silhouetted against the waxing and waning red glare from inside the mill. "Shall we inspect inside?"

Sumida studied the forest as if there might be some clue to the mystery. What is this all about? he wondered. No matter. Whatever — whoever — created it had his respect. One might hate the fox for sneaking among his chickens, but one had to admire the craftiness of the fox and his guile in the face of mortal danger.

They moved through the partially opened rear door of the mill. The sudden switch from the dark forest to the clangor of the mill was startling. To walk into the mill was to step into a section of hell. Sumida was struck suddenly by the feeling that he had stepped into a roaring battle. Yet he could see no human.

At the far end of the mill were two big, square electric arc furnaces. From there, a huge kettle, manipulated by a gigantic overhead rolling crane, was hauled into the presence of a furnace closer to them. This iron chamber squatted like a massive, round, black, and malevolent demon, mouth agape. Cables controlling the kettle tipped it. A plume of white-hot steel spouted into the gaping mouth. Even fifty yards away, the intense heat was scorching. Sparks showered into the darkness and fell glowing red to the mill floor. Every wall and every far-off recess of the roof high above was suffused in an orange and red glare. It was beautiful and terrible at the same time, like an artillery barrage.

He watched for a moment, then shouted over the din, "Kamasaki, this is a dangerous place."

"Yessir." The captain had been eager to get inside; now he was just as eager to go somewhere else.

"Let's go this way." Sumida swung his stiff leg awkwardly over jumbles of slag that had fallen to the floor and maneuvered around large, hot ingot molds that stood upright in ranks like so many iron soldiers.

They passed under a lattice steel deck into a vast roofed-in area flanking the one where the cranes and the furnace were at work. Most of the floor space was occupied by elongated tanks piled in tiers. Most were painted white, a few were black. They looked to Sumida like stacks of huge mortar shells. To their immediate left were the mill operations offices, insulated behind dirty glass and steel-panelled walls. Just beyond them were the heavy wire tool cages, like so many jail cells. Nothing was locked up at the moment. A rank of acetylene torches leaned against the cages, awaiting the scarfing crews who would come in with the morning shift. Inside one of the offices, Sumida saw Nakashita and his minions huddled around a big teapot, poring over some production schedules. Sumida and Kamasaki went inside.

"Is there anything going on?" Nakashita asked.

"All quiet," said Sumida. "I have posted my men at both the rear and front gates of the mill. I have only ten men, so we are splitting them in shifts of four hours of duty and four to rest. Captain Kamasaki or I will be present at all times."

"How long do you expect the danger to last?"

"Who knows? Until we investigate the whole incident thoroughly, it is hard to say exactly what happened," said Sumida. "After that we will know whether we are really in danger. In the meantime, we take what precautions we can with limited means."

"Whatever or whoever it was is gone," Nakashita said matter-of-factly. "Lightning never strikes twice in the same place."

"It never has any reason to," said Sumida. "But an enemy might."

V

Aboard *Grayfish* there was little to do now but wait until dark. Endo, Fujimura, and Hara played poker with the ship's crew in the forward torpedo room. Krag was napping. In the wardroom Borovitch, Hunley, and Marumoto watched Barton honing a thin, blue-steel stiletto with a long hilt.

"This time I go in with my tools." Barton grinned wolfishly. He held up the weapon. "This here's a Fairbairn knife."

"It looks like something Italian from the sixteenth century," said Borovitch.

"It's something British Commando from the twentieth century, Doc." There was a note tablet on the table. He took a sheet of paper and sliced it cleanly with the knife. "Like a razor."

Borovitch grimaced. "War forces us to use some terrible tools."

"A knife's not as terrible as a flamethrower, Doc. It's quick. It's quiet. It doesn't let you down. Like the man said: 'War is hell.' But everybody keeps on coming back for more."

"I fear you are correct, Sergeant."

"Why are you in this, Doc? You could be home running a war plant. Make big dough."

"The world is in a Manichaean struggle," he said. "A side must be taken."

"You lost me. What kind of struggle?"

"*Manichaean,*" said Marumoto. "The idea of religious dualism. It came out of Persia in the third century."

"This is the twentieth, Perfesser," said Barton.

"The idea," said Marumoto, "is that there's always a battle going on between God and the devil, good and evil, heaven and hell, light and dark, and so on."

"If you say so, Perfesser." Barton continued honing.

"The Japanese are in league with the Nazis," said Borovitch. "So they have chosen the side of the devil and darkness."

Barton sniffed. "They chose the side against the U.S. Marine Corps. That's enough for me. But what about you, Doc, you're a Russki."

"Members of my family are in Nazi concentration camps. I owe it to them to do what I can."

"Makes sense," said Barton. "Not a hell of a lot of sense, but some. What about you, Perfesser? You're a civilian. You could

152

be back at Yale talking about haiku and wood block prints. But you come along for this screw-up."

"Members of my family are in a concentration camp, too."

"Yeah? In Japan?"

"In Nevada."

"Come on." Barton looked skeptical. "The U.S.A. doesn't go in for concentration camps."

"They do now," said Marumoto. "My parents are in one."

"Hara's are, too, Barton," said Hunley. "The West Coast people of Japanese ancestry were put behind barbed wire. Presidential order."

"So you're here to make a point."

"I guess you could say that," said Marumoto.

Barton held up his knife. "This is the way you make a point with a Jap, Perfesser." He showed teeth in a rictus smile. There was no humor in it. "Quick. In the back. Into the kidney. Slice that big artery in there. Keep your other hand tight over the nose and mouth. No noise. They jerk a little and pee their pants. But they go fast. Very fast. They don't teach that at Yale."

"No. There's no course in murder at Yale."

"Ought to be. Death is what life's all about."

"You're a nihilist, Sergeant," said Borovitch.

"I'm a Marine."

11

The Working Mill, September 5, 1942

I

Telephoning from the plant office, Sumida had broken through a blockade of garbled connections only to become ensnarled in a thicket of bureaucracy. He negotiated his way through a choir of subordinates until, finally, he had a brigadier general on the other end of the line. The man identified himself as vice commander of the military district that included Ringo. It was clear to Sumida from the beginning of the conversation that the brigadier was not interested in anything that would upset the harmony and symmetry of his paperwork.

"But, sir!" Sumida said, trying to cool his temper. "It is not my imagination!"

"It is a civil police matter."

"But, sir, we believe it is saboteurs not vandals."

"Saboteurs? That is not Army business. That is for the *kempeitei*. Notify the police and file a damage report!"

"But, sir, the mill was damaged in a deliberate, professional way. It could very well be the work of an enemy landing party."

There was a disbelieving gasp. "Are you suggesting enemy troops are on the home island?"

"It had to be someone."

"Impossible! From where? The sea? The sky?"

"Yes, perhaps from a ship or submarine. Or paratroops."

"Ridiculous! The Americans are the last in the world to encourage such a suicide mission. And that is exactly what it would be!"

"Perhaps they came from China."

"The Chinese are incapable of such initiative."

"Some enemy came from someplace," Sumida persisted.

"How? When? Where?"

"I do not know the answers, sir. I only know that the mill was attacked somehow."

"But you said this mill was not even in operation."

"Yes, it's true the mill was not in operation."

"That does not make sense, militarily."

"I agree, sir. But it was done, sir, military or not."

The brigadier's voice turned cajoling. "Come now, Sumida. Let us think about this." There was a pause. "My clerk has brought me your record, and I see that you have been in a number of campaigns."

"Yes, sir."

"Badly wounded, I see."

"Yes sir, wounded."

"Where was this wound? Your record does not say."

"A leg wound, sir." Sumida wondered where this dialogue was going.

"Perhaps this incident is a return vision of your battles, Sumida. These things happen, understandably. Something exploded by accident and, naturally, you think of attack..."

"No, sir! It could not possibly have been an accident."

The brigadier was getting impatient. "But why attack an empty mill? Was there any attack on the neighboring plant that was working?"

"There was no attack on the operating plant."

"Now use your common sense, Sumida." The general's tone was almost pleading. "Is that a reasonable military action?"

"Sir, irrational or not, there *was* an attack. My duty is to report it to you for your action. Naturally, sir, if you order me to report it to others and forget the incident, I will obey."

Sumida knew that put the burden of responsibility on the general. There was an audible grumble at the other end. "Oh very well, I personally will notify the civil authorities to order an investigation. In the meantime post guards round the clock at the operating plant. Also, increase your patrols along the coast."

"But, sir, I have only ten men and an officer."

"So?"

"There are not enough to guard the plant and also patrol."

"Do your best."

"I should have more troops here."

"Be realistic, Sumida. The damage is done. If it was done by some enemy — if, indeed, it was an enemy — he has long since gone somewhere else. Remember, Sumida, lightning does not strike twice in the same place."

"Yes, sir," Sumida muttered. "Lightning does not strike twice in the same place." He was tempted to tell the brigadier what he had told the plant manager, but that would have smacked of insubordination.

Still he persisted. "But what if —?"

"Enough, Sumida! I will send you a ten-man squad by truck."

"Hah!" Sumida was relieved. "Yes, sir. Thank you, sir. Ten more men will have to do. Can they be here by dark?"

"By dark? Impossible! By noon tomorrow."

"Tomorrow?"

"The best I can do."

Sumida knew it wasn't, but he said, "Well, we will do the best we can."

"Do not worry. They — whoever they are — will not return."

"Yes, sir, you're right. Whoever it was probably will not be back."

"Do not forget to file a complete report, Sumida." The line went dead.

"Thank you, sir." Sumida bowed automatically at the telephone. "Good day." He hung up the phone. "He thinks I'm a fool," he said aloud to himself. "He doesn't believe me."

II

In the *Grayfish* control room Hunley updated his log to cover recent events. He turned to his sound man.

"Picking up anything at all, Chief?"

"Freighter. Way out. Going north. Destroyer passed a while ago."

"Yeah? I better log it. You note what time?"

The chief checked his note pad. "0722. About four thousand yards, on a bearing of 270 degrees, moving south."

"Anything moving in and out of Ringo?"

"Nothing that makes any noise."

"Can't complain about that."

"Seems odd, though."

"What does?"

"No reaction from the Imperial Navy. You'd think nothing had happened on shore."

"Yeah. Probably it'll take 'em a while to put the story together."

"Hell, if the Japs hit us with a landing party, there'd be a total alert. Everybody would be going every which way. Total confusion."

Hunley laughed. "I expect so. But apparently the people on shore here bought the whole story."

"Never thought the navy had such good actors. Do you suppose, Skipper, that the Japs are doing something like that to us? Hawaiian look-alikes running around San Diego laying charges?"

"Possibility, I suppose. I expect that's why they rounded up all those Japanese-Americans from the West Coast and locked 'em up."

III

Sumida's driver took him to the orderly room and waited. The major looked inside, but, of course, no one was there. All the troops were at the mill with Kamasaki. It meant there could be no coast patrols today. He went outside. It was a beautiful summer's day. He decided to walk home. He told the driver to pick him up in four hours at his home.

As usual, Ringo was quiet. Not even a dog barked. A few townspeople were about. He saluted them as he passed, and they bowed low in respect to his rank. Turning into his street, he could see down to the pier in the harbor. The inflated landing boats from the submarine were still tied up. No one in Ringo would disturb them. Some fishermen poled their boat out of the harbor. On the whole, he thought, it was as if nothing had happened the night before. It was as if there were no war anywhere. Ringo went through the same slow, time-honored paces it had taken every day for who knew how many centuries.

At his house Chiyo was waiting with a fresh pot of tea and a small meal of soup, pickles, and rice. She bowed a greeting. He struggled out of his boots.

"I will be out tonight," he told her. "Somebody attacked a factory building last night. We are posting extra guards."

"Who would do that?"

Sumida shrugged. "The high command thinks I am foolish, but enemy saboteurs is my guess."

"Saboteurs?"

"Looks like it. Either Americans or Chinese."

"Where did they come from? Where did they go?"

"We're all asking those questions." He said. All but the Army High Command, he thought. "The best guess is they came by parachute."

"I don't understand."

"None of it makes much sense. It is hard to convince my high command that this actually happened or that sabotage occurred. He thinks it is an accident."

"Did they do much damage?"

"Not very much, as far as I could see. But what they struck they destroyed completely."

"Where was it?"

"It happened in a mill that wasn't even completed. The one where the highway and the railroad tracks cross. Yet they ignored the mill next to it that was working." He attacked his meal with gusto. In some ways, he thought, it was good to have a little excitement for a change. "It is a puzzle."

"How odd."

"The real question is. . ." He held up his *o-hashi* for emphasis. "Why bother to hit this little mill at all? There are much bigger mills elsewhere."

"Is there something special about these mills?"

"Who knows? I'm not told these things. If there is a secret there, I have not been informed. Nor has my commander. To me it is just one of many steel mills, and a small one at that."

"Maybe they made a mistake."

"I hope so. The investigation ought to tell us something."

"But where could American saboteurs hide? Where would Chinese go? How can they escape?"

"Exactly! You saw those prisoners yesterday. How could people looking like that conceal themselves? They smelled bad, too."

A thought struck her. "Could it have been those Americans? Could they have escaped from Lieutenant Hara?"

"Hah!" Sumida scoffed. "I doubt that. He had five men. I wish I had them now."

"Lieutenant Hara and his men may be in Yokosuka by now. I hope he had no trouble with those Americans. They looked dangerous."

Sumida chuckled. "Hara's squad was armed as if they were going to attack Hawaii. Light machine guns, rifles, ammunition, equipment." He shook his head. "Too much. The Navy is not used to land requirements."

"Perhaps Lieutenant Hara thinks it is better to be prepared and overarm."

"Hah!" Sumida teased. "You defend him."

She blushed and looked down. "Please, Father."

"An attractive fellow. I like him."

"He was very polite."

160

"Do you like him?"

"What I saw, yes," she said softly.

Sumida was pleased. "I can make it my business to be in touch with him." He laughed. "After all, he has my truck. Of course I would prefer an Army man."

"Not Captain Kamasaki, please."

Sumida frowned at the notion. "Impossible. Sometimes I wonder about Kamasaki's character." Then he brightened. "I could tell that this Hara has character."

She nodded vigorously. "I think so."

"We could invite him back."

"But I am sure he is too busy to return to Ringo."

"Perhaps," Sumida mused aloud, "letters could be exchanged."

"There is a war, Father. He must be busy."

"War or no war, I must think of your future, Chiyo. And so must you. Besides, I want to be a grandfather."

"He may have no interest in me at all."

"He is a fool if he does not," Sumida said decisively. "But that is what we must find out."

She said nothing and kept her head bowed, looking at the tea tray.

"Well?" he prodded.

"There would be no harm in letters."

"Good!" Sumida slapped his thigh. "I will see to it."

12

The Cove, September 5, 1942

I

Once again Krag presided in the *Grayfish* wardroom. On the table was their diorama of Ringo and the approaches to the mills.

"All right," he said, "let's run through the music again from the top. In a nutshell: this time we stack the deck in reverse. We sneak in the back door through the cove and brass-ball our way back out through the front at the Ringo pier. Hunley?"

"After dark I take *Grayfish* in on the surface. All guns will be manned in case there's an enemy force on shore. We'll find that out quick enough. If we're fired on, we back off and get the hell out. Call it a day. If nobody's home, the landing party takes off. I'm lending you the *Grayfish* acetylene torch for backup. Please return it. McGlynn?"

"This time I go in with the landing party. Then I take a boat and a Bren gun down the beach and hide as close to Ringo as possible. I find a position near town covering the road to the pier and keep out of sight. Krag?"

"We're on the coast where we stashed the truck and we hope the hell it's still there. If it is, we drive to the mill. Hara?"

"If the truck's gone, or if it doesn't work, we go cross country. I set the pace. Nisei follow me. Barton and Krag on the tail. It's only two miles that way. Three by road. Barton?"

"Yeah. Truck or hike, we move in on the rear gate to the plant. Then me, the Perfesser, and Toda do a recon. Cut any telephone lines. When it's done, we signal the rest to come on in. Krag?"

"Inside the mill we round up the personnel. Doc says we should find about fifteen on the night shift. We lock 'em in the tool cage. Sakai guards 'em. Endo sets up a Bren gun position covering the main door. Toda and the Professor take rifle positions covering the entry we came through. Barton?"

"Now we've got the plant's acetylene torches. Fujimura and me get to work. Control room first. Hara?"

"I torch the furnace pinions and the power supply. Krag?"

"This time I climb the crane, torch the electric motors, cut the cables and the beam, then do the other one. Doc says there'll probably be hot metal in the ladle serving the furnace. So watch your backsides when it goes. I'll give you a shout. Sakai?"

"I locate the argon supply and either open the valves or torch 'em shut. After that, I'm swing man on the defense. Krag?"

"By this time we're probably attracting attention. Maybe drawing fire. Torching the plant's going to be slow since there are only a few of us to do the work. But we keep at it until the job's done."

"What's the signal to haul ass out of there?" asked Barton.

"The signal for withdrawal is when the big crane falls, so I'll do that last. Cover me until I'm back on the deck. Rally on the truck. We get the hell out best way we can. Then we make a run for Ringo." He gestured with his hands.

"At 0200 — or later — we run right out on the pier. McGlynn shoots a flare when he sees us coming, then gives us cover fire, if needed. Hunley?"

"I'm submerged in deep water until 0200. After that, I start moving on shore, watching by periscope. When I see the flare, I surface and run to the dock. When everybody's aboard, I back off, and we head for Pearl and the rum punch."

"Questions?" asked Krag.

"What if the job's done quick?" asked Sakai. "What if we're at the pier at 0100?"

"Very unlikely," said Krag. "We have to pin a time down for Hunley. If we finish early, we hide until it's time, then go for the pier."

"There's a reason," said Hunley. "I've got to wait in deep water and I can't see the flare if I'm that far out. So, just before 0200, I start creeping into shallow water, watching for the flare. When I see it, I come all the way up and we're in business."

"Question, Barton?" asked Krag.

"Yeah. I'd like to borrow one of the ship's boarding weapons. You carry submachine guns, Commander?"

"A Thompson and a dozen Springfields."

"I'll take the Thompson.""

"Welcome to it."

"Anything else?" asked Krag.

"You do not have enough men for this job," said Borovitch.

"We been through that, Doc. Hunley's only got twenty-seven men on a boat that crews eighty. He's bare-bones. He can't spare a man."

"But I have given this serious thought."

"So have we."

"I am available," Borovitch said firmly.

"Come on, Doc! That's nonsense! This is young men's work. You're not even a military man."

"Correction!" Borovitch stood and drew himself up. "I was an officer in the Army of the Czar."

"Appreciate the gesture, Doc, but . . ."

"And there is a more important point," Borovitch added.

"What's that?"

"I know steel mills. I can work a torch. In this kind of environment I can see weak points that you don't know. Extra eyes, ears, and hands that can work under pressure."

"He's got a point," said Barton.

Krag shook his head. "What if the truck's gone or on the fritz? Hell, he'd slow us down. What if we have to double-time back out. Can he run two, three miles?"

"If the truck's out of it, he can stay with me," said McGlynn.

165

"We can use him, Skipper," said Barton.

"You ready to carry him?"

"I'm ready to risk it."

Borovitch answered. "No one carries me. If it comes to that, shoot me. I stay behind dead."

Krag shook his head. "I don't think so, Doc."

"Please, I must go. It is important and I can help."

"Why not, Boss?" said Endo. "Hell, I'll help Barton carry him, if it comes to that."

Others nodded agreement.

"All right, Doc," Krag said reluctantly. "Just so you know what you're in for."

"I will do my part."

"Fair enough." Krag stared at them thoughtfully. "One more thing. Toda, I want you and the Professor to wear your Imperial Navy whites. You two are our local cover, in case we need it. We might have to pull a scam and you're the guys if we do. Don't get caught. Those duds make you spies. Sorry."

"Forget it," said Toda.

"What about the rest of us?" asked Hara.

"No Japanese uniforms. The rest of us go in wearing U.S. Navy blues. Carry your mine hat, but wear watch caps, black faces."

"Mammy!" Endo exclaimed. "I'm tired of being a Japanese sailor."

"Another thing," said Krag, "so they can't call you a spy if you're caught, each man, except Toda and the Professor, wears his navy collar insignia. Okay? Probably won't help you a hell of a lot, but it makes your blues a uniform. But no personal I.D. No letters, no wallets. Nothing. If they get us, nobody knows who we are. If it comes to that, make sure you're dead."

"If you ain't," said Barton, "they'll make you wish you were."

II

In the afternoon they strolled out to the shrine overlooking the

166

seacoast. Chiyo packed a small basket with *o-sushi* and a thermos of green tea.

"Now," said Sumida, "I can honestly report to my superiors that an Imperial Japanese Army patrol has scouted the coast today." He laughed. "You and me!"

It was a sun-filled day, steeped with the near tropical humidity of Japan in summer. But here on the forest path by the shrine the overhanging trees tempered the heat.

"Smell the pines!" she said.

Sumida took a deep breath. "Ah, life is so good among the trees. I like it here. One could rest forever."

The shrine was at hand. They bowed to it respectfully, then sat on boulders to eat their lunch. From the shrine the path continued down steeply to the rocky shore. There was barely any surf, but what there was stirred up a haze over the water and around the sea-washed rocks.

"Like a watercolor," said Sumida. "If I had any talent, I would sit here and compose a haiku."

"But you would rather fish," she teased.

"Yes, of course. But I am on military patrol. No time for such recreation. See? I carry my pistol. If an enemy steps out of the surf, I will shoot him. Several times, in fact."

She smiled. "Perhaps you could shoot a fish for our dinner."

He pointed. "See the big boulder there?"

"Yes."

"When the tide is high, that is the best place to cast the bait."

"I know. I have watched you."

"Important to remember. You might want to go fishing yourself sometime."

"Perhaps."

"Or perhaps lead Lieutenant Hara here. For fishing only, of course." He laughed.

"That is your duty, if he ever returns."

"He will."

"Do not overestimate his interest in me, if there was any at all."

"The man was not a fool. He was interested. I could see it."

"That does not mean he will return."

"One gets a sense of things," Sumida said thoughtfully. "I believe he will return. I hope so."

"Yes."

Some sparrows squabbled in the tree above them.

"What do you suppose they find to fight about?" asked Chiyo.

"Arguing over who gets to sit on the branch. It is the same with all creatures, even us."

"How long will the war last?"

"It depends on the Americans. If they persist in confronting us, it could last a long time. If they accept reality, it could be over tomorrow. In either case they must accept that we are the dominant nation in Asia, not them."

She said nothing, but wondered why dominance was so important.

"Soon I will go back to my regiment," he said.

"But your leg is not healed."

"Healed well enough. I wrote to army command. I got the reply today." He pulled a letter from his tunic pocket and handed it to her.

"Report at the end of this month. So soon?"

"Sitting here, I wonder why I am so eager to get back."

"So do I."

He shrugged. "I am a professional soldier, that's why. It is my duty."

"Of course." She looked at the letter. "It says your regiment is in New Guinea. Where is that?"

Sumida looked vague. "I do not know exactly. It is an island far south of the Philippines. I believe it is the staging area for the invasion of Australia."

"So far away."

"The world is very big." He looked at the sea. "If anything happens to me..."

"No!" she interrupted. "Do not speak of that." ...If anything happens to me," he persisted, "I would like my ashes to be put

168

right here at this shrine."

"We must pray nothing happens."

"But something could, and that is my wish. Promise me?"

"I promise."

"Good. Now it is time to go back. Our patrol is over and no enemy is in sight."

13

The Cove, September 5, 1942

I

Grayfish rigged for red an hour before surfacing. In a mood of gloomy fatalism, Hara felt as if they were bathing in blood. He wondered if the others had the same sense of foreboding. In any case, none of them expressed any sense of enthusiasm for the job ahead. They sat in virtual silence in the crimson twilight until Hunley took the vessel up at 2130 precisely. His own crew manned the deck gun and machine guns. Like the landing party they wore blues and blackface. They were virtually invisible against the dark hull.

Krag was on the bridge with Hunley. His group stayed below while the ship made a slow, quiet run toward the beach on electric power. Both officers scanned the shoreline with binoculars.

"Quiet," said Krag. "Don't see a damn thing."

"I guess that's good news."

"Yeah."

Hunley swung his glasses slowly along the tree line of the cove. "Negative this way, too. Almost wish I saw something," he muttered.

"Quiet as a tomb."

"Bad joke."

"Okay." Krag brought his binoculars down. "We're in business."

"Very well."

"You say the word, Skipper."

Hunley nodded. A few moments later he said, "Now! We're about as close as we can get without sticking." He spoke into the intercom. "All stop!" He heard the command repeated back. The faint hum of the electric motors ceased. Now there was only the sound of water playing against the hull.

"Landing party prepare to launch!"

The clanking of hatches sounded ominously loud. Krag's men shuffled into position. Quickly they inflated their boats and had them over the side. It was easier this time without carts of explosives or the arms that had been left ashore, stowed on the truck. When the boats were ready, Krag turned to swing down the conning tower ladder.

Hunley grabbed his hand. "Good luck, buddy. We'll see you on the pier at 0200 tomorrow."

"0200. I'll be there. You owe me drinks."

"If we get back to Pearl, I'll buy you a goddamn bar."

"You're on."

Krag went to the deck and boarded the second boat.

"Cast off." He didn't have to raise his voice. "Let's go."

In an instant the boats were on their way. The rocky beach was less than a hundred yards in, but it seemed a mile.

Hara's eyes were fully adjusted to the darkness. He could make out details with remarkable clarity. At the same time he felt as if his own details were being made out clearly from the shore by some hidden enemy.

It is, he thought, an irony that we were safer yesterday going ashore brazenly in daylight at a populated port than we are now sneaking through the darkness toward a silent shore.

For their part, Toda and Marumoto felt particularly conspicuous in their Imperial Navy whites.

We are, thought Marumoto, like the white go shells surrounded by black stones, about to be taken from the board. He made a note to himself to remember that metaphor for the book he would surely write about this adventure. The idea of a book cheered him. It was at least one good element to weigh against the bad, something to cling to during the hours ahead.

Through his binoculars Krag continued to study the shoreline and the inky pool of forest at the top of the bluff. The glasses were like a kind of insulating screen that protected him from truth, as if he were watching for potential disaster in another country. The impact of his boat on the beach jarred him back to reality.

"Take cover," he said to them softly, not that it would do them much good at this stage.

"Barton! Look around! See if anybody's up there!"

The marine dodged forward like a phantom, moving from boulder to boulder, working his way back up the path they had taken down the night before.

At the top of the bluff he waited silently in the brush and listened.

This was the lesson of the jungle. Mindanao had taught him how to tune his ears for different layers and qualities of sound. The call of birds, even at night, was normal. The soft chink of rock or metal or the snapping of a twig was not. He also sniffed the air like a wolf. Certain human smells would penetrate the atmosphere and linger on the damp air of hot nights like this. Cigarette smoke penetrated the farthest and lasted the longest.

He sensed no such odor.

Next would be the smell of fresh urine, the product of some lurking rifleman who would have relieved himself within fifty yards.

None of that either.

The dominant smell was the clean, familiar, reassuring aroma of pine.

And what was there to hear?

Only the cry of a night heron far away, the whisper of the faintest of breezes in the topmost branches of the trees, the dim slap of wavelets on the rocks below. This was a quiet place.

Satisfied, Barton edged toward the truck, concealed some

173

yards away. As he got closer, he picked up the smell of its gasoline. Again he waited. Nothing. He crept closer until, even in the darkness, he could see the truck under its layer of camouflage. He tried to remember exactly how he and the others had placed the branches. Nothing seemed disturbed. If the truck had been discovered, the enemy had gone to great pains to conceal it again as it had been. And why do that?

Finally, he crept directly to the truck and circled it warily. He recalled that he personally had placed the two Bren guns side by side on the truck bed. That wasn't because he had expected to return, but because he couldn't bear to see honorable weapons cast aside without dignity.

The notion, he thought, was strangely Japanese, as if he had, by some kind of osmosis, taken on some of their characteristics.

He raised himself at the tailgate and felt inside. The butts of the Bren guns were as he had left them. He turned on his flashlight and carefully played it around the truck bed. Everything appeared exactly as it had been. It made no sense that an enemy patrol would have left it alone. It was, after all, the only truck Sumida had.

He retrieved one of the Bren guns and a pouch of ammunition for McGlynn. Quickly now, he made his way back down to the beach and reported to Krag.

"Nothin', Skipper. Just the way we left it."

McGlynn came out from behind a boulder. Barton handed him the ammunition pouch. McGlynn belted it on, then took the Bren gun.

"All set, McGlynn?" Krag asked.

"Set."

"Got your flares?"

"Ready."

"Then you'll be near the dock about 0200."

McGlynn patted the Bren gun. "I'll be there."

"See you later."

"Make sure you do." He turned to Borovitch. He, too, was in blues and blackface. His white hair was hidden under a watch cap. "Doc, how you doing?"

"I'm fine. It makes me feel like a young man again."

"Yeah? Well, we've got to go up the bluff. The path's not too steep, but it's rocky as hell. Stay close behind Barton and watch your footing. He'll do the watching for the bandits. Okay?"

"I understand."

"Good. Let's go," said Krag.

Barton took the lead. It was easy going this trip. The pace was steady. The climb barely winded Borovitch.

"You're in better shape than I thought, you old goat," Barton told him.

"I might just outrun you, Sergeant."

"Keep thinkin' positive, Doc. We got a long way to go."

"And," whispered Marumoto, " '. . . miles to go before I sleep.' "

They were at the truck in five minutes. Quickly, they stripped away the concealing brush. They recovered their weapons and ammunition. Marumoto pulled himself into the driver's seat and hit the starter. It churned lethargically.

"Let's go, honey!" He pumped the choke. "Start," he snapped in Japanese. Called to life, the engine kicked over reluctantly. It sputtered a bit, then throbbed normally.

"On the truck!" Krag ordered. "Let's go!"

II

Sumida sat alone in his office adjoining his orderly room, composing a letter. This was only the first rough draft. The final version would have to be just right. He leaned back to contemplate what he had written:

MY DEAR LIEUTENANT HARA. . . [He would have to get the formal mode of address as well as a place to send the letter later.]

It was the greatest of pleasures to meet a sensible and progressive career naval officer such as yourself. . ."

[That sounded stuffy, but, on the other hand, appropriate.]

I trust that our Army truck served its purpose well in delivering the important prisoners to Yokosuka.

It was pleasing to me to have the opportunity to support interservice solidarity in the pursuit of our eventual mutual victory over the Americans and others.

[He liked that plug for cooperation.]

Now that you have done your duty regarding the prisoners, I suppose you will, with pleasure, return to your regular assignment in the exciting and significant submarine service.

[Was that a little overstated? he wondered. No. Better to err on the side of dedication.]

However, as a fellow Imperial officer, I know how useful it is to have time to refresh oneself before the next campaign. Therefore, I want to reiterate, most enthusiastically, my invitation to you to return here to Ringo and join me for fishing.

[Actually, he thought, I will be gone soon. Chiyo can take him fishing. In fact, that is the plan. He chuckled aloud.]

I hope this will be soon. By the way. . . [And, speaking of fishing, here was the hidden hook.]

. . . my daughter, Chiyo, joins me in this invitation. Though she had only a short time to meet you, I can tell you — just between us — that she was remarkably impressed. . .

That was as far as he had gotten. All in all, he liked the tone. Formal, but not oppressive. Friendly. Hara could not, of course, ignore the invitation. He would have to respond. Once there was a response, there would be a counter-response. Events would take their course from there. He smiled and picked up his brush to continue, but there was a tap at his door.

The door was open. He looked up to see Chiyo. Quickly, he put the letter away in a drawer.

"Ah! What brings you out?"

"I brought you some tea." She had her basket with the thermos, some cups, and cookies.

"Very thoughtful."

"What are you doing?"

"I was, uh, just going over some records."

"You are all alone here."

"The men are with Kamasaki out at that factory. Things are quiet."

"It is a beautiful night. No moon, but the stars light up everything."

"Yes." Too bad, he thought, that Hara could not come wandering by about now. He felt a fleeting pang for his own youth, long gone.

She poured tea and gave him a cup.

He studied her thoughtfully. "You know, Chiyo, when I go back to my regiment, I think it would be a good idea for you to stay here rather than return to Tokyo."

"I like it here, but there is little to do. If I go to Tokyo, perhaps they will let me work in a government office or a war factory."

"My daughter is not a clerk or mill hand," Sumida said emphatically. "You are a lady of the Samurai."

"I only want to help."

"Yes, of course," said Sumida. "I appreciate that. But, please believe me, you will help this old soldier the most by staying right here. We have a house. The village is quiet. The people are pleasant. Is that not so?"

"Oh yes, I like it here."

"Good. It is settled then." He sipped tea. Now it was only a matter of making sure young Hara was lured back. He half smiled. If only it all would work out...

III

They retraced their route with the truck and concealed it temporarily in the same place. But this time, when the time came, their approach would have to be over a service road leading to the rear gate entrance of the other plant. It was farther away and the road was visible almost all the way. Krag led the team to the same vantage point as before, where they could observe the working mill a mile away. He and Hara studied the plant through their binoculars.

Finally, Krag turned and handed the glasses to Borovitch. "Take a look, Doc."

He swung the glasses, looking at the working mill and then the previous night's target.

"They are virtual twins. I think they used the same plans. I doubt you will find any surprises there. At least not from the mill itself."

"And let's hope nothing else, either," said Krag. "Endo, you're the truck driver this time because we'll need the Professor up front."

"Okay."

"You and Doc stay right here until you see our signal. Clear?"

"Got it."

"I will watch, too," said Borovitch.

"Do that. Keep the binoculars. It'll take a while to work our way through the forest, but after that we'll be at the rear gate. When we're set, our two white sailor suits will come out on the road and raise their arms like so. . ."

He raised his arms high over his head. "When you see us wave you in, bring the truck down as fast as you can. We'll have the gate open and probably the rear entrance. Drive right inside. Got it?"

"Got it."

"Okay, everybody else follow me."

They moved through the fringes of the forest. Krag set a steady jogging pace that ate up distance. The pines made it easier because there was less undergrowth.

They continued jogging until Krag found an approach position that hid them near the rear entrance of the working mill. They had perfect concealment, aided by the red glare from the operating furnaces inside the plant.

"The physical setup is the same," said Krag, "only this time they have two sentries by that little guard hut at the rear gate.

Everybody see them?"

There was a murmur of assent.

"We have to take them out. But first, that. . ." He pointed at overhead lines leading from the plant on a path that passed them and led toward Ringo.

"They're not high-power lines," said Barton. "High-tension lines use big insulators. These got none."

"Sakai!" said Krag. "Get up on that pole! Cut those phone lines. Toda, you and Marumoto work your way in and take care of those sentries up front. Leave your rifles with us. No shooting. Barton'll back you up on the flank.

"The rest of you guys, listen. If there's a screw-up, we go in on the run and take 'em out with bayonets and rifle butts. Not a shot gets fired. Right?"

"Right," they chorused.

"What do you mean 'take *care* of 'em?' " Marumoto asked.

"Knife!" said Barton. "Up under the ribs, like so — "

"Christ! I'm no butcher," Marumoto protested. "I teach at Yale."

"No stomach for it?" Barton asked sarcastically.

Toda interrupted. "Just keep out of sight, Barton. We'll handle it."

"Cut the bullshit!" Krag snapped. "When the guards are out of it, Barton signals. Ready? Go!"

IV

Two of the off-duty guards were playing go in the main gate house at the front of the mill. Kamasaki, puffing one of the cigarettes captured from the Americans, watched from a distance. He would love to get into the game, but that was impossible with enlisted men. They were not very good anyway. The telephone rang. The sergeant answered.

"Sir! It is Major Sumida calling." He handed over the telephone.

179

"Kamasaki here, sir."

"Anything to report?"

"Nothing so far, sir."

"That is good. It is quiet here in Ringo, too."

"It is always quiet in Ringo, sir." It was as close to humor as Kamasaki ever got.

Sumida agreed. "Our saboteurs are probably back in China or Hawaii or wherever they came from."

"We are ready for them, if they return."

"Good. Listen, Kamasaki, I have a question for you: if you were. . ."

The line went dead.

Kamasaki jiggled the hook of the field telephone that connected the gate house with Ringo. He cranked the signal handle, then listened.

"Dead," he said to the sergeant. "The telephone line has gone dead."

"It is always doing that," the sergeant assured him.

Kamasaki felt his stomach tighten. "I do not like it."

"We can fix it as soon as it is daylight. It is a simple matter of splicing the lines."

"We are cut off from the major."

"But all the troops are here, sir. You command the unit."

"Of course." Kamasaki said it with more conviction than he felt. Without Sumida, he was responsible if things went wrong. Somehow he had to make sure nothing went wrong. But what should he do?

V

Barton, Toda, and Marumoto used the forest to screen them. They worked as close as they could to the gate. But there was still another twenty-five yards of open space between them and the sentries.

"What now, Sarge? What's the plan? Rush 'em?" asked Toda.

"Too far for a dash. They might get off a shot." He thought for a moment. "Tell you what. You and the Perfesser brassball your way so you get face-to-face with those guys. Bluff. Got it?"

"Yeah? What're you going to do?"

"See that patch of scrub? While you're distracting them, I scuttle in there. Don't let those guys look my way. Don't even think about me. At the right time, I'll be there. Got it?"

"You think this'll work?" Marumoto asked skeptically.

"Do you speak good Japanese?"

"Of course."

"Then it'll work. Give 'em a pitch in *nihongo*. You're the guy who said they inhale their own exhaust about Japanese culture and style."

"Hoist on my own petard," muttered Marumoto.

"What?"

"Never mind."

"We've got to have some kind of half-assed reason to show up in the middle of nowhere in the middle of the night," said Toda. "Let's do our drunk act, Professor."

"That might do it."

"Okay," said Barton. "Toda, Perfesser, that's what you do. Got your knife handy, Toda?"

"Yeah."

"Perfesser?"

Marumoto rubbed the hilt of his weapon, concealed in the belt under his sailor's blouse. "I have my knife."

"Okay. Do your drunk act."

Toda and Marumoto took deep breaths, then stood up and staggered more or less casually toward the gate. At first the guards didn't see them.

"Hey, soldier!" Toda yelled. He lurched against Marumoto, faking alcoholic tanglefoot.

The taller of the two sentries came to life. "Halt!" he shouted, bringing his Arisaka hip high at the ready. "Who goes there?"

"Friends! Friends!" the Americans shouted.

"Come forward! Hands high!"

"Friends!" Toda laughed hysterically. He didn't have to fake it. "Do not shoot!"

"Be calm, soldier," said Marumoto. "We need directions."

"Who are you?"

"Sailors," Marumoto slurred. "Do you not remember yesterday? Our patrol boat put into Ringo. Now we are lost."

The taller guard squinted. "Of course! I remember. The truck. What are you sailors doing way out here?"

"Looking for women and sake, of course," said Marumoto.

"Here?" the other guard asked incredulously. "But we saw you leave the truck."

"We brought your truck back a while ago and then we went looking for companions. We did not find any."

The short guard laughed. "This is a desert."

"Is this the way back to Ringo?"

"Ringo!" The taller guard relaxed. "You're crazy. That's five kilometers the other way. Go around to the front of this building. Turn right at the gate."

"Ringo's a dull place," said the other guard.

"You are telling us," said Marumoto. He rolled his eyes drunkenly. He edged closer to the guards, Toda beside him. "What is this place? A barracks?"

"Barracks?" laughed the smaller guard. "Obviously, you've never been in the army. It's a steel mill."

"How do sailors find their way in the ocean?" the taller guard teased.

"It's dark tonight," said Marumoto. "Cigarette?" He moved still closer and offered a pack.

"Ah." The guard grounded his rifle and took a cigarette. "Thank you."

The small guard accepted one, then grounded his rifle, too.

He's very young, thought Marumoto. Perhaps only seventeen.

"Thank you," the youth said, bowing slightly.

Marumoto held a match for both of them. He maneuvered to keep them from looking in the general direction of Barton's bush.

"Good cigarette," said the taller guard, inhaling deeply. The man glanced toward the mill yard. "I just hope Captain Kamasaki is somewhere else."

The guards weren't looking directly at Toda or Marumoto. They were thinking about their commander. Toda had his hand on his knife. It was time to act.

"Look!" he shrieked and pointed. "Over there! There he is!" The startled guards looked. "Wha...!" Toda grabbed the taller guard around the throat from behind and stabbed him twice in the back, in the kidney, just as Barton had coached. The man was finished just that fast, his renal artery pumped the rest of his life into the dust.

But Marumoto's man reacted. The youth swung away and faced him. He was terrified. His rifle clattered to the ground and he backed toward the fence. Marumoto stabbed ineffectually at his chest. It only slashed the boy. In pain he lurched away, rolling along the fence. Blood splashed Marumoto's white blouse.

"Why are you doing this?" the little guard cried.

Desperately, Marumoto tried again, but botched it. His knife caught in the soldier's tunic. "No!" the little guard whimpered. "Please! No!"

A black shape lunged out of the shadows.

It was over in a fraction of a second. The youth's dead open eyes stared at Marumoto, frozen in his terror-stricken face. The glaze of death dimmed them. His right foot twitched in a spasm, then stopped forever.

"Too slow, buddy-boy," Barton said matter-of-factly, wiping his blade on the jacket of the corpse. "Not enough oomph. Got to put your heart in it, Perfesser."

Marumoto was aware that his knife hand was shaking uncontrollably. He grabbed it with the other hand.

Barton put a hand on his shoulder. "It's over. Come on, boys," he said, almost gently. "Haul 'em back into the scrub."

'Marumoto was glad to do something, anything, to stop the shaking. He grabbed the small guard's body by the arm and dragged it into the brush. Toda did the same with the other man.

Barton brushed out the blood trails and heel marks. He looked into the guard shack. There was a field telephone. As he reached in to cut its wires, it rang. The jangling sound stopped him.

"Perfesser! Quick! Answer that bastard!"

"What do I say?"

"How the hell do I know? It's probably a routine checkup!"

Marumoto picked up the phone. His shaking had abated. "*Moshi, moshi.* Sentry post. . ."

"What kind of an answer is that, you stupid fool?" It was Kamasaki.

"Forgive me, sir. I did not know it was you."

"Whoever it is, you answer like a soldier, not like some idiot civilian. You understand me?"

"Yessir," Marumoto almost cried with relief at this lunacy. Kamasaki's men had just been murdered here and the man was complaining about phone procedure.

"I promise to answer with proper procedure in future. . ."

"You are a fool! I am putting you on report! What is your name?"

"My name, sir?" Marumoto waved at Barton. "Excuse me a moment, sir."

"Don't you know your own name?"

"Yessir, I know my name. But I think I see something outside."

Marumoto had Barton's eye now. He held his hand over the phone receiver. "Dog tag! Get me a dog tag!"

Barton raced to one of the hidden corpses, cut off an identity disc, and tossed it to Marumoto.

Marumoto unclasped the receiver. "I am sorry, sir. It was nothing, sir. Only a sudden breeze."

Kamasaki made an exasperated sound. "Name!"

"Sir! My name is. . ." Marumoto fumbled with the identity disc. He gasped audibly. His voice almost failed. "My name is Marumoto. Marumoto, Hajime. Superior Private."

"Are you drunk, Marumoto?"

"No, sir."

"You sound drunk."

"I swear I am sober, sir. It is only that we are concerned about the enemy, sir."

"Are you vigilant?"

"We *are* vigilant, sir."

"You are a disgrace!"

"Yessir, I understand my disgrace in not answering the telephone correctly."

"Enough of this! Is there anything going on over there?"

"All quiet here."

Barton mouthed instructions.

"Excuse me, sir. . ."

Barton whispered, "Ask him if he's sending a patrol."

Marumoto nodded. "Will you be sending a patrol around the perimeter?"

"Why do you ask?"

"We don't want to risk shooting our own men."

"With an idiot like you on guard, that is a good question. No patrol is planned now. I intend to keep the men together here in case something occurs. We will call and inform you if a patrol is sent."

"Yessir. Thank you, sir." The line went dead.

Marumoto leaned against the side of the shack and gasped for breath.

"Who was it?" asked Barton.

"Kamasaki. Chewed me out for not answering the phone right. Took my name for his discipline sheet. Christ! My hand's shaking. . ."

"You're doin' fine." Barton squeezed his arm. "You got to learn to relax, Perfesser." He sliced the phone line.

"What if he calls back?" asked Toda. "A dead line will make him suspicious."

"No choice. A phone that don't answer will worry him more than one that's dead."

"I asked him if patrols were coming around," said Marumoto. "And?"

"He said no. He wants to keep his men handy in case something happens."

"He's a damn fool. He should be patrolling. Sumida would patrol." Barton pointed at the forest. "Sumida would have his boys out there in the jungle hunting us."

"Wonder where he is," said Toda.

Marumoto went over to the concealed corpses. He tossed on a few more sprigs of brush. "This man had my name."

"So what?" said Barton.

Marumoto stared at him sadly. "You ever kill anybody with your own name?"

"Not this week. Let's get going. Let's give 'em the signal."

14

The Working Mill, September 5, 1942

I

Now it all came clear to Marumoto. This was the final elusive element in the loop of logic of this mission. It had been there all the time. They had entered Dante's fire and brimstone hell and they were going to burn. For Krag and the others the impression was less than poetic, but no less hellish. The mill held them all in thrall for a moment.

Krag and the others had seen the confrontation at the gate. They were already on their way when the signal had come. Endo drove without lights. Even so, it took less time than they had estimated to cover the distance down the service road to the rear gate. It was already open. Barton, Toda, and Marumoto waited by the big sliding door. The truck drove into the mill yard. Quickly, they pushed the door open. The truck roared inside.

Only Borovitch and Fujimura were really prepared for what it was like. They had spent parts of their lives in steel mills. For the others, especially Marumoto, it was a descent into the pit. The air was acrid with the smell of scorched steel and the stench of sulfur. The heat was pervasive and threatening. "Touch nothing here," Borovitch cautioned. "These ingots are still nearly red-hot."

Krag recovered himself and looked around. The only visible

human presence was a lone crane operator in his tiny cab high above. He either didn't see them, or paid no heed. Two heads were dimly visible through the grimy windows of the furnace control room, some distance away. There was nothing else except the pervasive clangor and threatening red glare of the electric arc furnaces pouring their cargo into the cauldron which would, in turn, haul it to the looming argon furnace. They were in free.

"Let's get on with it. Endo, get up on that crane and bring down the operator. Kill him if he gives you trouble."

"On my way." He jogged toward the crane ladder.

"Barton, get those guys in the control room. Hara, back him up. Rest of you go with me. We round up the people and get 'em into the cage. Keep your rifles at the ready. Anybody gives you a hard time, take 'em down. We got no time to play. Fuj, Doc, show us the way to those acetylene torches."

It took less than ten minutes. The surprise was total. The managers, foremen, and millwrights were shocked and frightened into docility by their black-faced assailants. There was no attempt at resistance as the mill personnel were herded into the tool cage.

"Ask 'em where the torches are," said Krag.

"Acetylene torches," Hara said in Japanese. "Where?"

A badly frightened foreman answered. "Supply cage." He pointed where. Fujimura and Barton headed that way.

"Who are you?" a manager asked. "What do you want?"

Sakai couldn't resist. "We are from the fuel company," he said sternly. "You have not been paying your bills. We are repossessing your furnace."

"What?" The manager was trapped between possibility and disbelief. "It is impossible!"

"Well, we're doing it anyway," said Sakai.

Barton shouted at them. "We got the torches!"

"He and Fujimura began wheeling them out of the supply cage. Each of the heavy tanks had its own barrow.

"Those are going to be sons of bitches to get up on the cranes," said Endo.

"I'll take the ship's torch up first," said Krag. "It's lighter. See if you can track down some rope or cable so we can haul up the others, if we need 'em."

"Okay."

"All right," said Krag. "Everybody know what to do?" There were nods all around. "Get going." He turned to Borovitch. "Doc, what's your plan?"

"I will first join Barton and Fujimura in the control room. After that" — he waved his arms expansively — "I will roam like an avenging angel, torching this, torching that." He slapped the side of a torch.

"Right. Okay, boys. Get to it!"

II

Kamasaki watched the main road from the window of the main guard house. He knew that Sumida would be along, especially after the telephone went dead. Of course, that was not unusual. Breezes, branches, and birds all conspired to pull down the flimsy military wire. Once something grounded the line somehow, it was always a day's patrol to find the cause. Sure enough, Sumida's car turned off the Ringo highway by the other mill and headed their way.

"Sergeant! Spruce up the men! Major Sumida is coming."

The go was put away. The teapot was refilled. The off-duty soldiers buttoned their jackets and stood by, ready to leap to their feet at attention when Sumida appeared. Kamasaki went outside to inspect his sentries. That's where he stayed until Sumida's sedan pulled up and the driver helped the major out.

"Kamasaki, what news?"

"All quiet, sir."

"Any clues about the telephone line?"

"No, sir. The other sentry post reports nothing. The telephone line has done this before."

"True. Only under present circumstances we must concern

189

ourselves about it more." He went into the gate house.

"Attention!" shouted the sergeant. The soldiers were on their feet in an instant, braced.

"What are these men doing here?" Sumida asked.

"In reserve, sir," said Kamasaki. "In case there is an attack."

"If there is an enemy out there, that is just what he wants you to do. You give him all the options to act while you wait. Put them on patrol! I want them moving around the perimeter until dawn."

"Very well, sir. I must tell the sentries at the other gate that patrols will be out so there are no accidents."

"I will do it." Sumida picked up the telephone and cranked the signal magneto. He waited. Nothing. He cranked again. "They are not answering."

"I talked to them just five minutes ago," said Kamasaki.

"You had better find out." Sumida felt the nibble of menace, like a small, but growing, termite biting inside him. It did not go away. "Take the patrol as far as the other gate and call me. If all is in order, the patrol can then go on by itself and you come back."

"Yessir!"

III

With Borovitch helping, Barton and Fujimura wrestled one of the torches inside the control room. They put on their miner's helmets and welder's goggles. Barton ignited the torch and tuned the flame to its nearly invisible maximum intensity.

"What first, Doc?"

"Allow me to save you some minutes," said Borovitch. Deftly, he unfastened wing nuts and removed the thin steel cabinet, exposing the intricate woof and warp of cable, wiring, and switching devices inside. He pointed. "Any and all of it, Sergeant."

Barton pointed his flame at a switch. In an instant its insulation flared away. The copper wiring fused, then dribbled away. Behind him, Fujimura welded some operating levers and shafts to their frames.

So they went, painting the destructive flame across the cables and gauges. The torches illuminated the space around them better than their helmet lamps. The flaring light sent shadows dancing like crazy goblins around the walls. Sparks leaped between grounds as lines parted. Molten copper ran like water into the farther reaches of the console. Outside a battery of illuminated red signal lights above the furnace flared, then went out.

"Good," Borovitch exulted. "The brain is dying."

"This is more fun than explosives," said Barton. "You get a better look at the results."

"I always liked torch work," said Fujimura. "Gives you kind of a creative feeling."

In short order the control console was a lumpy stew of melted equipment.

"What do you think, Doc? That do it?"

"These controls will never be repaired. Your work is done here."

Barton peered through the control room window. "There's the real Argon Furnace." He could see that the cauldron was partly filled with molten alloy. Heat waves agitated the glare-lit atmosphere above, all the way to the top of the building. At the base of the furnace he could see Hara torching the pinions.

"They had her loaded for bear, Doc."

"No question about it. I counted the ingots of material where we came in. There alone stands enough alloy to make a dozen or more engines."

"How do you know what kind of steel is in those molds?"

"I don't, in truth. But we must assume they were making high-alloy steel for something. Shall we move on, Sergeant? Fujimura?"

"Yeah. Guide me out the door with this torch."

Together the three of them maneuvered the heavy equipment and cart back down the control room ladder.

"How's it going, Commander?" asked Fujimura.

Hara pushed up his goggles. "See for yourself. They'll never get those gears unstuck."

Borovitch scrambled around and under the huge cauldron. The heat was intense, even on the exterior with a wall of double firebrick between them and the vast stomach full of white-hot alloy.

"There are some bearings there," Borovitch pointed. "If you melt them, this furnace is finished."

"I'll give you a hand, Commander," said Fujimura. He got his torch going. "They're sure going to have one big lump of iron sitting there."

"Life is full of travail," said Hara. He pulled his goggles down again and went to work on the bearings.

IV

Toda and Marumoto, each armed with a rifle, had taken up guard positions flanking the rear entry. They had pulled the huge door closed again, except for a slot they could watch through. Endo had taken the remaining Bren gun to a position guarding the front entry facing the main gate house.

They watched Krag up above, straddling the beam of one of the cranes while he burned his way through it. White-hot metal fell like a waterfall of fire.

"Hope he's not sawing himself off on a limb," said Marumoto.

"He's watching it." Indeed, as they spoke, Krag backed off from his cutting position to a more secure place on the crane tracks.

This particular crane had been idle. The other crane, farther down the length of the mill near one of the electric arc furnaces held a ladle of molten steel. The entry of Krag and his men had stopped the ladle furnace operations in the middle of an alloying procedure.

The work of destruction went apace.

Both of them could see Hara doing his chores. Borovitch was in evidence from time to time. So was Barton, hauling an acetylene torch cart behind him like some oversized pet.

Marumoto's thoughts turned elsewhere. We are, indeed, in a version of hell, he thought. Condemned, perhaps, because we have murdered. Or because the nature of the world dictates whimsically who lives, who dies, who goes to hell, who to paradise.

Toda interrupted his revery. "Let me have a couple of clips of ammo."

Marumoto came back to the moment. "What?"

"Ammo. I need a couple of extra clips."

"Sure, sure." Marumoto pulled some clips from his ammunition belt, but his hands still shook. He dropped the clips.

"What the hell's the matter with you?"

"I don't know." Marumoto sighed. "I guess... Oh...those guys."

"What guys?"

"Christ, we just murder two men and you ask 'what guys?' "

"Not murder. War. Push it out of your mind."

"How?"

"Snap out of it! You start thinking about that stuff and you'll wind up sick in the head." Toda tapped his temple with a forefinger. *"Baka."*

"Shouldn't killing make me *baka*?"

"This isn't the Ivy League, Marumoto. Forget it!"

"Am I just supposed to forget that I'm a human being" — he waved a hand helplessly — "or that they were? Do I turn off my feelings or something?"

"That's just what you do. Turn 'em off!"

"So, that makes us just like Barton now. A couple of killing machines. Give the victim a cigarette, then shove a knife into him. Professional. Like Barton. The world will never be the same."

"Never is."

15

The Working Mill, September 5, 1942

I

When they came to the service road leading to the rear of the mill, Kamasaki deployed his three men, alternately one on the left and the other on the right, with wide intervals between each man. He took the lead and the sergeant brought up the rear.

"Rifles at the ready!" he shouted. "Be alert! Forward!"

They followed the road toward the rear gate. As they got closer, Kamasaki realized there was no one at the guardpost. The shack was empty.

"Halt!" He stared at the wire fence with its gate ajar. "Where are the sentries?" he wondered out loud. "Sergeant!" The sergeant ran up from the rear of the patrol.

"Sir?"

"Where are the sentries?"

"They should be here, sir. You spoke with them only a while ago."

"That damn, drunken fool, Private Marumoto," he muttered.

"Marumoto usually is dependable," said the sergeant. "The other sentry is gone, too. Maybe they were called inside. . ."

Kamasaki knew it was more than that. He felt panic working on him. "This is very strange." He stared at the line of forest, jagged and black against the night sky. He remembered what Sumida had said about it.

195

"There is a smell of danger."

The sergeant looked around uncomfortably. He put his hand on the bolt of his rifle, ready to chamber a cartridge.

"I sense the enemy may be near," Kamasaki went on. "Deploy the men, Sergeant."

"Where?"

"Where do you think? Along the road to guard the gate."

"Yessir!" He shouted at the men. "Take cover! Spread out!"

The three soldiers sprawled along the berm of the road, facing the forest. Kamasaki went to the guard hut and looked around. No sign of them. He picked up the phone and examined it. He followed the wire from the leather carrier. He saw that it had been cut.

"Sergeant!"

"Sir!"

"This line has been cut. I'll remain with the men here. You go into the mill and telephone Major Sumida at the main gate."

"Very well, sir. Please be careful, sir."

"Don't worry about me. Look out for yourself."

II

Toda and Marumoto heard the shouted orders outside and got ready for action. They saw Kamasaki deploy his men, facing in the wrong direction. Then they saw the sergeant trotting toward them.

"Damn!" snapped Toda. He made a hand signal to Marumoto to hang back, then pulled out his knife. He crouched behind a stove-hot ingot, ready to pounce on the Japanese soldier after he came through the door.

The sergeant came up to the entry. The slot was too narrow for him. He dragged the big door along its tracks. But before moving inside, he hesitated. Some instinct, the evil red glare, perhaps, made him stand and wait. The fountain of sparks falling from Krag's torch made him look that way. He started to make a tentative move forward.

Toda braced.

But just then the air was pierced by the shriek of tearing metal. The crane beam, cut nearly through, twisted and fell with a clanging crash to the mill floor.

The sergeant pulled back. What is this? he wondered. What is going on?

He stared at the devilish figure on the high track behind the warped stub of the crane beam. It was a man like some black-faced demon in his goggles, seeming to writhe and dance in the shadows and flickering heat waves of the crimson glare. The man reached and pushed up his goggles. His face was gleaming with sweat. It streaked the black on his face like zebra stripes. But this devil's face illuminated in the garish light was no Japanese face!

"American!" the sergeant gasped. He backed away, then turned suddenly and began running back toward Kamasaki.

"Son of a bitch!" shouted Toda. He cast his knife aside, picked up his rifle, and fired. The shot caught the sergeant high on his shoulder and he went down. From his backup position, Marumoto ran forward, rifle ready.

The sergeant worked to his feet and staggered toward Kamasaki.

"Captain!" he screamed. "Captain!"

Toda tried to chamber another round. His bolt jammed on the cartridge. "Get him, Professor! Shoot!"

"Americans," shouted the sergeant, lurching toward the rear gate. Blood gleamed on the back of his tunic. "Americans are inside!"

Marumoto, hands shaking badly again, hesitated. Then he raised the rifle quickly and fired. It was a snap shot, but the bullet caught the sergeant in the back of the neck. He was dead before he hit the ground. As if still running, the victim's leg kicked and jerked spasmodically for an instant, then stopped. Marumoto felt hot tears welling in his eyes. "Just like Barton," he whispered.

III

Kamasaki turned when he heard the first shot. He saw the sergeant fall, then pick himself up. The sergeant was at the gate before the second shot hit him.

Kamasaki dived behind the low cover of the road facing the plant and drew his pistol. "This side! Quick!" His men needed no prodding. They had seen the sergeant die, too. "Stay down!" he told them. "Don't fire unless you have to. Americans are inside with our people." He pulled himself lower. He checked to make sure there was a round chambered in his pistol.

"You!" he shouted at one of the three. "Go back and tell Major Sumida what has happened! Tell him we have them trapped! Stay low!"

"Yessir!" The man started to scramble off on all fours.

"Run, dammit! As hard as you can!" He turned to the other men. "You, take cover there! You there! Keep watch on that entrance!" Kamasaki slumped against the low embankment. Now he just had to hold out against the enemy until Sumida gave instructions or reinforcements arrived.

IV

Up on the wrecked crane Krag also heard the shots. He shouted down. "Toda! How many?"

"Army patrol! Kamasaki! We nailed one of 'em. He's got four left."

"Don't let 'em in." Krag looked into the shadows below. He could see other torches at work in the semi-darkness. Hara was making scrap out of the furnace machinery. The control room already was wreckage. Somewhere out of sight Sakai and Borovitch were doing terrible things to the powerhouse and, he hoped, the argon supply.

Krag felt certain now that with just a little bit more luck they could complete the work. Getting back out again was something he preferred not to think about right now. It was time to get on with the job.

The first crane had gone down with a marvelous crash. The other one was a different story. For one thing, it was more massive, with a thicker beam. The cutting would take longer. And, for another thing, there was the unknown.

This crane was holding a monster ladle of molten steel. When that stuff fell, who knew what would happen or exactly where. How high would it splash? He was all too aware from the torch cutting he had done so far that his clothing was no match for white-hot sparks. But then, there really wasn't any choice. He started to maneuver his acetylene tank along the catwalk beside the crane track toward the next target.

V

Sumida knew something was wrong as he watched the soldier gallop toward him. The man clearly was running as if he had demons after him. The man got to him gasping for breath.

"Major!"

"Calm down!" Sumida said gently. "What is it?"

"Sir, Captain Kamasaki says" — the man gulped for air — "he says Americans are in the plant. They are armed. Sergeant Kondo has been shot."

"Is he alive?"

"I do not think so, sir. He was shot in the shoulder and then in the head. The bullets went through him."

"How many?"

"Two shots," said the soldier.

"No! How many *enemy* did you see?"

"None, sir. They are hiding."

"But our own people. . .workers. . .are in the plant?"

"Yessir. None came out."

Sumida grabbed the company telephone that connected with the mill offices and rattled the hook. Nothing.

"Telephone lines have been cut." He glanced at the messenger.

"Now, soldier. You say the sergeant has been shot and he is dead."

"I think he is dead, sir."

"So that leaves Kamasaki with two men and you here." He looked around. "I have four."

"Yessir."

"Go back to Captain Kamasaki." Sumida checked his watch. "Tell him to attack the rear entrance at exactly 2400. I will attack this entrance at the same time."

"Sir, Captain Kamasaki said the Americans are trapped in there."

Sumida snorted. "The enemy is not trapped. He is in there on purpose. He is trying to wreck the plant. We must prevent that. Repeat the order back to me."

"Captain Kamasaki begins attack against rear entrance at 2400. Major Sumida will attack the front entrance at the same time. Prevent the enemy from damaging the plant."

"Very good." Sumida patted him on the shoulder. "Go!"

"Yessir!"

VI

Barton still carried the Thompson and ammunition pouches he'd brought along from *Grayfish*. He dodged around ingots and equipment until he got to Toda near the rear entrance.

"What're they doing?"

"Sitting tight. Probably waiting for reinforcements."

"That won't last long. They'll be coming in. Wish to hell we had that other Bren gun we left with McGlynn."

"Don't worry," said Marumoto loudly. "We'll get 'em, Barton. Dead. We're kill-crazy."

Barton stared. It was totally out of character for Marumoto. He turned to Toda. "What's with him?"

"Yale meets Reality."

200

"If he's cracking up," Barton whispered, "we got to get him off this door."

"See that corpse out there?"

"Yeah."

"It was the Professor's shot. He'll be all right for now. Later on, I don't know."

"Yeah. Well, I don't care about later on. Now's when it counts. I'm going back on the torch, but I'll be near by. Give me a shout if you need help."

"See you 'round the campus."

VII

Sakai was working on the powerhouse when Borovitch found him.

"How's it going, Doc?"

"One crane is down already. The control room is destroyed, and Hara is doing the furnace. I think he's done enough already to stop it for good."

"That's great." He pointed at the diesel engines. "The work of the master. They'll never get the heads off those engines."

"Did you do the drive shafts?"

"Yep! See for yourself."

Borovitch inspected. "It is not necessary to be so neat, you know."

"Artistic pride. I think I'm done here. Let's go find that argon."

"I have found it. It's stacked waiting for us in the storage area. Follow me."

The little man wheeled his torch cart behind the old man. The storage area, unlike the other mill, had sheet-metal partitions. The big, white argon tanks were stacked in low tiers like cordwood with thick wooden wedges inserted to keep them from rolling.

"There it is, Sakai. The monster's blood. Enough to keep the Argon Furnace working for a month."

"You still think I should weld these suckers shut?"

Borovitch had found some large crescent wrenches. "Now that I've inspected the scene, I have a better idea." He clamped a wrench on the valve of one tank. "We will do them this way. We will open the valve. But be careful of the gas. It's extremely cold until it expands. As it escapes, it will freeze you in an instant. After that, it is no problem."

He wrenched open the valve. A jet of white gas burst from it. "It'll take a long time for the gas to escape. So, to prevent our enemies from possibly coming back and saving any, we will weld the valves open!" Borovitch laughed at his own ingenuity.

Sakai pointed at the jet. "Is it poisonous?"

"No, it's inert. But it can smother you. So be careful. Make sure you get air."

Sakai went to work. He wrenched open a half dozen valves, then backed up and welded them in place. The cold argon gas hissed loudly. Heavier than air, it poured to the floor, then as it expanded it crept rapidly across the floor of the mill.

Sakai felt as if he were working in the clouds. He climbed across a low tier of argon tanks. On the other side he found a stack painted black instead of the white of the argon tanks.

"Hey Doc!"

"What is it?"

"I found some other tanks. These babies are painted different."

Borovitch was melting a fuze box with his torch. He turned his flashlight Sakai's way, picking out black-painted tanks with Japanese characters painted on them.

"I don't know what they are. Can you read those kanji?"

"That's kata-kana, not kanji. Let's see. Says, uh, 'liquid petroleum gas.' Mean anything to you?"

"My God! Don't open those tanks! We would have an explosion. Petroleum gas is very volatile."

"What's it for?"

"It's probably the gas they use to preheat alloy materials in special chambers."

"How do we wreck it?"

Borovitch shook his head. "Let it alone. It's very explosive. We can't risk dealing with it."

"Hate to leave a good tank untorched. But whatever you say. . ."

VIII

Hara found Endo bunkered behind a pile of scrap steel used to charge the electric arc furnaces near the main entrance. The huge front door was closed, and Endo had secured the hasp with a piece of steel rod.

"They're on to us, so look sharp."

"Yeah. I heard shots back there. Anybody hurt?"

"None of ours. One of them dead. Any activity out this way?"

"Can't see a hell of a lot from here. I was watching through one of those little windows a while ago. I did get a glimpse of Sumida's car driving up. Maybe if I hunker up closer to the door. . ."

"Stay put. You're too exposed up by the door. Wait'll they try to break in."

"You think they'll try."

Hara shrugged. "If they wait for reinforcements, they're letting us do our job. If Sumida figures out what we're up to — and he's got to have a pretty good idea — then he'll have to act. From here you can keep 'em off our backs while we finish up."

"How much longer?"

"We got the control room and we've fused the pinions on the furnace. Krag's got one crane. He's working on the other one, but he's got a way to go."

They both looked toward Krag, invisible in the flickering red glare and shadows cast by the molten steel in the cauldron. But they could see the shower of sparks falling from his torch.

"Doc and Sakai have aced the powerhouse and they're working on the argon now," Hara said. "I'd say we have maybe ten more minutes of work."

"Long ten minutes! Especially when they're on to us."

"Long as we're inside, we can mangle the mill. That's what we're here for. As for them, they can't get around us or over us, so they have to come straight through. It'll cost 'em."

"Think we'll get out of this?"

"Sure," Hara lied. "You'll be back at U.S.C. throwing a football a year from now."

"No."

"Why?"

"I'm a running back."

"See you later."

16

The Working Mill, September 5, 1942

I

Sumida deployed his handful of men carefully. They cut access holes in the fence, rather than maneuver directly through a potential field of fire at the main gate. They covered their approach from behind the heavy equipment parked in the mill yard. The major studied the closed main door carefully. There was no choice but to go in that way while Kamasaki would do the same at the other end of the building. Sumida disliked the idea of a direct assault. Rows of small windows flanked the door on both sides. But he had seen no face peering out. Nor was the glass broken — that would have been a sure sign that someone intended to shoot through. Only the reflected glare from molten metal showed. Yet he knew that behind that wall there were enemies.

How many? How armed? How deployed?

How ready to die?

Even as he asked himself, he knew the answers: too many; too well armed; too well deployed.

And too ready to die.

Why else would they be here in their enemy's land?

He drew his pistol from its holster, checked the magazine, then chambered a round. The sergeant had left his whistle behind in the gate house when he went on his fatal patrol. Sumida put it to his mouth and checked his watch.

The second hand swept into the final minute, then the final seconds. At precisely 2400 he blew the whistle.

The men moved quickly toward the main door in classic infantry fashion, one covering as another leaped ahead. Quickly they were at the door with no shot fired.

"Open that door!" Sumida shouted. "Stay low!"

The men yanked and banged. Obviously, the door had been barred on the inside. Sumida knew what to do. Swinging his bad leg as best he could, he hobbled to one of the big tractors. He ignored the windows. The enemy was too clever to use them. The big machine had a well-equipped toolbox, including wrenches and a crowbar kind of instrument used to work on the tractor treads.

"Hey!" The men turned to look. "Use this!" He hurled the crowbar to them. One of the men stood bravely and stabbed the bar between wall and door and pried. The hasp inside broke away. He should be decorated, thought Sumida. I will recommend it.

Still no shot from inside.

The others crouched as the crowbar man braced his shoulder against the heavy door and shoved it aside. The hellish glare from inside flooded out. At the same time there was the staccato thud of a machine gun. The crowbar man jerked upright, twirled, then dropped. A rivulet of blood streamed from his body, found a crevice in the tarmac, and ran toward Sumida like some ruby messenger. It gleamed in the unearthly light of the mill. Bullets clanged into the parked tractors, then whined off into the night.

"Inside!" shouted Sumida. "Quick! Quick! Take cover!"

His men fired shots back into the mill. Sumida hurled himself behind the cover of the mill wall, then edged his way to the entrance. There he bolted inside and threw himself to the floor in the shadows. Shots snapped overhead. He crawled over to one of his men, secure behind a wall of thick bags of mill material.

"Corporal, help me move this bag."

"Yessir."

They tugged one of the heavy bags aside, allowing Sumida to peek through a narrow gap and study the scene. Despite the pervasive red glare from molten steel in a huge cauldron hanging midway down the mill, it was difficult to make out actual features. It was a volcano world. Rising waves of heat distorted everything. The one great source of light cast livid rays of red that made the shadows seem darker. High above this, Sumida saw a fountain of sparks falling in a stream from the still darker shadows near the roof of the mill. The sparks would fall in a rush, then subside, then fall again in a torrent.

Sumida knew a man was there, maybe two, doing something, but he couldn't make out forms. Assuming they were saboteurs, someone — or two or three — would be covering them. But from where? The bizarre light cast surreal pools of light and dark that made concealment simple. Indeed, the features of the mill floor itself were strange. Sumida was glad he had inspected the area before. He knew that the ranks of huge soldier-like forms were molds. The pile of material to one side of the molds was scrap steel.

He had been told by the managers that the scrap was put into the electric arc furnaces, melted, and then transported in that huge hanging cauldron down there to the other furnace. It, in turn, was like a gigantic cocktail shaker to mix and purify the alloys. Sumida stared intently at the heap of scrap. It was the one vantage point that could cover the mill door with no impediment between.

"Corporal, you see that pile of iron? Look carefully."

The man edged to the gap in the bags and looked. "I see it, sir."

"I think an enemy is posted behind it. Throw something that way. Make a noise to see if he fires."

"Yessir." The man found a chunk of cement. "Will this do, sir?"

"Good. Throw hard. I will watch."

"Yessir." The corporal lobbed the fragment in a high arc over the barricade. Sumida saw it land near the scrap heap.

Instantly, there was a three-round burst of fire toward the door.

For the briefest of instants, the gun flashes showed the black silhouette of a man, then the figure was behind cover again.

"He is there! He is down behind that scrap heap! Give me one of your grenades."

The corporal rummaged one from his pouch and handed it to the major. Sumida spoke earnestly to the young man.

"Now listen. I will throw this grenade at the scrap heap. With luck we will wound the machine gunner. Even if not, he will be blinded for an instant by the flash. You understand?"

"Yes, I understand."

"Good. Now remember. The very moment the grenade explodes, you and the others rush him. You must not waste a fraction of a second. Run your hardest. Understood?"

"Yessir."

"Good." He patted the corporal on the shoulder reassuringly.

"Crawl over there and tell the others. When you are ready, give me the signal."

The man stayed on his belly, scrabbling crablike on elbows and knees, rifle cradled in his arms. Sumida nodded approvingly. These were men untested by battle, but if they remembered their training, it would work.

Sumida saw the corporal get to the others. He pulled the safety pin from his grenade. A moment later, the corporal raised his hand and nodded "yes" vigorously.

Sumida returned the sign, then crawled to the end of the stack of bags nearest the scrap heap. His leg nagged him. He had been doing too much to it, and it was complaining. No matter. This was action, and his leg would just have to put up with the inconvenience until the matter was settled. He reached the end of the stack and peered carefully around the edge.

He saw part of a man's shape and the steel glint of a light machine gun. The enemy saw him! Sumida ducked back just as the machine gun fired. Bullets clipped pieces from his barricade. Dust went into his eyes. Close call! So be it. He knew where to send his message now. He glanced back quickly at his men.

They were crouched, set to go, rifles at the ready. Sumida banged the grenade against his chest to pop the fuze. He held it for two seconds, then lobbed it toward the scrap heap. He heard the iron shell of the grenade clank on the scrap. Then there was a bright flash-bang! He turned to see his men rush forward, then looked back at the scrap heap.

The enemy had been hit! The man, dressed all in black, sprawled backward from the scrap, blood rushing from wounds on his head.

But he wasn't dead!

Sumida fired his pistol and hit the man. But, obviously dying, the man staggered to his feet. He pulled the trigger on his machine gun and kept firing until the magazine was empty.

Ricochets slapped and whined in all directions.

Sumida's men were on top of him!

The enemy swung his machine gun like a club, knocking down one of his attackers. It was to no avail. The other two soldiers bayonetted him. A shot from somewhere else spanged into the scrap. Sumida's men dived for cover on their side of the heap of steel.

They did well, Sumida thought, but I have no time for satisfaction.

He looked back at the body of his own man by the big door. The still corpse was, like the scrap heap itself, only wreckage. Human, but wreckage none the less. I have lost one man for one of theirs, he thought. Who could win with this kind of attrition? And this is only the beginning.

II

Krag heard the thud of the Bren gun, but didn't look. The job at hand was more demanding. It was crushingly hot work. Even with yards of distance between him and the molten steel in the cauldron, the heat was scorching. His dark clothing seemed to absorb it all. The vertical member of the beam was slow going.

But he was making progress. He had about a third of it eaten away. Soon the weight of the vessel would make the difference.

Krag didn't like to think about that. The molten steel, he knew, would fall spectacularly and it could happen at any time. He kept at his work.

After those initial shots he heard nothing for a few minutes. Then came the unmistakable blast of a grenade. This time he looked. Just at that moment Endo loosed his final, long, defiant burst of fire before the bayonets found him.

Just below Krag there was a rifle shot at the Japanese. Probably Hara. It forced the attackers to cover. Krag could see that one of them had been hit, a huddled shape in the main door opening.

He shouted down, "Hara! Barton! Cover me!"

"We see 'em, Skipper!" Barton shouted from the shadows. He tapped off a few rounds from his Thompson. Krag slipped his goggles down and went back to work. Soon the shower of molten steel resumed.

III

It was a different story at the back of the mill. The moment of 2400 came and went, but Kamasaki still had not ordered his attack. The reason was simple: his people didn't have cover. As soon as they stood up, they would be easy targets. While he tried to figure out what to do, his men stayed in the shelter of the road bank. While they couldn't attack, they could shoot.

Though Toda and Marumoto were well covered, the shower of steel sparks marked Krag's place. Every once in a while one of Kamasaki's men would wing a harassing shot in his general direction. Marumoto or Toda would answer with a shot. Barton worked up behind them again.

"We got to shut that sniping off. They get Krag and we lose the crane."

"Any ideas, Barton?" asked Marumoto.

"I thought Japanese were hard chargers, Perfesser. Where's that old banzai spirit?"

"Banzai?" Toda laughed. "There's only a few of 'em. If they rushed, we'd get 'em all."

"Tell it to Kamasaki," said Barton.

"That's a good idea," Marumoto said. "Load a fresh clip."

"Huh?" said Toda.

"What's your idea, Perfesser?"

"Load up. You too, Barton."

"Barton checked the magazine of his Thompson. "Okay."

"I'm loaded," said Toda.

"Stand by." Marumoto cradled his rifle and started inching on his belly toward the door opening.

"What the hell's he doin'?" Barton asked.

Toda just shook his head.

Marumoto found a chink in the steel siding of the wall. With the barrel of his rifle, he pried the opening a bit wider.

Suddenly he shouted in Japanese: "Charge! Everybody up! Banzai! Rush the door! Charge!"

"Yeah!" Toda and Barton shouted at each other.

Two of the Japanese soldiers leaped up and came racing through the gate straight at the door opening. Behind them another voice, Kamasaki's, began to shout: "Stop! It is a trick!"

Toda saw him yank one of his soldiers back to the safety of the embankment. But it was too late for the other two. They stopped when Kamasaki shouted. Barton put two .45 caliber slugs into the chest of one. The man flipped backward as if pulled by wires. Marumoto knocked the other one down with a bullet in the thigh. Toda put the finishing shot into him. The man staggered and fell beside the corpse of the sergeant. It was over.

"Good goin', Perfesser," Barton exulted. "We'll make a marine out of you yet."

Marumoto slumped back against the wall of the building. His hands were shaking violently. He clutched them together, as if in prayer, and hung his head, trying to catch his breath.

"I don't think they'll be coming in from this side," said Barton.

211

"They only got Kamasaki and what? One man? Two?"

"I only saw one," said Toda.

"Okay, we're under control here. I'm going back the other way."

On the other side of the fence Kamasaki lay prone beside his remaining soldier.

"How does the enemy know Japanese?" the soldier asked in wonder.

"I don't know." Kamasaki felt inept, useless. He had lost three men and, as far as he knew, the enemy was unharmed.

"Maybe it is our own people," the soldier said. "What shall we do?"

Kamasaki accepted the reality. "There is nothing we can do here. We must join forces with Major Sumida at the front. Come on!"

Together, the two of them wormed their way to the cover of the forest to begin their roundabout journey to the front gate.

IV

It was a dream world. The storage area was knee-deep in spreading clouds of argon. Where they drifted into the reflected glare from the furnace chamber they returned an ethereal pink light. As he returned to Sakai, Borovitch was struck by the unreal beauty of it.

One looks for angels, he thought, but one is more likely to find devils.

"Hi, Doc. I heard shots. How's it going on the other side?"

"The enemy knows we're here. There has been fighting, but he hasn't broken in yet." Borovitch looked around. "This reminds me of a ballet I once saw. The beautiful women in their tutus danced in clouds of carbon dioxide."

"Too bad. None of 'em here."

"I half hope to see a ballerina leap out of the wings."

"No such luck." Sakai's torch bit through a valve connection.

A violent jet of gas escaped in a spike of white.

"Be careful with those valves!" Borovitch snapped. "There's a lot of pressure in those tanks!"

"I know." Sakai nodded. "All under contr. . ." A rifle shot stopped him in midsentence. He slumped heavily against the mound of tanks, then slid to the clouded floor. His torch hissed angrily.

Borovitch crouched down. Quickly he shut off the torch, then turned to face the other end of the room. As if watching in slow-motion, he saw a Japanese soldier working the action of his rifle. The man seemed to be rising out of the gas like something from Olympus. The soldier brought his rifle up. . . But then another shot blasted from just behind Borovitch. The Japanese soldier dropped his rifle and clutched his chest. He swayed for an instant, then collapsed. He disappeared under the argon. Borovitch turned again. The rifleman was Fujimura. "Sakai's hit. Help me get him up."

Borovitch motioned Fujimura to where Sakai had fallen. They rummaged in the vapor until they got a good grip on him.

"Get him up out of the gas. It can smother him," said Borovitch.

Together they hauled Sakai up and stretched him out on a tier of tanks well above the vapor. Sakai clutched his midsection with his arms. Blood seeped through his blues and ran in streaks across the white argon tanks.

"How bad is it, Fuj?" Sakai gasped.

"Can't tell when you got your hands over it, Murray."

"Let me look," said Borovitch.

"Don't bother, Doc. I don't want to let go of my gut. I'll be okay. It don't hurt too bad."

"Let me look."

"No!"

Gently, Borovitch pulled Sakai's hands away and inspected the wound. Even in the best of circumstances it would have been a dangerous injury. Here it was mortal. "Let me fix you up. . ."

"Get out of here, Doc. You too, Fuj. I'll be okay." He reached, groping for something. "Just got to torch a few more of these tanks. Get out. Hara and Barton need help."

Fujimura glanced at Borovitch. He knew, too, that the wound was mortal. He looked at Sakai and nodded. "I'll leave a rifle with you."

"Sure. And, Fuj, listen. . ." He gasped as a spasm of pain gripped him. "Listen, pull my torch up here on the tanks beside me."

Fujimura wasn't sure he'd heard it correctly. "Torch?"

"Yeah. Put it right up on these tanks beside me."

"Okay. Doc, give me a hand, please."

"Certainly."

They lifted up the heavy acetylene cylinder and torch and nested them on the tier of argon tanks beside Sakai.

"That do it?" asked Fujimura.

"Thanks." Sakai reached out and patted the tank. "Get goin'."

Fujimura clutched his arm, then turned away. Borovitch squeezed his hand. "*Sayonara,* young friend."

"*Sayonara,* Doc."

Fujimura and Borovitch headed for the main floor of the mill. They didn't look back.

V

Creeping fingers of white gas were what had caught Sumida's attention. That was why he sent one of his men to investigate what was on the other side of the wall behind the electric arc furnaces.

Watching from his barricade, he saw his man aim, fire, and — mistakenly — bring his rifle down to chamber a new round. He should have kept firing as fast as he could. He paid for the error. Sumida saw the man hit and fall, swallowed totally within the clouds.

Now, he thought, the clouds are reaching for me like the tentacles of some clammy ghost. He didn't like the omen.

Worse, another of his men was gone.

Kamasaki crept up behind him. "Major, I've come to join you."

"What are you doing here? You are supposed to be attacking the other end of the building!"

"We did attack, sir. All were killed except me and this man." He pointed at his remaining soldier. "We could do nothing more there, so we came to join you."

"Very well." Sumida counted his casualties. "Two dead here, three gone at the other end. An unacceptable attrition."

"I apologize, sir," said Kamasaki. "I. . ."

"You did what you could. It cannot be helped."

"What is the plan?"

"Plan?" Sumida almost laughed out loud. Still, something had to be done. "The plan is to stop the enemy in his work. See those sparks up there?"

"Yessir."

"A man is cutting down the crane. We must stop him, but we cannot hit him from here."

"Perhaps, if I took a man around the other way." Kamasaki pointed at the cloudy storage area.

"Not that way. It is defended. One of my men was killed there." He pointed instead at the argon furnace.

"I think the best route is to circle around that furnace. Try to get him from the other side."

"How many are defending?"

"I do not know. We killed that one over there."

"What uniform is that?"

"I have not been able to get close enough to inspect. It looks like some kind of special night garb, like a *ninja* might wear."

"He is a *ninja*?"

"I did not say he was a *ninja*, only that his garb is black like that."

Kamasaki focused on the clouds of argon gas creeping toward them. "What is that?"

"I do not know. Carbon dioxide, perhaps. Be careful of it. It does not seem to be poisonous, but it might be volatile."

VI

Keeping low, Fujimura and Borovitch maneuvered their way back to the main mill floor. They met Marumoto.

"They got Sakai, but we got one of theirs."

"Sakai?" Marumoto shook his head sadly. "That poor little man."

"He died as big as any man around," said Fujimura.

"Death is with us," Marumoto murmured.

"How is it back there?" Fujimura asked.

"They gave up on our end. Toda's staying to watch."

"Barton ran in a crouch over to them. "We can use you, Perfesser. You, too, Fuj. We lost Endo and the Bren Gun up front. Hara's covering for the moment."

"Where you want me?" asked Marumoto.

"Find a spot where you can cover Krag. Sumida's boys are trying to get at him."

"On my way."

Barton grabbed his hand. "Take care of yourself, Perfesser."

The gesture surprised Marumoto. "Thought you hated Japs."

"I do. But you ain't one. You're a good marine, Perfesser. When we get back I'll personally pin the globe and anchor over your Yale heart."

"Better than a Ph.D." He turned and started working his way closer to Krag.

"Man, when that crane comes down, there'll be one hell of a splash of hot stuff," said Fujimura. "Hope the Professor's got an eye on it."

"Damn right! And make sure you're well away from it, too."

"Count on it. Where do you want to post me?"

"Back up Hara. He's over there. See him?"

"Got it." He started to go.

"Oh, Kid."

"Yeah?"

"Dreaming up the torch trick was pretty goddamn smart."

"This time I think I'm so smart I'm stupid."

"No. You done right. This mission is what it's all about. With you, we're able to do our mission."

"The mission, yeah. And it's cost us Endo and Sakai."

"That's worth an awful lot. But the mission is all there is in life."

"And death."

"Die happy."

17

I

Slowly, painfully, Kamasaki and his lone rifleman inched their way across the mill floor. Sharp fragments of slag shredded their clothing and scraped the skin from their knees and elbows.

But, thought Kamasaki, scraped knees are better than a bullet in the head. His rifleman had similar thoughts. Both were diligent about their progress. An occasional shot rang out as Sumida kept up suppressive fire to keep enemy heads down. Seconds turned into minutes, minutes into a quarter hour. But, in time, they worked their way directly under the hot, grimy shelter of the big furnace. At last Kamasaki had an unimpeded look at the source of the showering sparks.

"See him?"

"I see."

"Can you get a shot at him?"

"Perhaps."

The rifleman snaked forward a few inches. A bullet spanged against the furnace just over his head and went humming away like some angry hornet. The rifleman was aware of a dark shape moving somewhere close by. But, intent on his assignment, he took aim at Krag and fired.

II

Krag was trying to maneuver his work so that more of the crane would be between him and the attack party.

It was no good.

The rifleman's shot caught him in the right chest. The shock of the impact froze him for a moment. He knew the wound was bad. The worse they were, it seemed, the less they hurt at first. His right side was numb. Blood pooled on the top of the crane beam. He gathered his energy and shouted.

"Barton! I'm hit!"

"Hang on!" the marine called back. "I'm coming up!"

"Stay put, Barton!" Marumoto yelled. "I can get to him quicker."

On the beam Krag used his remaining strength to stow his acetylene torch so it wouldn't fall. Then he started to edge his way backward. A thick trail of blood followed him. His thoughts chased him through a wall of pain. This is the way it ends, he thought. My blood pours out on the floor of some dirty factory and I'm dead. And that's all there is.

Slowly, as if swimming with one arm against a heavy tide, he crawled for the shelter of the crane's cab. Keep going. A foot, then only inches to go. Just a little more. Maybe, he thought, just maybe. . .

A second shot blew away the top of his head.

Krag's body dropped from the crane. It bounced once against an angle beam in the mill wall then thumped to the mill floor amid the red-hot slag of his own work.

Marumoto was only twenty feet away. There was nothing anyone could do for Krag. But the base of the ladder was even closer than the body. He called to Barton, "Cover me!" He slung his rifle crossways on his back, then started scrambling up the ladder to finish Krag's job.

A bullet clanged into the steel ladder. Another snapped by and punched a hole through the sheet-iron wall of the mill. Hand over determined hand, he moved up.

Barton opened up with the Thompson. Borovitch joined in. Hara and Fujimura moved to cover them. The volley forced the Japanese soldiers under the furnace to get down. As Marumoto worked higher, Borovitch slipped into the vantage point he had vacated.

At the top of the ladder Marumoto pulled himself to the crane, then locked his arms around the thick beam. Trying to keep out of the line of fire, he tugged himself toward the torch Krag had placed so carefully out of harm's way. Its flame still burned with a kind of amethyst purity, ready and waiting. The professor's hands slipped in Krag's blood. It was difficult going, crouching the way he was. Finally, he reached the torch. Cautiously, he inspected the beam. The vertical member of the "I" was nearly half cut. It couldn't take much more. He put the point of the flame at the bottom of the cut. In an instant the steel glowed maroon, then cherry, then white. The shower of molten steel resumed.

III

Sumida saw some of this action from his barricade. He saw the enemy fall. That was something, but the important thing was that the shower of fire had stopped. Then, after a time, to his chagrin, the sparks began to fall again. There had been a lapse of only minutes. He could make out this man a little better.

This one was wearing dirty white. The man had gone up the ladder, apparently unimpeded. The fall of sparks had resumed a short time later. Obviously, from the volume of shooting, Kamasaki and his rifleman had been pinned down. Something else would have to be done.

Sumida edged out from behind his barricade. No shots came at him, though an occasional stray bullet went by with its characteristic whip-crack sound. So he wasn't drawing fire. Boldly, he limped up to the scrap heap. The dead enemy sprawled there, bloody-faced, eyes staring angrily at the top of the mill.

It did not seem to be a Caucasian face, but who could tell with all that blood on it. Sumida didn't care about that. There was no time for investigation. He wanted the machine gun and the dead man's ammunition. He picked up the weapon and examined it in the shadows. It seemed to be a Nambu or something very like it. He threw away the empty magazine and found a fresh one in the dead man's ammunition pouch. He took a spare magazine and tucked it into his belt.

"Soldier!" he called to one of his reserves. "Take this. And here's an extra magazine. Put it in your pocket. Join Captain Kamasaki. Keep the big furnace between you and the other end of the mill. Go! Quickly!"

In a crouch the soldier scurried forward. Some random overhead shots sent him to the floor, but he kept going in a frenetic scramble. In a few minutes he had managed his way to Kamasaki. "Captain."

Kamasaki, intent on the rain of sparks, turned.

"Ah! A light machine gun! Where did it come from?"

"It is the enemy soldier's gun. Major Sumida ordered me here with it. Where do you want me, sir?"

"See that rifleman? There. Fire at the man on the crane."

"Yessir." The gunner ran forward and dived into position. Instantly, he fired a long burst in the direction of the sparks. He saw movement. A man in dirty white garb. He fired a short burst. The molten metal continued to fall. The gunner fired a burst that emptied the magazine.

IV

The machine-gun fire was wild, but a spinning ricochet from the last burst hit Marumoto in the upper part of his right arm. His hand lost feeling. He couldn't move it. He knew the arm bone was broken. He couldn't work any more.

"I'm hit!" he called below. "Coming down!" Like Krag, he placed the torch where it wouldn't roll. He left the flame burning. Some kind of symbol there, he thought through the haze of shock.

We pass the torch and keep the flame alive.

But why?

Sheltering himself as much as he could, he crept backward on the beam. No more machine-gun bullets, but rifle shots banged the metal around him.

Barton and the others opened up, silencing the Japanese.

In a way, he thought, it was easier going down, but now he felt agonizing pain growing in his smashed arm. Bone splinters grated nerves.

"Come on, baby," Barton shouted from below. "Let go. I got you."

Marumoto slid the last ten feet into Barton's arms. He gasped with pain.

"Oh man, I'm finished."

Barton glanced quickly at the wound. "Hell, you only got an arm nick. We'll get you back in shape in no time. A little cruise on the sub and you'll want to come back."

Barton pulled Marumoto's good arm over his shoulder and hauled him toward shelter. Shots snapped and hummed around them. Hara and Fujimura laid down covering fire. Marumoto collapsed. Barton slung the smaller man over his shoulders and lumbered behind cover with the others. He stretched Marumoto out.

"Bad?"

"Arm," Barton puffed. "Take a look!" He slumped against an ingot mold, trying to catch his breath.

Hara glanced at the wound, felt for pulse, then flicked up an eyelid. "He's done."

"You're kidding! He's only nicked in the arm."

Hara pointed. "What you call that?" A random shot had bored through Marumoto's thigh. The bullet had severed his femoral artery. "They got him while you were getting him over here."

"Son of a bitch! The only Yale man I ever knew."

"Yeah. We'll talk about it later."

223

Fujimura had been covering them. He glanced over and saw Borovitch climbing the ladder to the crane. "What the hell's Doc doing?"

Barton looked up from Marumoto. He shouted at the old man. "Doc, get down off that goddamn ladder!"

"Cover me, boys! There's only an inch to cut!"

"Christ, look at the old goat!" Barton exclaimed in awe. Shots began to strike close to the ladder.

"Lay down some lead for him!" Fujimura shouted.

"I'll do better than that!" said Barton. He raced to an exposed vantage point where he could see the rifleman and machine gunner under the furnace. He sprayed slugs at them. One caught the machine gunner between the eyes, but the rifleman had a chance to aim and fire. His shot hit Barton squarely in the chest. The marine fell backward.

Hara and Fujimura stared in shocked disbelief. It was as if some truth had been overturned; as if a slab of granite had turned to sand in front of their eyes. It had not really occurred to them that Barton wasn't bulletproof.

Now they knew.

"My turn," Fujimura said grimly. He ran to a point near where Barton had fallen, firing from the hip as rapidly as the bolt on his Arisaka allowed. For an instant the firing forced Kamasaki and his last rifleman to back away. It was all the time Borovitch needed to get on top of the crane.

But for Fujimura there was no more time.

Kamasaki had reloaded the Bren gun. A burst of fire laced Fujimura's body. He spun and fell, nearly on top of Barton.

"Fuj! Fuj!" Hara screamed. It was a futile cry against fate. He knew Fujimura was dead. He looked up and saw the relentless shower of sparks commence again.

Hara cupped his hands and called, "It's up to you, Doc!"

"Stand away, Hara," the old man shouted. "Get far away!"

Hara realized that the cauldron now could fall at any instant. He ran toward the rear entrance of the mill, near where the truck was parked. He turned to look at Toda, still guarding the

224

rear entry. Then he looked back at Borovitch. The old man's white hair glinted in the sparkle of his torch. Relentlessly, the shower of molten metal fell.

Aloft, Borovitch spoke to his torch as if it were a tired and flagging friend.

"Only a little to go. Fall," he muttered. A bullet snapped nearby. Then another struck the crane beam close to him. Tiny splinters of metal nicked his face. He ignored it. His goggles saved his eyes. The work went on. But now he began to feel a strange sense of desperation, as if there were no more time left before the end of the world. He thought the beam was well past its point of stability, but it didn't bend.

"Fall, damn you, fall!" he cried.

A bullet snapped so close to his torch it put out the flame. This was bad.

He rolled behind the full shelter of the beam as more shots clanged around him. Frantically, with fumbling fingers, he worked to reignite the torch.

"Dammit," he shrieked aloud, "flame!"

His lighter sputtered futilely. The torch gasses hissed in derision. Then with a last flick the lighter struck. The gasses flared to life. Quickly, he tuned the fat yellow flame to the correct mix. He had a sharp lavender point with which to eat steel. He resumed his work. The crane was stubborn. It fought the flame.

"Fall!" he cried. "Fall! Fa...!"

A bullet caught him in the temple. Borovitch and his flaming torch together tumbled end over end and crashed into the floor of the mill.

V

Kamasaki was jubilant. He pounded his rifleman on the shoulder.

225

"You got him! Well done!"

But there was no time to rejoice.

There was a new, piercing sound, like a soul in hell. Then came the high-pitched shriek of rending metal. The last bare inches of steel supporting the weight of the cauldron gave way. The huge vessel slammed to the mill floor with a sound like a cannon blast. It burst open like a black melon full of violence and sunlight. Kamasaki and his soldier had no time to react, not even to cry out.

A tidal wave of molten steel inundated them. Their bodies exploded into steam as the torrent of 2,300-degree metal engulfed them. The molten steel raced like falling water across the mill floor. It found the bodies of others — Krag, Barton, Borovitch, Marumoto, Fujimura — all were vaporized in an instant. Then the only sound amid this ghastly light was the crackle, sputter, and hiss of gasifying objects — human bodies, puddles of grease, scraps of wood. Everything was bathed in a brilliant, horrifying dawn.

At the far end of the mill Sumida shielded his eyes from this nearly staggering brilliance and searing heat. Finally, he ventured a look. The great chamber was as light as day. The lake of steel spread. But even then, as the huge, reaching pool of metal spread toward him, it slowed and cooled. The bubbling surface began to fade to an orange-red.

Sumida was aghast.

All was consumed.

All were dead but him, devoured by molten metal.

"My men!" Tears streaked the grime on his face. "My men!"

18

The Working Mill, September 6, 1942

I

Like Sumida, Hara cringed from the stunning heat and almost overpowering light from the collapsed cauldron. The explosive pop and sizzle of his comrades' bodies assaulted his ears. Their shriveling corpses bounced and rolled as they vaporized amid the hellish shimmering waves. The violent sounds registered, but it would not be until long afterward that it would dawn on him what horror he'd seen and what ghastly sounds he'd heard. And they would haunt his dreams forever.

When he finally was able to look back at the hell-lit scene, all he saw were rivulets of white-hot steel running into declivities, probing open places. The flowing tide turned, reached its limit, turned yellow, and stopped. Cartridges in rifles abandoned near the heat exploded. Casings twirled into the luminous air like celebratory firecrackers.

There was no time to think about all this. He pulled himself together. He turned to see Toda gaping in shock at the flickering devastation.

Hara climbed into the truck cab and started the engine.

"Toda! Get in! We're pulling out!"

"Where are the other guys?"

"Dead!"

"All of 'em? Doc? Barton? Fuj? Endo?"

"Everybody! Endo was killed in the first rush. Fuj and Barton got it near the ladder. Doc got it topside. . ."

"Christ!"

"Let's go!" Hara gunned the engine.

Toda ran over. He started to climb into the cab. A shot, seemingly from nowhere, thudded into his body. He fell to one side, clutching the truck door.

"They got me, Tomi."

Hara reached and grabbed him. "Come on, buddy." Even as he let the clutch out and the truck lurched forward, he hauled Toda into the cab. As he did he looked back through the side mirror. Far away, starkly illuminated by the lake of hot steel between them was Sumida. The Japanese officer had a rifle. He brought it up, aimed. Hara ducked. The bullet starred the windshield.

Toda was bleeding badly and in pain. "It's over, Tomi," he groaned. "All over."

"Like hell it is! You're too mean to die." Hara gunned the truck out through the rear entry of the plant. The truck lurched and bumped over the corpses of the Japanese soldiers killed earlier. Without slowing at the gate, he twisted the wheel. The truck skewed onto the access road.

"On our way, buddy!" he shouted at Toda. "You'll be on the sub soon. Get you fixed up. Home to Hawaii."

Toda slumped against him. Hara looked. He realized Toda was dead.

Now he truly was alone.

II

As the truck fled, Sumida fired one more shot. The firing pin hit an empty chamber. He threw the rifle aside and yanked out his pistol. He fired a shot and another, but it was futile. The truck was gone. There was no way to get to that end of the building through the furnace chamber. The pool of steel glowed as red as the setting sun.

Sumida turned back to the entry into what he now thought of as the Chamber of Clouds. Dozens of great long cylinders, stacked in tiers of three, hissed like serpents.

"This is Major Sumida!" he shouted. "Corporal!" He listened. "Anyone!"

He heard shouts far away, at the other end of the building. He ran that way down a lane between tiers of argon tanks. The hissing cylinders screened him from the other parts of the chamber, but they pointed straight to the tool cages where the plant personnel had been penned up during the excitement.

Sumida picked up a pinch bar and smashed the lock.

"Get out of here!" he shouted. "It is very dangerous. The enemy may have planted explosives. Go!"

"Major! The saboteurs are our very own people!" said the plant manager. "How could it be?"

Sumida shook his head. "It is some kind of trick! Do not worry! Reinforcements are on the way! Please leave! Everybody is in danger here! Out the back! Quick!"

The plant personnel all ran out as ordered. But even as they ran past the bodies at the rear gate, they bowed in honor of the dead. Sumida limped behind them until all were out.

He watched the refugees scurrying down the access road to safety. Then he turned to survey the smoking mill from this side. The air danced and swayed above the gradually hardening steel.

"What can be done?" he wondered aloud. At this point all he could do was try to get word to the authorities. But the telephones were dead, too. Then he remembered his car. Of course, his driver was dead with the others.

But I can drive, he thought. Bad leg or not, I must drive. He began the long, painful march to the other side of the mill.

III

The thundering crash of the cauldron had jarred Sakai back to consciousness.

I'm still alive, he thought. These are the same old clouds.

The pain that had filled the place where his stomach used to be was numbed by shock. He turned his head. The argon gas had crept up nearly to the level of the tank he was lying on. He turned his head the other way. There was his torch. He took some breaths and thought, One of these will be the last. If this is dying, it's taking too damn much time.

He closed his eyes and waited. He lost any sense of time. But then he heard shouting in Japanese.

"Father?" he asked aloud. "What are you doing here?"

Then his brain told him that was impossible. His father was in a concentration camp in California.

Suddenly and surprisingly, he was awake. Moreover, despite weakness, he was fully alert.

He listened.

He heard another shout. He knew that voice. Sumida!

He listened again. Far away he heard the rattle of the tool cage, excited voices. They faded. They were going away. What now, he wondered? What's it going to be? Bleed to death from a gut shot or suffocate in the gas?

He squeezed out a laugh. I am, he thought, delirious. But what are the options? He thought hard about it. An idea occurred to him: I don't have to die either of those ways. I am master of my fate.

He liked that notion.

Something could be done. He knew what it was.

He began.

Slowly, Sakai edged his legs over the side of his tank. The weight of them falling pulled him painfully upright into a lounging, sitting position. He cast his gaze around the storage chamber. Incredibly, everything seemed brightly lit. The clouds of gas glowed reddish orange. He realized that the light was streaming from the furnace chamber through doors and chinks in the superstructure. But what made the light? He concentrated on that. Then it struck him: the big cauldron must have fallen and spilled. That was the loud sound that had called him back, not some heavenly temple gong. The molten steel would run every which way and light things up like a gigantic floor lamp.

Sakai listened intently.

He heard no more sounds. Nothing. Had anyone from his group survived? Were they all dead? Or had they gone? The cauldron, after all, was the last big job. Whichever it was, it would not affect the idea he had.

Painfully, he tore away his bloody shirt. He wadded it up and made a thick compress. Then he stripped off his belt and strapped the compress around his middle. He gasped at the pain, then he chuckled sardonically. At least I know I have guts, he mused. I can see 'em.

Satisfied that his compress would hold him together, he slid his feet down into the cold gas, now almost waist deep. Then he dragged the heavy acetylene tank and torch to the floor. The drop of the heavy weight almost knocked him down. His innards felt as if huge hands were twisting them. He waited until the pain passed.

When it subsided a little, he began to drag his tank down the length of the room to where he had seen the black petroleum gas tanks. It was agonizing going. He had to stop every few feet and fight back the pain and dizziness. But he was determined. It was, he knew, the last thing he would ever do.

But that last thing would be a beauty.

He really had no idea how long it took him to find his mark. Three minutes? Ten? Twenty? He didn't care. He made it. He found it. Struggling the last few feet, he stumbled against something soft, something in the path of his tank. He fumbled in the clouds and realized he had tripped on the corpse of the man who had shot him. Using his feet, he rolled the body out of the way.

"No hard feelings, buddy," he said. "We're all in this together."

Sakai propped his acetylene tank against the huge petroleum gas cylinder. He rummaged his lighter from his pocket. He opened the valves on the torch and with trembling, feeble hands lit the flame.

Even as he adjusted it to the lavender hue he wanted — the hottest — he knew, as if bells were announcing a special message, that his end was near. Meticulously, he placed the torch just so — its amethyst tip just barely touching the side of the propane tank.

Now, he thought, the last laugh.

He tried. No laugh came. Instead, tears streaked his face. Life, he thought, if there were just a little more life.

"Still, brother," he murmured aloud, addressing the dead man in the clouds below, "it'll be one hell of a" — excruciating pain clutched his middle — ". . .one hell of a. . . Hell. . .!" Sakai sank beneath the clouds into the embrace of the man who had killed him.

Above the two corpses the almost invisible flame burned on, just kissing the side of the cylinder. After a time, a spot of maroon appeared. Then a redder, brighter glow. . .

IV

Sumida was nearly exhausted by the time he reached the main gate. But his car was just where it had been. No damage to the car, he thought, only to me.

The pain in his bad leg was agonizing. He felt as if he were wearing molten steel from inside the mill. He stumbled into the gate house, hoping against hope that the telephone had been repaired.

The hope was futile. He looked through the window toward the mill. The body of his brave man lay just as he had fallen by the big door. The glare from inside had faded now to bright red, but still it was intense. It would be days before it was completely cool. He went out and struggled painfully into the driver's seat of the sedan. The keys, fortunately, were in place. For once his driver had done the right thing by violating orders.

As Sumida started the car, he wondered where the nearest

telephone might be. There was, of course, a telephone in his office in Ringo. But that line had been sabotaged, too. Up the railroad line a few kilometers there was a freight siding and station. It would have some kind of communications system. That would have to be it.

Sumida put the car in gear and drove off down the plant road. He had not gone more than a hundred yards when there was a gigantic explosion from inside the plant behind him.

The shock wave from the blast battered his car almost out of control. He braked the car and dived for cover. Debris showered around him. A huge orange and yellow ball expanded rapidly overhead. Then the building was wracked by another explosion and another. Corrugated siding was stripped from the upright girders.

The mill stood like a skeleton in the light of its own flames, its girders glowed red and warped with heat.

The explosions stopped. The ball of fire above dispersed. In shock, Sumida crawled on his hands and knees. He pulled himself back into the car and continued his mission.

19

Ringo, September 6, 1942

I

Hara was less than a quarter mile from Ringo's main street when the exploding gas lit up the town with a stunning flash followed in seconds by the sounds of heavy detonations. Startled, he stopped the truck and looked back. A ball of fire rolled upward into the sky, expanding as it went like some titanic balloon. More blasts followed with even more violent orange and yellow fireballs. Hara had no idea what could have caused the blast. But there was no doubt in his mind that, somehow, the mill had blown up. Whatever had happened, he knew it was a mixed blessing. While something had unquestionably obliterated the mill, it also had awakened every soul in Ringo. Lights went on. People wandered out into the street, gaping and pointing at the sky. This was a complication. The plan had counted on a sleeping town. He glanced at his watch. 0120. Forty minutes to kill — or forty minutes in which to be killed.

Hara paused to take stock.

More troops? God only knew if there were any more troops around. If Sumida had more men, where were they? And what about Sumida himself? Had he gone up with the mill? And if not, what would he do? All the telephone lines were cut. Or were they? Had one been missed? Was there another nearby?

One thing for sure. He couldn't sit here in an army truck and hope for the best. There was nothing for it but to bluff on. His truck had been seen. He put it in gear and moved ahead, beeping his horn.

"Please!" he shouted from the cab. "Go back into your houses! There is grave danger! Go back into your houses! It will be all right! The Army is sending reinforcements!"

An elderly man ran up to the truck. "What is it? What happened?"

"The enemy has attacked a plant. There are parachutists everywhere. Huge blond men."

More people gathered. They stared into the cab and saw Toda's body.

"Hide!" Hara shouted. "Get back into your houses! Hide!"

"What will happen?" somebody shouted.

"There will be shooting! Keep lights out! Hide and lie flat on the floor! Do not move until you are told it is safe by the Army! Do it! Hurry!"

They believed him. People fled back into their houses. Lights went off, lanterns went out. Hara drove further along the main street toward the pier. How the hell could he hide himself? In his anxiety to get aboard the truck, he'd dropped his rifle behind in the mill. Toda's had fallen when he was shot. Of course there was the pier, covered by McGlynn. But he didn't want to go to the pier yet. That was his ace. That would be his last-minute move when covering fire could help. Any shooting now would only give them away prematurely.

No, he had to stall, to wait until the last minute when McGlynn's Bren gun would have backup from the guns of *Grayfish* — far more firepower than any infantry platoon could muster, if such were around.

In the meantime he had to find a place to wait.

The truck ground on.

Suddenly ahead of him in the darkness he saw a familiar silhouette, like a witch princess who might have dropped from the fading glow of the fireballs. He stopped and swung out of the cab.

"Chiyo!"

"Tomi? You?"

"Yes, me."

"What is going on?"

He rummaged his mind for some plausible story. The truth was at hand. "The enemy has attacked. You must go inside. It is very dangerous for you."

"You have been in the fighting?"

"Yes."

She looked at him in the dim light. "You are hurt."

"No, I am all right."

"But you are bloody. Your face. . ."

"It is nothing. Please go inside. I am all right."

"Oh!" She saw Toda's body inside the cab. "This man is badly hurt."

"He is dead."

She turned back to Hara. "Please, Tomi, come inside. Let me help you." She put her hand on his arm.

Hara wanted nothing more than that. But he didn't want to put her in danger, either. He started to push her hand away. Suddenly, he couldn't. His hand tightened on hers. Why not spend these dangerous minutes with her? They might be his last minutes on earth. Why not steep his soul in beauty for those minutes? If any troops came to Ringo, he'd run through the dark, winding back streets for the pier and McGlynn. What better place than here with her to keep out of sight for a time?

"For a little while," he said. "The enemy may be near. Does your father keep an extra pistol at home?"

"Perhaps. He has a box he keeps some of his army things in."

"Good." Hara looked up and down the street. All seemed quiet again. In fact it was eerily quiet. The good Japanese citizens had followed their orders to the letter. He looked up. The fireball had burned itself out. The lingering smoke cloud was only a smudge of black now, like a mourning band across the stars.

"Come," she said, tugging his arm. "This way."

"You are very kind, Chiyo."

"I worry about my father."

"Of course you do. But he is a good soldier." Too good, thought Hara. "I am sure he is doing fine."

"Where is the fighting taking place?" She slid open the door of the house.

He wondered what to tell her. "The, ah, mill. Out by the railroad tracks."

"Ah? That happened last night, too." She closed the door and dropped bamboo blinds. She lit a small lantern. "Come inside, please."

"I had better stay here by the door, Chiyo. I must keep my shoes on," he said. "In case I have to run outside quickly."

"It is all right. Please put your feet up on the tatami. It is an emergency." She looked into his eyes. "I am glad you have come back — so I can help you, I mean."

"I enjoyed my visit with you last night much more."

"Thank you." She thought of something. "My father. I think he went to that mill. His men are there. Have you seen my father?"

"Yes." Hara hesitated. "Yes, I saw him a while ago. At the steel mill."

"Was he all right?" she asked anxiously.

"I think so." At least that's not a lie, he thought. "He was very busy."

She went to the other room. "Those big explosions, what were they?"

"Bombs. The enemy made bombs."

"Where did the enemy come from?"

"The sky."

"Did they drop from airplanes?"

"Yes. From airplanes. I think," Hara said with more than a tinge of sadness, "that your father's men destroyed all of the enemy in the mill."

"Really? Then he will come home soon?"

"There may be other invaders. That is why everyone must stay inside."

238

"It is amazing that such a thing would happen here in little Ringo."

She brought a bowl of water and a cloth from the other room. She wet the cloth and dabbed delicately at his face. He winced. "I am sorry, Tomi." Her eyes sought his again. "I am clumsy."

"No." He smiled softly. "Your hands are very gentle. It is worth a little pain to have you touch my face."

She caught her breath, then went back to work. "How did you get hurt?"

"A bullet hit the windshield of the truck." A bullet from Sumida meant for him. "Fragments of glass cut me."

"You are lucky. The cuts are very small." She giggled abruptly. "Your face is very black. Like a demon."

His throat tightened with sudden anguish. Tears burned in his eyes. He tried to smile at her, but it twisted. "Tonight I *am* a demon."

"But I do not understand." Her brow puckered. "How did you get here? We saw you go away in the truck."

"Of course," he lied glibly. "We delivered the prisoners without trouble. I was bringing the truck back. Petty Officer Toda was driving." He touched her hand. "I was hoping to see you again, Chiyo." It wasn't a lie.

She looked at the tatami. "See me?"

"Yes. I enjoyed our visit so much last night. I thought that. . ."

"Yes. . ."

"Well. . ." He didn't know how to pursue it. He switched back to his story. "Anyway, as the truck was going by that mill there by the railroad, we were stopped by your father's men. They told us that there were enemy parachute troops in the woods. They were attacking the plant."

Her eyes widened. "You were right there?"

"Yes. Right there. I decided the least I could do was to help your father since he had lent us the truck."

"Very generous. Very brave."

"I had an *ohn* due to him. So we went to help. Your father told me to drive here to Ringo and tell the town to stay inside, out of danger."

"How did your man get shot? How did your face get all black? How were you hurt?" She listened raptly.

"As we were driving this way, the enemy fired at us. A bullet hit him. Another went through the windshield. The fragments hit me." The lies came easily, and the idea saddened him. "A nearby explosion blackened our faces."

"I am very glad you are not hurt so badly. But how sad for your petty officer. The war. It cannot be helped." She soaked the cloth again.

Hara looked at her perfect profile, skin soft as a petal glowing in the light from the little lantern. "You cannot know, Chiyo, how sad it really is," he said. He looked at his watch: 0146. "I must go soon."

"Stay." She didn't look at him. "Please. Just a few minutes longer."

"Thank you, Chiyo." He remembered something. "You said your father might have a spare pistol."

"Oh yes." She went to a cupboard by the *shoji* and brought out a wooden box. She brought it to him. "It might be in this."

"Thank you." He opened the box. Inside were several medals, decorations for valor. There were photographs of Chiyo and another woman. "Your mother?"

"Yes. It was taken only a year before she died."

"You look like her."

"Thank you." She fingered a bundle of notes. "These are her last letters to Father and some poems."

"I see." There wasn't much in the box. But, clearly, these were the things Sumida cherished — love letters, some poems, special pictures. Honors for valor in some pointless battle somewhere. Not much to show for a whole life. Hara moved the items respectfully to one side. In the bottom of the box was a Nambu automatic pistol. He removed the magazine. "Empty. Does he keep ammunition for this, Chiyo?"

"He carries his ammunition. I am sorry. Perhaps if you see him, you could get some from him."

"I am sure I could," Hara murmured dryly. He put the pistol back into the box and closed it. "It cannot be helped." He smiled. "I will have to fight with my bare hands."

She knew he was teasing. She smiled back, then her face turned serious. "I hope you never have to fight again, Tomi."

"I will be very honest with you, Chiyo."

"Yes?"

"I never want to fight again. Ever." He squeezed her hand.

"I will be very honest with you, too."

"Yes?"

"I have thought about you."

"I am glad. I think about you, too." He looked again at his watch. It was time. "Now I must go. It is sad because this is just the very moment when I want the most to stay."

"I wish it were so."

"Put out the lantern, please."

She did. He went to the door and slid it open. Things were still quiet. He went out. She followed. "Go back inside," he said. "Hide!"

"Will you write to me?"

"If I survive this war, I will come back."

She grabbed his arm and clung to it. "Do you promise?"

"I promise." He wanted to leave her with something, anything. He felt inside his blue navy sweatshirt. There were collar insignia on the officer's shirt underneath. He ripped the insignia from one collar. "Here. For you. It is not very much. Only an officer's insignia. A token. Hide it."

"I will treasure it."

"Remember me."

She threw her arms around him. "Stay!"

"I cannot." He pushed her away and turned her to face the house. "Do not look after me. Inside! Quick!"

"I will remember you. *Sayonara.*"

"*Sayonara.*" He watched to make sure she went inside. When the door slid shut behind her, he went out on the main street. He started to approach the truck, but headlight beams swung

241

across his path from the far end of the street.

He lunged back against the wall. With a jolt he recognized Sumida's sedan. Staying in the shadows of houses, he ran hard for the pier.

II

It had taken far too long, Sumida knew. But this time he had some luck. The freight station telephone not only worked, it connected with military headquarters. And this time the higher-ups had taken him seriously. It took dead soldiers to convince them.

Reinforcements were on their way both by express train and by truck. The train troops would deploy around the plant sites. He was ordered to return to Ringo. An army convoy would pick him up at 0400, and he was to deploy them along the coast in squad-size patrols. Headquarters promised to alert the navy, but who knew what they would or could do. And, thought Sumida, everyone — Army, Navy, *everyone* — were all too late and too confused. The damage was done. Maybe later someone would explain why his army, so superbly effective in Malaya, was so inept at home. Perhaps someone would tell him what this night's events had been all about.

The drive back into Ringo had been uneventful. He had doubled back past the mill. Steel girders and chunks of siding still glowed dark red, a somber image of blood pooled against the night sky. Itinerant flames chewed at scraps all around. Whatever the mill had been before, it was only glowing embers and wreckage now.

Wherever the enemy had gone, they were completely gone, even the bodies of their men had been destroyed by the molten steel. Not even ashes would be left. It all seemed very thorough, very final.

On the drive to town he kept his pistol at hand in case some of the attackers were lurking on the road. For much of the way he had kept the car lights out, driving by starlight and instinct.

242

There was nothing to be seen except the shadowy form of an owl coasting across the dark sky.

The town itself seemed remarkably still, he thought, considering all the excitement and explosions. Where was everyone? Were they deaf? Frightened? He shook his head. Civilians were always either a problem or a puzzle.

He turned the headlights back on and drove slowly toward his house.

What was that in the street near his house? A truck? It was far too early for the reinforcements. Sumida doused the headlights again and stopped. He opened the car door. With difficulty he climbed out, clutching his sheathed sword in his left hand and his pistol in his right. There was no mistaking that it was an army truck. But was it the same truck that had fled the mill?

Staying in the shadows, he edged toward it. There was no sound. As he drew nearer, he could hear the soft gurgle of water in the radiator. That meant the engine was still hot! The truck had not been here long!

Sumida flicked his pistol safety off and crept up on the truck cab. The driver's door was ajar. What was that? A hand? He moved closer. Yes, a hand. It didn't move.

Despite his bad leg, he leapt quickly into position to shoot into the cab. The figure didn't move. He looked more closely. Dead eyes stared at the roof of the cab.

They were Japanese eyes. The man wore a dirty white blouse, a Japanese sailor's blouse. Sumida moved the dead man's head and looked at the face again. The unmoving face wore an almost insolent half-smile. Dead men often wore that smile. Sumida wondered what they knew at the last instant.

As for me, he thought, I know nothing. What is happening? Suddenly, Sumida realized he knew this face!

Yes! It was one of Hara's men from the night before. But why here? Sumida backed away and pulled the truck door closed. The numbers! It was his own truck! The one Hara had borrowed! Sumida looked up and down the silent street in puzzlement. This was no coincidence. This had to be the truck that had been at the mill. The dead man; the bullet hole in the windscreen. But...

He looked inside the cab again. It was obvious the dead man hadn't driven the truck. He had a massive wound, and he had bled on the rider's side. So the truck had been driven by someone else. That someone had to be nearby. But where? In one of the houses?

Sumida looked up and down the street, wondering what to do. His own office was useless because the telephone was dead.

Slowly, his gaze focused on the harbor glittering softly, reflecting starlight. The pier!

Of course, he thought, I am a fool. The enemy could escape by boat. Perhaps he already had done so! But if not...

Grimly, Sumida began to hobble toward the pier, clinging to the shadows.

III

"McGlynn!" Hara called hoarsely at pierside. "McGlynn!"

"Over here!" came a voice from down the shore.

"It's 0200! Give 'em the flare!"

"Right." An instant later a red ball of light flew up, then settled into the harbor.

"Where are the others?" McGlynn called out of the dark.

"Gone. Dead."

"*All* of 'em?"

"All but me."

Offshore there was the sound of waves breaking, then the dull rumble of diesels. "I hear the sub out there."

"Hold your position," said Hara. "Sumida's coming up any minute. I don't know how many men he has. I'm unarmed."

"Right!"

Hara looked out into the dark harbor. Far away he could see the silhouette of *Grayfish*, black as death against the horizon. Soon he could see the wake of the vessel sliding his way. It seemed to move with agonizing slowness.

"Who is there?" The shout in Japanese startled him. "Who are you?"

Sumida moved from the darker shadows. Hara could see a pistol in his hand. The major wore his sword, clutching it with his other hand. Between Sumida and McGlynn were walls and a beached boat. Hara had to lure Sumida into an exposed position.

"Come closer," he shouted.

Sumida limped to the shore end of the pier. "I can't see you."

"Come ahead. I'm unarmed."

Sumida limped still closer, pistol ready. "Do I know you?"

"Yes. I think you do. Come closer and see."

Sumida moved a few more feet and squinted. Hara's face had been scrubbed clean by Chiyo. "You?" he gasped.

"The same. Hara."

"You? A saboteur? How can this be?"

"My only regret is betraying your hospitality, Major. The war. It cannot be helped."

Sumida moved still closer. He shook his head. "You work for Americans?"

"I *am* American."

"But. . .you are Japanese."

"I am an American naval officer. All of our men are. . .were . . . Americans."

"But you are Japanese," Sumida insisted.

"My parents were Japanese forty years ago. Not any more. I am American. Born and bred. I am here for my country."

"But you talk, you think Japanese," Sumida said in disbelief. "You were a guest in my house. . ."

"I am sorry, Major."

Sumida seemed near tears. "I even thought of you for my daughter. . ."

"I regret that most of all, Major. She is a fine woman of great character. But she is a victim of war. So are you. So am I."

Sumida's face suddenly contorted in rage. *"Traitor!"*

245

"American!" Hara shouted back at him. "Don't you understand?"

"Traitor!" Sumida shouted again. He limped forward a step, brought his pistol up, and fired a shot. It was wild. Sumida took another step forward and started to aim again. A staccato burst from McGlynn's Bren gun knocked him down. Sumida's pistol fell into the harbor.

McGlynn ran from his hiding place and down the pier past Sumida. "He was alone," he panted. "But there probably are more on the way!"

The throb of diesels was louder. "Ahoy!" Hunley called through the bullhorn.

"Come on in!" McGlynn shouted.

Hara turned to watch the maneuver. Behind them Sumida rolled to his stomach, then slowly pulled himself to his hands and knees. He struggled to his feet, then drew his sword.

Hara saw him. "Give it up, Sumida!"

"Never!" He staggered down the pier trailing blood.

"Dammit!" McGlynn whirled to fire, but Hara pushed the barrel aside.

"No more shooting."

McGlynn turned the weapon butt side up.

It was obvious to both of them that Sumida could accomplish nothing. They watched transfixed as the Japanese officer swayed and staggered toward them, sword in hand.

Ten feet away he took his sword in both hands and confronted them. Blood streamed from his mouth.

"Why?" he whispered. There were tears on his face. McGlynn was there, but Sumida stared only at Hara.

"Why?...Why...?"

Epilogue

". . .Why?"

Hara pulled himself back to the present. "He fell at my feet. That was his last word: *Why?* And I don't know the answer."

She was crying gently. "At dawn," she said, dabbing at her eyes, "we crept out to see what had happened. There was no one there except the dead man in the truck and. . .father. Dead on the pier. Where you left him. His sword in his hand."

"I came back to tell you the truth, Chiyo. You had the right to know. . .about your father. . .about me."

She turned away from him abruptly and looked out at the sea.

"I know this is very hard for you," he said. "But I think, somehow, he would understand. At least now he would understand, even if he did not that night."

She turned to look at him. "He liked you. He said you had good character."

"But my character is American, Chiyo. I am dedicated to another cause. He did not understand that then. Perhaps now. . ."

"Cause?" she cried. "I do not understand 'cause.' My father died."

"And so did a million more Japanese soldiers and seamen. And tens of thousands of *my* people. It was a terrible war, a horror. But it is over. My country won. I helped. We were right, and I ask no forgiveness for doing what was right. But for me

247

and you, two people, I do ask. That is all I can do, ask you to forgive."

She shook her head bitterly. "How can I?"

"I understand." He nodded sadly. "In another world and in another time your father and I would have gone fishing together. He would have talked about you, about the future. You and I would have met in another way."

"Perhaps," she said, thinking back. "Just before he died, we came here together to the shrine. He spoke of grandchildren. I think, perhaps, he sensed the presence of death even though he did not recognize that you were his nemesis." Her tone was bitter. "Not many men get to talk face to face with their nemesis."

"Or," mused Hara, "none of this might have happened at all. Who knows? The fact is that the three of us *did* meet just the way we did. War is not a matchmaker. It *is* fate."

"It is death."

"It is over." He left her facing the sea and went back to his jeep. "Goodbye, Chiyo," he called. He started the engine.

She turned suddenly and shouted after him, "And now? What happens now?"

"We live on. You and I. Everything will be all right."

"Where will you go?"

"Home."

"Home. . .? America?"

He nodded.

"Will I never see you again after fate has put us together?"

"Do you want to see me again, the man who caused your father to die?"

"You were my dream!" She wept. She shook her head in anguish and confusion. "But now you tell me you are my nightmare."

"Truth can be a nightmare."

"I do not know what is true now. Is fate true?"

"Fate lies. But the spirits are real. Think! Would the ghost of your father stand between us?. . .Or help us?"

"How could he not be there?" she cried. "I do not know. I am so confused."

Hara stopped the engine. He couldn't leave her weeping. He got out and came back.

"The war was cruel to you, Chiyo."

"But cruel to many others, also."

"To millions. We all lost."

"The war — " She looked up at him as if understanding something that had been incomprehensible before. "In truth, it was war that made my father die. Not a person. Not you. War! Only war! He was a warrior. A mirror that reflected war. The mirror shattered. He died in war. It was his code, his destiny. . ."

"His tragedy. And mine!"

"But now the war is over," she said softly. "His tragedy is no longer mine." She looked into his eyes. "That is how I feel now. It is as if a weight has been rolled away."

He nodded and allowed a small, encouraging smile. "Come on. I'll drive you home. We will talk. Perhaps we can find some meaning in this after all."

She hesitated, looking back at the shrine.

A whisper of breeze riffled the tops of the pines, encouragement enough. Together they went toward Ringo.

Author's Note

The problem that plagued early development of practical jet aircraft engines was, as indicated in this novel, the production of heat-resistant alloys.

Although the German Luftwaffe flew the first successful squadrons of jet fighters, the Messerschmidt Me.262As, they were not able to optimize performance of their best engine design, the BMW 003, because they could not produce adequate heat-tolerant alloys. This led to relatively inefficient fuel consumption by the engine and reduced speed and performance of the aircraft. Using today's alloys, the Me.262A engine, with some modification, probably could achieve another hundred miles per hour of speed, vastly greater fuel performance, and higher altitude.

Obviously, the existence of exceptionally advanced steelmaking technology, such as the argon-oxygen decarburization furnace, in the 1940s would have revolutionized not only jet engine development, but also would have altered history. It did not exist then.

Although the theory of the AOD process had been worked out, no furnace was built until long after World War II. The first commercial AOD furnace did not go into production until 1973.

Even though specialty steel technology had advanced enormously since 1945, the results of the AOD were astounding in terms of quality, speed, and low cost of production. This technology is critical in the production of today's exceptional steel alloys.

During the final year of the war, the Japanese did, indeed, finally build jet engines: the NE-12 with 748 pounds of thrust and the NE-20 with 1,045 pounds of thrust. A jet airframe was developed by Nakajima Company engineers; it was similar to, but smaller and lighter than, the German Me.262A. The Nakajima plane was called *Kikka* or "Orange Blossom." The prototype was built during the summer of 1945. *Kikka* made its successful first flight from Kisarazu Naval Air Base on August 7, 1945...one day after the first atomic bomb destroyed Hiroshima.